The Success of Suexliegh

Zack Keller

The Success of Suexliegh
by Zack Keller
www.zackkeller.com

Edited by Ben Tuller, John Dusenberry & Karen Keller
Cover by Lindsey Lydecker

Special Thanks
Lindsey, Percival, Abigail, Henrietta, Oslo,
Karen, Ken, Megan, Nick, Rich & Henry

Pen, Pint & Pyre Publishing
www.penpintpyre.com
ISBN: 978-0-9858827-1-6

To wine. And my mother.
(for buying me such good wine)

A Note to the Reader on Pronunciation

"Swoo" as in the sound of spinning rope
✿

"Lee" as in the side away from the wind
✿

"A" as in the first letter of the alphabet
✿

"Swoo-Lee-A"
✿

Suexliegh

I.
Pearl

Chapter The First
The Greatest Man To Have Ever Lived

NOW, it is not every day that you meet a person better than yourself. However, for one man, every day he most certainly meets someone worse. This man is not a great political figure, nor gifted creative spirit, or someone who changed the world for the better through his achievements. He did not become famous for saving a life, or even taking one. He never fought in a war or stood up for what he believed in. He was not right when others were wrong, nor did he rise against impossible odds. In fact, he did little of anything truly important. Yet, he was everywhere. He owned everything. Man of the Year, twice. A walking, talking, smiling page of Encyclopedia Britannica. Even when he looked in the mirror, that man in the reflection was only his equal, never better. For quite simply, Suexliegh was the greatest man to have ever lived.

"Come now, Quincy, it will only be a few ticks more," shouted Suexliegh over the plock-plock din of racquetball as he smashed a winning forehand past his cursing opponent, Victor Yardsley, a solid oak of British upbringing and a wonderful drinker. The two were heating up the racquetball pitch so greatly that the windows were beginning to fog from the effort.

"With respect, sir," followed Quincy, a kindly, old bald eagle of a man, with feathers of gray hair and a gentle smile, "your guests are waiting."

"With even more respect, my dear Quincy, a sporting man never leaves until he bests or has been bested. That's the mark of a true gentleman. Advantage!" With a graceful pose only Michelangelo could recreate, Suexliegh lofted the ball and sliced a spinning ace off the wall directly into his opponent's gut.

"Oof!" grunted Victor as his breath escaped him, "Foul! Foul I say!"

"The only fowl here is you playing like a turkey, my good man!" chuckled Suexliegh before tossing the racquet to a fumbling Quincy. "I do believe that is game, set, and match, old chap. I've worked up quite a Niagara of a sweat in our bout! Good form! Same time next week?"

Victor only grumbled as he threw his sporting shoes into the trash and scuffed his way off the court. Suexliegh snatched a towel from Quincy's waiting arm and vigorously rubbed the sweaty shine off of his face.

"You know what they say, Quincy," smiled Suexliegh.

"What's that, sir?"

"It's not about winning or losing, it's about how much money you bet on the match! Haha!" Suexliegh pantomimed several of his memorable strokes causing Quincy to duck out of the way as his master whipped the racquet around at concussive speeds.

"Quite right, sir, now if you really would follow me out to the veranda," said Quincy as he escorted Suexliegh, an exactly six-foot-tall-man with slick, oil-black hair, into a tailored suit, every stitch measured precisely to length. A piece of clothing that fit only one man on Earth.

"Yes yes, it is that time I suppose," mumbled Suexliegh as he refreshed himself with a spritz of mint water straight to the tongue. "Now, Quincy."

"Yes, sir."

"Remind me again," Suexliegh raised a well-groomed eyebrow, "why are all these lovely people at my manor?"

Quincy flurried with delight as he clasped his hands together and chuckled, his age countable in the creases of his smile. He pushed open the double doors with a heavy creak to reveal a veranda filled with hundreds of guests all holding glasses of champagne.

"Why, sir, don't you know? It's your birthday!"

Chapter The Second
A Carousel Of Cotillionites

"HAPPY BIRTHDAY!" they all cheered. Thousands of faces, all of them knew his name, how many zeroes his bank account held, his life story. When Suexliegh looked out into the crowd and smiled, it was like he knew every single one of them too.

"Thank you, one and all, for being here this fine evening and sharing the day of my birth," boasted Suexliegh, knowing just when to pause for applause, and just when to start speaking again. As always, when eyes were on him, he was flawless.

"When I was but a plucky tike, my father said to me, 'Son, one day you will grow up before you know it, but always remember, keep your heart young, for then you will never grow old.' Everyone, a toast, to old friends and young hearts," monologued Suexliegh, with every ounce of charisma he could conjure.

It was more than enough; not a dry monocle in the house as the guests lifted their glasses and sipped to their champagne futures.

"Now, I do hope you would accept my sincerest apology for being tardy this evening, I was playing racquetball," the crowd roared with laughter, thinking his quip to be in jest, as Suexliegh egressed off the deck to immediate envelopment by alacritous guests.

"So tell us, Mr. Money," chortled a piggly girl-raised-in-the-south, whose sparkling golden pendant strained to hold her jugular together, "just how old *are* you?"

"Oh well now, can't we just celebrate my survival of another twelve calendar pages? Isn't that enough?" swooned Suexliegh. Though he would look forever young, the only number Suexliegh didn't like was the one currently affixed to his being. For time was the one thing he could not purchase more of.

"No!" came a roaring cheer, all enjoying the game.

"With wit like that, you must certainly be the devil!" snapped

Grits. "What's the big secret? Forty? Fifty? Come now, one hundred and eleven!?"

"Yeah, afraid ya might be gettin' over the hill, or one step closer to goin' under it?" retorted Grits's sun-torched, grinning husband, a Texan; he remembered the Alamo.

Suexliegh paused, counting to five on the metronome wheezes of Mrs. Grits's post-guffaw recovery.

"Why, I'll tell you," began Suexliegh, "I am, to the day, to the minute, to the second, exactly one year older than I was last year." As the guests pointed their mouths skyward to eject an uproar of laughter, Suexliegh disappeared further into the crowd. Past oil tycoons and dot-com kids, past debutantes and heirs, past credit limits high enough to buy Australia.

These socialites, blue bloods, patricians, crème de la crèmers, they were a mix of money. Many inherited. Some marry into it. A few created their own. Regardless, they all had it, and they all spent it. They loved it. They hated it. They gossiped about money like it was a person. The Almighty Dollar was his name, and it was a pleasure to know him

But Suexliegh, he was different, for he was, quite literally, in the business of making money: he owned the world's largest mint and printed green for the red, white and blue. It was rumored that the "S" in the American dollar sign was even created in Suexliegh's honor. Though like many men of money, there was not much that he actually did for the company, other than be its number one customer. Suffice it to say, as much cash flowed out of his account as into it so even if every single person in the world went suddenly and unequivocally broke the mint would still need to be in operation twenty-four-seven. Tender, legal or otherwise, was Suexliegh's game, and he played it very, very well.

Chapter The Third
The Frankenstein Manor

SUEXLIEGH MANOR had been converted into a wonder of the world for his birthday celebration: glittering gazebos stamped the yard depicting uniquely continental pleasures with names like Secret of the Orient, where silky Japanese concubines shiatsu'd away your nine-to-fives, and the African Affair, a private, savannah petting zoo Mother Nature herself would envy. To say the estate was gargantuan would be an understatement, for it was at least twice that. One hundred rooms, nearly as many baths, kitchens and libraries, manicured gardens that stretched beyond the horizon, enough butlers to fill the downs of a horse track and its own private dock, airstrip and zip code. A game of Hide-And-Seek played by a troupe of traveling dignitaries once lasted over twenty-two days and required the use of sophisticated global positioning systems and satellite arrays to track everyone down. Many claim it is the only man-made object visible from space, much to the chagrin of the Chinese populous.

The manor was a Frankenstein of sorts, imperfect in its perfection, but very much alive and well. A man as well traveled as Suexliegh, and a man who traveled in such circles, would undoubtedly come across abodes that he rather fancied. Instead of having an architect replicate the magical masonry of the original, Suexliegh would simply purchase it, extricating wood, wallpaper and all, and graft the new appendage on to his own house. It was the only way; Mr. Suexliegh did not want to be a copycat, you see. As such, everything from hand-tiled Roman baths to the scarred, creaking cellar door of a 13th century Belgian trappist, adorned the house like so many organ transplants.

"Suexliegh! Over here now Suexliegh!" shrieked a positively telephone pole of a woman. Living on nothing but caviar and compliments left her skeleton a common presence. She spoke his name with harsh incorrectness forgetting the "x" was silent.

"You simply *must* meet my daughter, Deidre," Janet, as the skeleton was known, put so much stress on her words that they nearly had a nervous breakdown. With bird-like zeal she scanned the party-goers back and forth and called out, "Deidre, dear! Where *are* you?"

A brace-faced young girl, Deidre presumably, two knuckles deep in a bowl of guacamole, snapped her head around and smiled a metal, mottled green smile. Deidre stuffed a handful of crumbling chips into her purse before making her way back towards her mother while licking the salt off of her fingers.

"She's simply *lovely* isn't she? Her cotillion is next week no less so I do say my little rose bloomed at just the right time. I think she'll look lovely in lavender. Lovely in lavender, listen to me, a born Dickens," squeaked Janet. She eagerly motioned for Deidre to hurry over who had been distracted by a passing butler carrying a platter of deep-fried olives. She popped a few in her mouth and a few more in her purse.

"You have quite the gift of gab, Madam, perhaps you shouldn't have French kissed the Blarney Stone. A friend of mine did so and now he even talks in his sleep!" Suexliegh shook his head. "His poor wife."

Madam Skeleton's bones rattled as she laughed. She was a coat hanger for her dress.

"Handsome *and* funny. You're quite the catch," she sidled up to Suexliegh with the grace of a sack of potatoes but Suexliegh ignored her and scanned the crowd, searching. "As of yet Deidre is unescorted to her cotillion, not that there haven't been ample suitors mind you. We were merely looking for the right one… and I think I've found him."

"Congratulations, I'm sure he's a wonderful man," slipped Suexliegh, not caring, nor realizing her borderline statutory implications. He was preoccupied, and rightly so, for all he wanted right now was a piece of his birthday cake.

Chapter The Fourth
Quincy Sr., Quincy Jr. & Musings on Quincy the Third

AND THERE it was. Like the tower of Babel reaching skyward to the heavens, a multilayered nirvana of chocolate decadence. Cake that would make God himself forget his diet. A spindly blond butler, Quincy Jr., eagerly handed over a wedge of delight, careful not to spill a crumb, and within moments Suexliegh had fractioned the dessert. Quincy Jr. was the son of Suexliegh's long time butler, Quincy Sr., who had known the master since before he was in diapers. As Quincy Sr. spent every waking hour looking over the manor, and with the unexpected birth of his son and the even more unexpected death of his wife, he was a widower and raised the boy to butler too. The boy's, Quincy Jr.'s, only dream was that one day Suexliegh would have a son of his own, a Suexliegh Jr., one that Quincy Jr. could sign a life of servitude to before the young master could even control his bowels. Being a butler wasn't much of a life for some, perchance even loathsome to many, but it was all Quincy Jr. ever wanted: to be needed.

"How are we, QJ? That's Quincy Jr. for short," chuckled Suexliegh, licking his fingers with culinary delight.

"We are most good, sir. The warm summer air should settle any conniptions the guests may have this evening. It will be a night to remember. How are… we?" stumbled QJ as he adjusted his posture back to perfection.

"So divine," mumbled Suexliegh between chews. "So tell me, Junior, considering any college universities for matriculation?"

"I wouldn't dream of it, sir," started Quincy Jr. who nearly toppled the tray of cake in his worry. "My place is here with you."

"Yes yes, very good but how will you ever meet a wife to make *you* Quincy Sr. and make you a Quincy Jr. of your own?" Suexliegh reached over and began forking bitefuls of cake as he listened.

Quincy Jr. blushed, he hadn't thought of that, what with all the work to be done around the manor.

"I hadn't thought of that, what with all the work to be done around the manor," said Quincy Jr. astutely. "There will be time for that eventually, but for now, I just want you to have the happiest of days. It is your birthday after all, you only get one per year so you shouldn't worry yourself one bit about my feminine troubles."

Suexliegh became suddenly serious, a rarity for the man, for he, like many reputable doctors, believed laughter to be the best medicine and decided to overdose on such prescriptions as often as humanly possible.

"If I am standing between you and the fairer sex that is just... unfair!" roared Suexliegh who finally put down his chocolate-covered fork. "Why, Quincy Jr., you're fired!"

Quincy Jr. gasped, his face *The Scream*. His life before his eyes.

"Bu-bu-bu-but, sir!" stammered Quincy.

"Don't bu-bu-bu-but me, my good man. Go out there and find a girl with a nice bu-bu-bu-butt of her own and live happily ever after!" he said, slapping a bewildered Quincy Jr. on the backside as he stumbled, catatonic, into the crowd.

"Give it the old college try, lad!" chuckled Suexliegh who immediately delved into his next slice of manna.

"Ahem, sir?" said a nervous little voice.

"Ahem, yes?" Suexliegh spun around, showing the chocolaty geological record in his toothy grin.

"Sorry to bother you, sir, but we need to talk," squeaked Ernie Grosser, who carried tissue paper in all his pockets, used on the right, virgin on the left. Suexliegh never saw his accountant unless there was bad news, and this was the first time he had seen the man since he was hired.

Chapter The Fifth
April 15

"CAN'T YOU SEE I'm quite busy," masticated Suexliegh as he forklifted another mound of enlightenment into his mouth and tried to ignore Ernie. The party had reached paragon conviviality and this was no time to talk business: the champagne bubbles were fizzling higher, the tall tales were growing grander. It was a night to see and be seen for everyone except Ernie.

"But sir, it's April fifteenth," Grosser whispered the date, as it was considered by many a terrible *faux pas* to even mention. A Black Tuesday come once a year. If even one person heard him say those words, the entire night's festivities would collapse like a house of cards under Thor's mighty hammer. Tax Day was always a period of great mourning for people like Mr. Suexliegh who often had to part with much of their beloved riches. Many created fake charities and opened off-shore bank accounts to keep "the Man in Washington" at bay, whomever that man was in particular no one knew.

"Yes, yes, so I've heard, my birthday," clearly not amused by his accountant's incessant interruptions. Suexliegh marched at a direct angle away from Ernie in hopes the crowd would somehow form an impenetrable barrier between them, but Grosser was surprisingly lithe and weaved through the human obstacles without a false step.

"And tax day. You never sent me your receipts, nor your earnings. You said you would, but you didn't, so I called, but you didn't return, so I came by, but Quincy said you were bathing, so I waited."

"Is it a crime to be clean?" mused Suexliegh, picking up a fluted glass of champagne off the tray of a passing butler.

"For six hours, and you still didn't show, so I left."

"I don't want to catch the bubonic plague now do I?" huffed Suexliegh before turning away. He snapped his fingers and the closest butler immediately fell onto all fours creating a perfect surface upon which Suexliegh could step. Using his new height advantage to survey the party, his eyes finally found Quincy Jr. who was attempting to converse with a female of the opposite sex in the Darwinian hopes of arriving at or near knowledge of a carnal nature. It was quite obvious he might soon be extinct.

"Good man," Suexliegh stepped down and allowed the butler his leave, two grassy footprints marking him square in the back.

"This is a serious matter. You owe the government," Ernie looked around suspiciously then leaned in, "a lot of money this year. All the cars, the planes, the parties, that city you bought in Scandinavia, not to mention the flights to France just to get those crêpes you like.

"I told you never to speak of that again."

"Sir, the IRS could audit you."

"Oh IRS, what you need is a good helping of IBS. Here, have some cake," Suexliegh lifted a black triangle of perfection right under Grosser's nose. "I'm sure by tomorrow morning everything will be just fine."

"All the experts agree, the United States has slumped into its worst recession since the Great Depression. And these same experts agree it is all because of one man, no not the President, but a globe-trotting entrepreneur named Suexliegh, leaving a wake of wealth along his many travels from Prague to Portland on his numerous private jets, whose failure to pay taxes on his enormous fortune has cost the government untold sums and caused the beginning of a world market meltdown."

Suexliegh stared at the television in shock, "That's just preposterous; I've never been to Portland."

Chapter The Sixth
The Beamish and the Barrister

"HOUSE ARREST! How can they keep me under lock and key like some sort of animal! I'm a human man!" exploded Suexliegh as he paced back and forth in his lawyer's office. Wendell Almond, like most lawyers, had an office with a respectable library filled with respectable books that respectable people would nod at respectfully when they saw them. A grandfather clock swung lazily in the corner as Wendell flipped through a hefty stack of documentation three feet high concerning Suexliegh's purchases from his birthday spectacular the night before. Wendell poured over every single receipt from "applewood smoked bacon" to "zoo keeper" and felt as if he experienced the party himself, though he was never invited.

"Well, wait just one moment... did they mention which house?" Suexliegh started, his mind racing as he strode around the room. "I do fancy a few months off in my Bavarian cottage right now. Those black forest ham sandwiches would much improve my current disposition."

Suexliegh licked his lips at the memory.

"You were just on a six month sabbatical," grunted Wendell as his hands idly opened a locked drawer where he hid his vices of fine whiskey and butterscotch toffee. He quickly slammed the drawer shut so as not to show a sign of weakness in front of his client. Almond had been Suexliegh's lawyer since he was the ripe young age of eighteen and regretted the decision ever since. It took an entire, fully staffed office and a monthly ulcer just to keep the finances of this one man in order. If Suexliegh didn't overpay him so graciously every month Wendell would have jumped ship a long time ago.

"Yes, and I'm still recovering from that," huffed Suexliegh who crossed his arms and turned away. He began pulling on each and every book in the library to see if it might unlock a trap door.

Wendell looked blankly at Suexliegh, "I believe they mean your estate here, in this city, where you are currently standing."

Suexliegh gave up his search and slumped, dramatically exasperated, into a welcoming chair that "foomp-ed" upon his impact. Wendell approached Suexliegh, pulling up a seat beside him.

"You must be careful from now on. This is the U.S. government we're talking about: if there's one thing they know how to do it's prosecute American citizens. Just hold off on any wanton spending while the IRS goes through your records. It should only be a few weeks."

"Weeks! I thought we'd be done by lunch! I'm hosting a caviar tasting at Lake Como tomorrow! Wendell, you know how much I love caviar and how much I don't love eating it in the United States. Isn't there anything you can do?" Suexliegh pleaded. Though Suexliegh was the reason for Almond's receding hairline he couldn't just hang his one and only client out to dry, especially one so horribly ill-equipped to deal with the nuances of life in the real world.

"Perhaps our good friend Salmon P. Chase can help us out!" said Suexliegh as he jumped to his feet, removing an out-of-print $10,000 Federal Reserve note bearing the bust of the late U.S. Treasurer, Salmon Portland, from his wallet. He never carried what he considered "peasant money," or anything below one hundred dollars. Coins were especially out of the question as he believed in the principle of rounding up to the nearest hundred.

"Or perhaps Woody," he pulled a similar note for one-hundred thousand dollars with the late president Woodrow Wilson on it. Rumor had it the bill was haunted.

"Are you suggesting we bribe the U.S. government?" Wendell sighed as he crossed his arms.

"Only a smidgen," cooed Suex, clearly content with his plan.

Chapter The Seventh
Pennywinkle

"QUINCY, amuse me."

"Yes, sir. How would you like to be amused?"

"Oh, I don't know, surprise me."

"Yes, sir... just how exactly would you like to be surprised... sir?"

"Bring me my gun."

"Pull!" BANG! "Pull!" BANG!

Quincy delicately placed another Fabergé egg into the cannon and sent it spinning cloud-ward before it burst into a meteor shower of priceless nothing.

"Well shot, sir, that's the last of them." Quincy said, applauding.

"There must be something else to shoot. This is America is it not?"

"It most certainly is."

"I tire of these trifles. Come along, Quincy."

And Quincy did. Suexliegh tossed him the massive elephant rifle which nearly toppled the feeble old man. He hopped in his golf cart and sped around his property searching for amusement, yet he was bored by the endless hedge maze, yawned at the jet ski obstacle course, scoffed at the private yacht on the private lake, and turned his nose up at the human-sized chess board. He was not in the mood for Scrooge McDuck-esque shenanigans as, sadly, a dive into a pile of money would be unable to cheer him up.

"Quincy! I need you!" Suexliegh flopped onto his Quad-King bed; four regular king beds fused together to create a surface large enough on which to play tennis.

"Yes, sir. Anything, sir? What is it, sir?"

"I can't take this, I'm likely to be committed to a mental institution for cabin fever at any moment."

Quincy checked his pocket watch.

"But sir, it's just 9:35, you've only been up thirty-five minutes."

"9:35! My whole day wasted already. Damnation to the man in Washington! Someday I will find him and give him the what for. Perhaps I should take matters into my own hands. Yes, I've been thinking."

"You shouldn't do that, sir, it might tire you out."

"Perhaps, with your help, the two of us could tunnel our way right out of the mansion. You dig during the day and I'll take the night."

"That's one idea. Or maybe you'd prefer this."

Quincy displayed a newspaper article about the opening day for a centennial horse race known as the Corona Crown.

"The Corona Crown is today!? I'm going to miss Pennywinkle's race! I paid my prettiest penny for that horse."

"Sir, why not just watch it here from the comfort of your home. I'm sure you can call in your bet," Quincy said, picking up the rotary dial.

"But it's not the same, Quincy," Suexliegh lamented as he leapt theatrically onto his bed. "I need to hear the roar of the underprivileged crowd who set aside their measly earnings for one chance to taste greatness through winning a gamble. That and the good old scent of sweat and manure."

Quincy paused, "I'm sure that can all be arranged."

"Quincy, get my checkbook, I know how we can get to that race."

"The checkbook is in your pocket, sir."

"And?"

"Oh, very well, sir."

Quincy shuffled over and reached into Suexliegh's side pocket, taking out the checkbook and pen.

"I'm coming Pennywinkle!"

Chapter The Eighth
Cheque Mates

SO SUEXLIEGH WALKED, further than he ever had on his own two legs, to the edge of his property, some eight furlongs yonder, until they reached a two-story high hedgerow which acted as a buffer for both sight and sound from his neighbors.

"Quincy, ladder," ordered Suexliegh, ringing a little golden bell to get his attention, and promptly there was a ladder placed in front of him. Like a practiced circus monkey, he clambered up the rungs until he could just peer over the bustling hedgerows into his neighbor's territory.

"I do say, Worthington, my good man," shouted Suexliegh to a portly fellow with curly black hair clamped under a swim cap who glided through his pool, displacing water like an orca.

"Quite…busy! Come back…later!" choked Worthington through gasps of air. Suexliegh climbed fully onto his hedgerow and took a sit on the edge, surveying the property. It was nice, monocle and top hat nice, but to Suexliegh, it might as well have been manufactured by Mattel.

"If you'd stop your flapping for a moment, I have a proposition for you," chimed Suexliegh who idly crossed his legs as he peered down.

Worthington fluttered to a stop and bobbed in the deep end. His supple, trophy of a wife, watching with mock interest from a chair set to "lounge."

"Oh really?" snapped Worthington, angered that his BPMs had dropped below regulation. This rise in blood pressure wouldn't help anyone.

"Quite really. I would like to buy your property."

"You would what?" gurgled Worthington.

"Your property, I want it. How much?" Suexliegh removed his checkbook and pulled out a fountain pen, ready to sign.

"This was my father's house, and his father's before that, there's family history here," Worthington seemed to be in a state of disbelief at Suexliegh's braggadocios behavior. His wife sacrificed her precious tanning time to sit up and watch the two negotiate.

"History, huh? Well, I'm going to write a one, followed by zeroes. You just tell me when to stop," Suexliegh began to write zero after zero until it seemed Worthington's eyes would bug out of his head. His pen quickly ran out of ink causing him to remove a portable well, unscrew the cap, dip then fill the pen, and continue writing as Worthington watched in amazement.

"There's only so much room on one piece of paper, oh well, perhaps I'll go over to the back."

Suexliegh continued writing zeroes onto the back of the check with a steady progression.

"Looks like I'm almost out of room, perhaps I should just tear this up and bid you good day," Suexliegh ripped out the check and motioned to split it in twain.

"Wait wait!" shouted the exasperated man as he splashed about, paddling his way over to Suexliegh, one arm outstretched to shake. "You've got a deal!"

Suexliegh smiled his pearly whites.

"Grand! Now get the hell out of my pool."

So on they went, Suexliegh and Quincy, and in their wake left a trough of newly acquired land, technically now Suexliegh's property, and therefore he was still technically under house arrest. Not a single homeowner could resist Suexliegh's charm, or his charmed bank account. In no time at all they had cut a swath straight through Acropolis Heights, an uber-bia at the end of the rainbow where the rich and famous wish they lived, all the way to Uppington Downs, Pennywinkle's luxury stable.

Chapter The Ninth
For Better or Horse

"PENNYWINKLE!" shouted Suexliegh as he rushed up to his prized racehorse and embraced the massive beast as best he could.

"From one stud to another I think you'll take the carrot on this race no sweat! But I want a good clean trot, no funny business, you hear? Oh you must know I'm joking, Penny! Stand up straight, let me have a good look at you," Suexliegh giggled like a schoolboy.

Pennywinkle snorted and stamped her feet as Suexliegh paced around the majestic beast, eyeing for imperfections but finding not a one. He fed Penny a handful of peppermints, her favorite treat, which she eagerly lapped up. The four-legged mustang stood over six feet tall, the color of an ancient oak, with muscles that Hercules himself would envy. Pennywinkle was the heralded offspring of two of the winningest horses ever to have graced the track, Honeydew and Bloodlust, whom Suexliegh fed and bred to create a racer of such supreme caliber that it might run down Mercury's chariot were it ever given the chance. All these years of training had led up to today's race of all races, the Corona Crown, that which Suexliegh desired above all else.

"Mmmmmmsuexliegh," rang out a voice pitched high due to a lifetime of self-satisfaction. Suexliegh knew that voice. The voice of a man whom he hated more than most. In fact, more than all.

"Hello, Dingle," seethed Suexliegh.

The man was Dingle Steeds, Equestrianaire, as much a thoroughbred as the horses he raced, born with a silver, honey-covered bit in his mouth. For a living, he raced horses, the very best. He loved to win, and win he did. Suexliegh would never let on, but if he could be beaten at one thing by one man, it was this man and it was horse racing.

"It's going to take more than a two-bit pep talk for my stallion to be beaten by your walking glue factory," he laughed receptively at his own joke. Dingle sauntered over to his private stable where his horse, Winchester, was held, humming all the while. It was rumored that the name Winchester came about for the horse's qualities of both starting off like a shot and speeding faster than a bullet down the track. Winchester had never lost, for you see, Winchester had never raced Pennywinkle, and Pennywinkle had never lost, for Pennywinkle had never raced Winchester.

"Well, Suexliegh, you're a betting man are you not?"

"Depends on the bet and whom is betting."

Dingle sauntered over to Suexliegh and squeezed his chubby baby hands into tight, white riding gloves.

"The Corona Crown is all well and good and it will look smashing above my fireplace, but I say we up the ante: whomsoever loses must act as the other's butler for a fortnight. Doing dishes, taking out trash, using the telephone, and all manner of other unmentionables."

Dingle shuddered at the thought.

"What say you we up it even further," said Suexliegh standing up to his full height and quickly dwarfing Dingle.

"Oh?" whimpered Dingle, stepping back a bit.

"Oh yes," Suexliegh paced slowly around the stable, letting the moment sink in before locking his gaze on Dingle. "The loser may never race his horse again."

"Never?"

"Ever," Suexliegh said as they played a game of chess with their eyes until Dingle stepped cautiously up and extended his hand.

"I look forward to seeing Pennywinkle at the local petting zoo."

"I look forward to seeing *you* at the local petting zoo when you have been forced into manual labor after a thorough and decisive trouncing by my horse-friend. Cheers."

Chapter The Tenth
A View From On High

"AND THEY'RE OFF!"

Gates snapped open. Hooves churned soil. Onlookers leapt to their feet. Nostrils flared. Jockeys whipped. Bobbing snouts. Teeth gritted. Suexliegh walked into his private viewing suite just in time to see the first race of the day. His luxury box, placed atop all others, had prime real estate aimed squarely at the finish line. Every race was a heart-wrenching photo-finish. Lining the walls were massive television displays, one per horse in the race, which made sure Suexliegh could keep the closest eye on his competition. Checking for signs of fatigue, of malaise, of buttress foot.

The floor to ceiling wood paneling was dotted with golden trophies from Pennywinkle's past exploits, all save for a single case, empty, but already marble engraved with his horse's anticipated winning of the Corona Crown. Some might think that presumptuous, but the same some didn't know Suexliegh for with each and every other trophy case in the room he had done the aforementioned. They say fortune favors the bold, but Suexliegh says the bold favor fortune. It seemed his winning streak was incorruptible, as if Lady Luck herself had taken the man as a permanent gentleman caller.

"Could I get you a drink, sir?" chipped Quincy as he made ready his master's favorite lounging chair, placing before him the most luscious olives, cheeses, and dried meats intricately arranged on a silver platter. A separate, smaller platter held his prized dark chocolate, 100% pure South American cacao, prepared and distributed by a specially funded and organized team of planters, pickers, scientists, and delivery men, all adults mind you, no child labor, for the sole purpose of creating chocolate as dark as the heart of Africa and matching in richness to Suexliegh himself, for you see, he was a connoisseur of sorts, with a wolf's nose that could smell succulence a mile out.

"A bit of Glacial would hit the spot just about now," Suexliegh reclined and breathed deeply, content for the moment due to his past success with getting to the race, his present success with the bet, and his soon to be future success of owning the Corona Crown.

"Right away, sir!" Quincy darted off to a private nozzle, where, on tap at all times, ancient glacier water was piped from the South Pole. Water so pure and wonderful that Suexliegh believed it to be the elixir of life. Liquid heaven. One sip would kill the devil himself. While there were still glaciers left to be drunk, why not drink them? It was a pleasure he reserved for the finest occasions, of which today was one.

Suexliegh settled deep into his leather chair and swiveled his spotting scope race-wise, scanning the crowd, stopping only to visually heckle. The bleachers were made up of all walks of life from the dismally poor to the absurdly rich for everyone enjoyed good, healthy competition to forget about their worldly troubles. Besides, everything is much more fun when there is money at stake.

"Oh look at that man, Quincy, wearing a hat during the daytime, what a cad! Who does he think he is, Theodore Roosevelt?" Suexliegh snorted with glee.

"Would you like me to have him removed?" stated Quincy in all seriousness.

"No no no! Let him have his cake. I do so love coming here, it makes me feel like a commoner," he said as he sipped of his glacier water and ate of his Grecian olives.

The day passed, fortunes were won and lost, hearts broken, a lifetime of stories told about animals running in circles. Then, just as the sun took a seat on the horizon, Pennywinkle and Winchester strode out onto the field to meet their destiny.

Chapter The Eleventh
Race Relations

"THERE HE IS, oh would you look at him," fawned Suexliegh as he gazed longingly through his viewing scope at Pennywinkle, who stood majestically at the starting gate. "Like a wingless Pegasus."

At the next stall over appeared Winchester, his black body rippled in muscular glory like a twisted tree trunk. Though in reality there were eight horses racing, there were actually only two. And though thousands were betting, it mattered for only two.

BANG!

The starting gun fired with a crack causing Suexliegh to jump out of his seat and rush to the window.

"This is it, Quincy! Can you feel it!" chanted Suexliegh.

"Feel what, sir?"

"That I'm going to beat Dingle into a penniless pulp!"

"Yes sir, I feel that."

And was it ever a sight to see. Equus Caballus. Two near-mythical animals paced neck and neck around the ellipse, quickly spacing several body lengths ahead of their competitors. The crowd roared with biblical fervor as they spoke in tongues, shouting the horses' names.

" P e n n y w i n k l e ! "   " W i n c h e s t e r ! "   a n d   s o   o n .

"I don't think I can watch anymore. It is too much for my heart. Quincy, tell me what's happening," Suexliegh fell, exasperated, into the chair, his arm draped melodramatically over his eyes in a mock faint.

Quincy, scopeless, squinted out the window attempting to distill such a grand moment in mere words.

"Pennywinkle is ahead. Now Pennywinkle is behind. Winchester is losing ground, now he is just losing. The two horses are neck and neck. I think one just bit the other."

Suexliegh leapt out of his chair as the horses rounded the final turn shouting, "Oh I have to watch! Come on Penny!"

The louder the crowd roared, the more tied the race became until they were only a few seconds from the finish.

A knock at the door. Suexliegh whipped his head around: no one knocked on his door during a race. Such an offense was like telling an executioner that you had an itch on your neck, one that should be scratched by a guillotine.

"Quite busy!" shouted Suexliegh as he snapped back to the race.

"Open up, it's the FBI," shouted a gruff voice.

"Whom?"

"The FBI, sir, we have a warrant for your arrest."

"I don't know an FBI, call again later," Suexliegh returned his attention to the horses as outside the door there was momentary muffled chatter then silence. Suexliegh's eyes locked on the race, Winchester was slowly creeping ahead.

Suddenly, the door ripped off its frame and a portly gentleman, presumably from the Federal Bureau of Investigation, stumbled into the room and fell face first on the floor. Several more men followed and quickly secured Suexliegh in handcuffs, pulling him out of his chair as the meaty man ungracefully got to his feet and dusted himself off.

"What is the meaning of this! How dare you interrupt in the middle of a sporting event!" cried Suexliegh. "This is a race between animals!"

"You men can't be in here! He has done nothing wrong!" defended Quincy, attempting to bat the invaders off with a baguette.

The crowd burst into cheering and before Suexliegh could catch a glimpse of the outcome, the men tackled him.

"Did he win? What happened? Did Penny win?" Suexliegh was on the verge of tears as the men dragged him away. His answer would have to wait, for now, he was going to jail.

Chapter The Twelfth
A Jury of His Peers

SHOWING ONLY perfectly straight teeth and no fear, Suexliegh stood before a judge awaiting his verdict. It was decided that his failure to pay taxes this year cast the economy into a rampant downward trend costing an untold amount of people an uncountable amount of money. He had also broken the terms of his house arrest though his lawyer argued beautifully in his defense, first claiming Suexliegh did this knowingly to show the government the perils of their own system, secondly claiming the government sought to refill their ailing coffers with a good old-fashioned arbitration, and lastly claiming insanity, not on Suexliegh's behalf, but on the entire U.S. government. None of it worked, but it sounded so damn good. Yet, through all the verbal battery and disciplinary assault from the Judge, Suexliegh wore a smile, hoping to charm the jury with a heart of gold and eyes of Neptune blue.

The Judge was unremarkable both physically and otherwise, or so Suexliegh's rare glances in his direction would lead you to believe. Though whenever there was a lull in the courtroom, or he could manage a distractionary sneeze, he would sneak a small handful of M&Ms into his mouth. Cough-chewing to hide his addiction.

"Don't worry, we'll get you out of this thing," whispered Almond, leaning in close. "They don't have any hard evidence."

"Don't you think these seats are a bit uncomfortable?" Suexliegh said, shifting side to side as he tried to gain a more pleasant purchase with his buttocks. "You'd think they could afford some pillows around here what with all the taxes I'm paying them."

A side door opened and out walked the jury, knowing Suexliegh's fate but showing nothing. He managed to catch a young female juror's eye and petitioned her with a subtle wink and nod. She returned the action, much to Suexliegh's delight.

"In the case of the United States of America versus Suexliegh, how do you find the defendant?" asked the Judge.

Suexliegh managed his biggest grin yet, one tooth per juror. The young juror looked from Suexliegh to the Judge, hiding all emotion.

"We find the defendant guilty on all charges."

The courtroom burst into an uproar as Almond launched a barrage of objections and further pleads of insanity. How could this have happened? This man had an airport named after him! But it was decided, and the Judge's gavel fell like Mjollnir, silencing the room.

"Suexliegh," coughed the Judge, "because of your rampant disregard for the well-being of those around you, not to mention numerous, blatant attempts at bribery-"

"Those offers still stand, your honor," interjected Suexliegh.

"I sentence you to ten years in prison," the final words hit Quincy like atomic bombs. The bailiffs approached Suexliegh with handcuffs, but he just kept smiling. With all that had gone on, the fact that Suexliegh was still smiling made the jurors think he might actually be insane.

"That's actually a pretty fair sentence," mumbled Almond as he packed up his briefcase while the bailiffs escorted Suexliegh out of the room, "but I'll get you out within the week."

Quincy rushed through of the crowd, tears streaming down his face, his slender frame shaking.

"Sir! Master Suexliegh! Stay strong! Just remember that you're better than them and you can do anything!" Quincy shouted, fearing for his master who was going to spend nearly a fort-year in a room smaller than the closet on one of his planes. Not only that, he had to share that room with another human.

"I'll be just fine," exclaimed Suexliegh with a subtle hint of uncertainty in his voice. "Just fine. At least Pennywinkle won."

From there, Suexliegh did not pass go, he did not collect two hundred dollars, he went directly to jail.

Chapter The Thirteenth
The Big House

THE SUEXLIEGH Minimum Security Facility. Yes, he owned that building too. One of his many "charitable" donations built for his friends who dabbled on the dark side. It was called a prison, but that's not what it was, what with its vaulted ceilings, vintage Scotch collection, a squash court, two Olympic-sized pools, Sunday bruncheons, even a Swiss masseuse from Switzerland. Everything a gentleman could want, and no minorities. A paradise prison. Though, again, that is not what it was.

Suexliegh was escorted through the foyer where chandeliers dripped from the ceiling like stalactites. One might think they were checking into a spa, not a place where white-collar criminals with golden parachutes lounged away their sentences sipping Mint Juleps and working on their calf muscles.

The Concierge, a well-groomed and dressed man, gave Suexliegh a matching set of clothes, one for sleeping, one for working out, and one for just traipsing around. Suexliegh was escorted into a private changing room where he immediately slipped into his sporting clothes, eager to challenge his old friends to a heated game of racquetball. After forfeiting the remainder of his worldly belongings to the custodials, he was ready to say goodbye to the world he once owned in order to pay back his literal debt to society.

Quincy blubbered and wheezed, blowing foghorn sounds into his kerchief as he watched his longtime friend and employer cruelly taken from him. The tears flowed through the wrinkled deltas at the corners of his eyes before cascading down over his cheeks. Without anyone telling him what to do, Quincy was simply lost. A boat without a rudder. The only other time the two had been parted for a considerable amount of time was while Quincy waited for Suexliegh in the womb. Those were the longest eight months he had ever endured, and had the young master not been so eager to conquer life and induced his own labor early, he would have had to wait at least one month more for gestation. It was then that Quincy decided to break his master out of prison.

Suexliegh was marched down the hallway past the other inmates who looked on with an expression comprised of amusement and fear; if Suexliegh could be arrested, what was this world coming to? Instead of the usual barrage of playful badgering aimed at recent arrivals, he was met with silence which he returned with a smile, a wave and a polite "hello" to his new neighbors.

He recognized many of them either by acquaintance or front-page scandal. Verne Dempsey made a fortune when his company, claiming to have cured the common cold, went public until the FDA realized he was just selling ground up Skittles. Jules Reneau eliminated his competition at a French newspaper by tossing him into the paper press while it was running. Needless to say, the story was all over the front page. And most notorious of all, Hans Haddinger created a line of supremely popular children's toys made entirely out of asbestos ripped from the walls of derelict buildings. These men didn't commit heinous acts; the people they ordered to commit them did. They weren't doing it out of vile, but because their stockholders demanded a green upward trend. Regardless, all had one thing in common: they were untouchable. Even the long arm of Lady Law could only keep them contained in cushy confinement for a couple of years. Tops. And after that they would be back on top again.

So it was without a second thought that Suexliegh made his way to his suite, was handed his key, and told that dinner would be promptly at seven. Chilean Sea Bass. He unlocked the door and was greeted, not only by a lavishly furnished bachelor pad, but by Willard Austerio, his old college roommate.

Chapter The Fourteenth
The Burgundy Scoundrels

"THOUGH A LIAR," started Suexliegh, barely containing himself.

"He was true to his word," Austerio grinned a forest of white teeth as he reached out his hand to shake. Willard was a big man with tanned skin who always wore a polo shirt regardless of the situation. Suexliegh took his old friend's hand, shook it, then the two performed an intricately complex series of finger, palm and wrist grapples. The ordeal concluded with a hearty double-handed handshake as the glint of forgotten memories stirred in Suexliegh's eyes, "The Burgundy Scoundrels meet again."

During their collegiate matriculation, Suexliegh and Austerio had formed an exclusive tea-and-crumpet society known as the Burgundy Scoundrels, a consortium of only the finest gentlemen destined to becomes barons of industry and golden parachuted before they could rent a car. One simply couldn't apply to the secret cabal, either you were a member, or you knew nothing about them. Legendary for their invisibility yet overpowering appeal, the Scoundrels were often linked to many of the greatest pranks to ever grace the school's quadrangle.

In the fall, a few unlucky freshmen would arrive, already feeling the chemical withdrawal of homesick malaise, to an unexpected roommate in the form of a liberated lab animal, recently shaved and angry as thunder. In the winter, the dean, on more occasions than he cared to remember, would attempt to leave his office only to find himself trapped behind a wall of ice blocks erected whisper quiet in front of his door, sprinkled with salt to seal the cracks into an impenetrable frozen fortress. Egyptians couldn't have built it better. In the spring, rival sporting teams would mysteriously run off the field in the middle of a match and begin climbing trees in an attempt to lick the sun, a common side effect of LSD-spiked water bottles. In the summer, all of the clocks were reprogrammed to run ten percent faster making each class ten percent shorter. It was a small victory, but a victory nonetheless. Now, the Scoundrels would never claim any of these pranks as their own, mischiefing is unbecoming for such sophisticates, but everyone knew they were the culprits.

"Willard, you old so-and-so, your hairline hasn't changed a hair! Still giving Ms. Nettersworth a jolly rogering?" said Suexliegh with a wink and a nudge.

"I am," smirked Willard, "and it's 'Mrs.' now."

"Made an honest man out of you did she?" elbowed Suexliegh.

A slow grin spread on Austerio's face, "But I'm not the Mister."

Without missing a step Suexliegh burst into congratulatory, adulterous laughter, "You salty dog, you!"

"What about your love life? Is there a love of your life?" Austerio pulled out an elegant smoking pipe and began to puff away on a pinch of earthy Albion tobacco as Suexliegh admired his reflection in the antique mirror. "Or are you looking right at him?"

Austerio's pipe crackled as he took a long draw then exhaled a plume of swirling smoke through the open window. Outside, the setting sun glistened off the rippling tide of an inland bay which surrounded the facility's one hundred acres of spoiled sanctuary.

"Willard, my good man, she's out there, and I'll find her. Everything is destined to go well for me. Quincy even said there was a movie based on me called *It's a Wonderful Life*. In the end, the guy makes a lot of money, betroths the girl and something about Christmas I can't remember."

"Destiny? Don't tell me you believe in God now?" Austerio chuckled, coughing dragon's breath through his nostrils.

"I gave up Catholicism for Lent," said Suexliegh as he locked the door. "So what do you say, should the Scoundrels ride again?"

Chapter The Fifteenth
Nicked

AT PRECISELY 7:15 every morning, each gentleman received a complimentary straight edge shave.

At precisely 7:14 this morning, the two remaining Scoundrels replaced all the shaving cream with sour cream.

At precisely 7:16, the first men were shaven, sniffing at the pungent aroma tickling their nostrils, confused by the flecks of green chives falling into the sink.

At precisely 7:17, everything went completely and horribly awry. A beyond comically obese man for whom the denomination "morbid" was invented, named Bentley Ore, who ironically made his fortune excavating precious gems from the Earth, was nicked ever so slightly on his neck by an errant razor strike.

Now, normally there is no reason to be concerned. An apology, the shaver is reprimanded, perhaps his tip withheld, firm pressure applied until the cessation of bleeding, and life goes on. But not for Mr. Ore. He was lactose intolerant and the moment the soured cream entered his bloodstream, whether through the cut on his chin, or the incessant licking of his lips, he began to bloat, belch and strain like the Hindenburg, at any moment threatening to erupt into gastronomic St. Elmo's fire from the front of his body or the back. Unfortunately for everyone involved, it was both, which quickly offended all of the senses and sent the shave-ees scrambling away, still dripping creamy beards like rabid Santa Clauses. Within seconds, the barbershop had emptied leaving the barber with his gastronomic client fighting not to explode all over the linoleum.

"My belt," moaned Bentley. "Loosen my belt!"

The horrified shaver looked as if the struggling, gassy man had just asked him to hug a pile of TNT that was counting down from three. Holding the shining razor, a tiny drop of blood on the tip, the shaver knew it was in part his fault, but no one deserved the fate that befell him. He reached towards Bentley's bulbous gut, closing his eyes to picture a better world for himself, when a hot, rumbling eructation slowed his progress.

"Here, your tip," said Bentley who wiped his mouth and reached into his Napoleon pocket. He produced a sopping wet fifty as his gut heaved up and down. The shaver hesitated, then shakily reached over for the bribe, a look of pity for his peer and himself, and started fumbling with the sweaty man's leather belt which was stretched tight across his ballooning stomach. With every yank, Ore threatened to Vesuvius all over the poor man, his innards gurgling like a drowning lion. The fat man and little boy struggled in a ballet of torque as the additional notches cut into the belt to accommodate Ore's stature left little room for finagling and a lot of room for the horror that was this man's inability to absorb a simple, dairy-derived sugar molecule. Then, finally, with much strain, the shaver snapped the belt free and toppled to the floor, rolling for cover, as whistling flatus followed by an overwhelming volume of vomit escaped from the man-porpoise who slackened with exhaustion after such a catastrophic failure of human decency.

Suexliegh and Austerio watched the entire event unfold, stunned, from the safety of the hallway. Willard lit his pipe to cover the stench, his eyebrows furrowed as he contemplated everything that he stood for in life. Suexliegh, the man who had seen everything, had never seen this.

"Looks like we're off to a good start," chimed Suexliegh, shaking his head at the horror they had just created.

"That, or we're off to a very bad one," Willard swung the door closed and rubbed his eyes but knew there were some things you cannot un-see.

Chapter The Sixteenth
Ain't That A Sham

"CAN YOU keep a secret?"

Willard pushed up his sunglasses and leaned close to the table, gesturing subtly for Suexliegh to do the same. He did so, cautiously, as before them lay an exquisitely prepared brunch bounty complete with all manner of jams, crêpes, and truffles which threatened to taint his attire with rainbow splotches should he get too close. Around them, other men were doing the same: eating a little and talking a lot. Even though one was away from society, one must watch one's figure or one's suit may not fit anymore.

"On my parents' grave," whispered Suexliegh, gravely.

"Aren't your parents still alive?"

"Yes, well, I hope they would die already so they can use the headstones and plot of land I bought them for their fiftieth wedding anniversary," Suexliegh bit furiously into a preserve filled croissant which squirted menacingly towards his white shirt.

"I don't belong here," a smile appeared on Willard's face. "I didn't commit a crime. I'm just here for the free food while this whole economic dilly-dally blows over. More mimosa?"

"Please," said Suexliegh as Willard topped off his glass, "but I heard you embezzled money from your company?"

"I heard the same. Truth is, I don't even know what embezzlement means," Willard pointed across the table. "See Roger over there?"

Suexliegh followed Willard's finger to an uncomfortably tall, vested man with curly black hair that draped across his forehead like open curtains who was playing cricket with several Indians. The bowler, Mandip, a barrel-chested Middle-Easterner who could easily be mistaken for a pharaoh, bowled a ball too close to Roger's nethers for his liking, causing him to charge towards the other end of the pitch, brandishing his bat twirled above his head. As it was a pleasant, sunny morning for such sporting all over the facility's numerous fields similar scenes of sportsmanship and ill-conceived honor erupted with regularity.

"The government nabbed Roger for racketeering, but because of his wealth and connections he got off with just a slap on the wrist. Now he's here where he has it easier than ever before! He could have his food pre-chewed if he so desired!" Willard exclaimed and he tossed down his fork and knife. "That's what I want! And this is the best part: you know who's footing the bill? The taxpayer. It's brilliant, can't you see? I'm living the life of Riley and not spending a single penny. More people really should consider going to prison."

Suexliegh contemplated this, but found it difficult to concentrate with all the "criminals" shouting "Marcos" and "Polos" from the pool.

"What do you have out there that you don't in here?" Willard remarked as he stuffed a pastry with snail caviar.

"Money," Suexliegh sighed. "How I miss seeing the faces of all those old, dead, white men. The touch of it, the smell of it, the taste..."

While the rest of the world had moved to plastic credit cards, Suexliegh couldn't resist the sensation of freshly inked notes lining his coat, pant and butler's pockets. Every purchase he made was in pure cash, which often caused considerable consternation to anyone ringing him up and everyone waiting behind him in line. Money couldn't buy Suexliegh happiness because money alone is what made him happy. He still claims his greatest business negotiation to be trading the Tooth Fairy one of his teeth for a whole union dollar. With that single bill in his pocket, he was one gram heavier, one gram happier, and able to drink milk through a straw without opening his mouth.

Suexliegh's daydreaming about the subtle green hue of his favorite c-note was shattered by the pierce of a woman's scream. From the sound of it, she was French. And she was pissed.

Chapter The Seventeenth
Croquet Madame

VALERIE PETIT. As respected as a botanist could be; creator of ornate bouquets for Paris's elite bourgeois who requested only the best in beautiful, dying plants. Her husband, a man of old money, died mysteriously of a croquet mallet to the cranium. All signs pointed to Valerie as the culprit: fingerprints on the mallet, blood on her dress, a seething, demonic hatred of her beau, and her intense affinity for the sport of croquet. Yet she wore a different flower in her hair every day to court, cried with such saccharine conviction, and led everyone to believe that a lithe French damsel couldn't possible wield enough force to deliver a crushing blow to a full grown man's skull. Could she? No, thought the jury, so she was set free, only to find herself in prison not three weeks later for telling a police officer where to stick his baguette. For a man, it would have not been a very nice thing to say, but for a lady to do so would be damaging to the reputation of the entire female population.

Valerie Petit was the only female at the facility. It's not that women don't commit crimes; that's just how it worked out. As such, an entire wing of the grounds belonged solely to her; it was originally created for what one would assume to be a decent sized femme fatale populous complete with separate living areas and water closets, the whole shebang. Instead, a lavish female ghost town with just one resident.

Valerie Petit did not sleep, and she hadn't since her fifth birthday having passed out into a sugar coma, which then became a real coma after eating an entire marble bundt cake. Since then, nothing. No dreams. No nightmares. No sheep. To keep herself somewhat sane, she glued her life to a rigorous hourly schedule with metronome precision. At this hour, eleven in the morning, she would always play croquet.

Left and right, bystanders were standing back as Valerie glared at them with disgust, the croquet mallet slung menacingly across her shoulders. Apparently there had been a disagreement over a large sum of money: a foolish man had bet that he could best her, but when Valerie executed a thrilling sextuple peel (a perfect game), the man revoked his claim and tried to wash his hands of it. Being beaten by a woman and losing money was too much of an efface to his masculinity; he would rather be dishonest than dishonored. Suexliegh marched towards them, wearing his winningest grin and combing his hair flat against his head, as he prepared to play arbiter. The man, Finnegan Tufts, held his mallet up like a cross, warding off the evil spirit of Valerie.

"What seems to be the trouble?" Suexliegh stopped and put his hands on his hips, surveying the crime scene.

"No trouble, no trouble a'tall. I was just leaving."

Finnegan casually strolled back towards the bruncheon, hoping to make an escape in broad daylight, but was halted by Valerie who hooked her mallet through his suspenders, trapping him. He struggled to continue walking, and after exercising all the slack he could muster, was rebounded back to his starting place.

"This man made a bet, and he lost," she yawned, her dark, sleepless eyes half closed, "and I expect him to make good on it."

"Yes of course, that is only fair," Suexliegh stated.

"This is between me and the missus," Finnegan stepped up to Suexliegh, puffing out his chest. "Who do you think you are?"

"I think I'm Suexliegh, in fact I know I'm Suexliegh, but I'm disappointed you haven't heard of me," he stuck out his hand for a formal introduction. "My name is Suexliegh, the pleasure is mine."

As Finnegan accepted, Suexliegh pulled him to whispering range.

"Let me show you how it is done," Suexliegh released his grip on the confused man and walked up to Valerie, all smiles.

"Madame, I wish to take over this man's bet, double or nothing."

Chapter The Eighteenth
Double or Nothing

SOMETIMES TAKING A BET one knows they will lose is half the fun. One has the altruistic satisfaction of helping another with their ego and can just enjoy the game for what it is: a game. Competition is the spice of life: a Greyhound race without wagers is much like a deviled egg without paprika. Decent, agreeable, but not thrilling. Betting is what made Suexliegh's clock tick, and for him it was always double, never nothing.

"Seeing as you seem to possess some degree of skill in this recreation, I propose a challenge," Suexliegh snatched Finnegan's mallet and proceeded to engage in a series of strenuous calisthenics. "Points and 'firsts to' are all well and good, but we all know one really judges a person's character by how far they can hit something. So what say you, whomever's ball is whacked furthest wins?"

"Typical American response: whose is bigger, whose is longer."

"Are you saying that yours won't be longer?"

Eyes locked on her opponent, Valerie deliberately reached out and dropped a blood red ball onto a tuft of grass. Suexliegh stepped back, crossed his arms, and smirked. A crowd had formed, unsure whether they were going to see someone lose a lot of money or someone get killed. Either way, they stayed. Valerie sidled into position, stepped her feet to shoulder length, and gave a few practiced strokes to warm up.

"It looks like she's trying to crack an egg," Suexliegh perked up, enjoying the attention. "Don't worry, a chicken won't hatch out of it!" With that Suexliegh began to absurdly mimic a chicken, "clucking" and stamping about. The crowd erupted into cheers and jeers as Valerie gritted her teeth, trying to regain composure.

"I'm sorry, that was quite rude," chuckled Suexliegh, "but sometimes I just can't help myself. Please, continue."

Valerie gave him one more daggerous look, drew back, and then struck the ball with the ten-ton force of rage behind her. The little red ball went sailing, at first skimming the grass, then lifting into an arc through a flock of flailing geese headed South for the winter before bouncing once, twice, three times over a bridge, through a chauffeur's bowed legs, and down into a gully almost out of sight. Hushed, the onlookers turned their gaze from the devastating drive to Suexliegh who idly picked the morning's brunch from his teeth with his pinky finger and tongue.

"Very good, that caviar was very good. My turn?" Suexliegh said, tasting around inside his mouth for more morsels as he lofted a green ball a few times before dropping it with a solid "thud" onto the grass. He stood erect and, blocking the sun from his eyes, gazed out onto the terrain, scrutinizing the landmass for signs of advantage.

"And it looks like he is searching for his lost puppy," Valerie's thick French accent making the insult sound even more condescending and bizarre. "Come home, lost puppy, I want to be in your arms again!"

Valerie smiled, clearly content with her convivial jibe. No one laughed, and it was awkward for everyone.

"Nice," mocked Suexliegh. "I'm kidding it wasn't, but this will be."

Instead of repeating Valerie's success, Suexliegh turned and cracked the ball through the crowd of onlookers who dove out of the way as it rocketed down the pathway on a collision course with a hedgerow.

"Looks like you are about to hit a dead end," she smirked.

Just then, a van on its way to pick up a fresh supply of pillow mints crossed the ball's path as it jumped the curb and ricocheted through an open window, taking refuge in the trunk as the vehicle exited the gate and headed into the city. Suexliegh patted Verena's shoulder.

"That automobile is driving to the Falkenstrom Chocolaterium on the other side of town, twenty-two miles from here. I would say yours is about sixty-five yards. Looks like I win."

Chapter The Nineteenth
Visitors in Triplicate

AND FOR A TIME, Suexliegh enjoyed himself. As much as he loved Quincy, Quincy was only one man. One old man. While in prison, he had an entire staff to wait on him. Torching his crème brûlée, brushing his teeth, pre-heating every chair he was about to sit in. When people talk about prisoner rehabilitation, this is to what they are referring. Not denigration, but vacation. In less than a week, Suexliegh was feeling as chipper as a squirrel searching for a place to hide his nuts. He was relaxed, he was happy, and then he had a visitor.

Suexliegh walked, unescorted, down the winding, tapestry-lined hallways with ambient, recessed lighting, nodding to old friends, smiling at potential new ones, until he reached the visitation room. Forgone were the lonely countertops, telephones, and safety glass windows of standard, replaced instead by two arching applewood chairs positioned to split one's attention between the visitor and the roaring fireplace.

So there it was, the reason Suexliegh loved prison more than chocolate, for the one person he never wanted to see again wasn't in there, but somehow he was sitting right in front of him.

"Hello, Dingle," scowled Suexliegh, who sat and directed his entire attention into the fire.

"Suexliegh," nodded Dingle, who was, without fail, sporting his full riding attire. Either he had arrived on horse, planned to leave on horse, or was simply the most obnoxious human being to have ever lived.

"I thought I'd come by to see how you were holding up in here?" Dingle lazily stoked the fire with his riding crop which singed from the heat. He blew out the sizzling end like an overdone marshmallow.

"I'm fine. Are you dying yet?"

"How blithe," Dingle attempted to scoot his massive seat closer, but the seven stone throne was too heavy and he was left scuffing the ground as he ran in place. Instead, he leaned in.

"I'm fit as a fiddle," seethed Dingle, "but everyone has been talking about how you're a criminal now. Your shine has finally tarnished."

"Oh good! You know they say any publicity is good publicity. Plus everyone likes a bad boy," Suexliegh said with his baddest smile.

"Not everyone! You can't be a jailbird and a gentleman. It's really unfortunate. I do so hope you'll be invited back into society if you ever get out of here."

"If you're going to be there I'd rather not," spat Suexliegh, indignantly. Dingle jumped to his feet in anger but a knock on the doorframe snapped the two gentlemen from their bickering.

"My apologies, sires, but Master Suexliegh you have another visitor," said the droopy-eyed, basset hound of a butler.

"I'll see you at the races," Dingle trotted away. "Good day."

"Why don't you get in some trouble and join me here?" remarked Suexliegh. "Or would you miss your precious pony too much? Say hello to him for me. Now that he can't race anymore I'm sure he's quite lonely."

Tap tap tap tap. Succinct, rapid footsteps betrayed their origins. Quincy had come to see his master.

"Master!" Quincy exclaimed, exasperated, as if he had seen the ghosts of Christmas past, present and future manifested all at once. He rushed to his master's side, taking a creaky knee and holding Suexliegh's hand to his cheek. Soft, the way a baby's manicured hand would be. Quincy pulled a nail file from his coat pocket.

"Sir, I've come to break you out of prison," Quincy's hushed tones echoed off the cavernous sitting room walls. Each oil painting of a prolific quail hunter or foxing hound was an accomplice.

"That won't be necessary," said the sudden voice of Wendell Almond, "you're free to go."

Chapter The Twentieth
Man About Town

THE THING ABOUT PEOPLE of wealth is that they are lucky. And the thing about Suexliegh is that he is wealthy. While he was paying his debt to society, society had gone further into debt. Banks failed. Businesses collapsed. Arrows pointed downwards. The economy was on the tip of everyone's tongue, and they were all parched from talking about it. There simply wasn't enough money in circulation to keep the heart of the country beating. It was anemic, and an overseas transfusion would only delay Wall Street's cardiac arrest long enough for it to die in the ER, instead of in the gutter. What the country needed was a donor, one who was pulsing with cash.

So the courts reconvened, verdicts reconsidered, and sentences were rescinded. Suexliegh was pardoned from all of his prior crimes, but only under the strict condition that he spend money like a lonely trophy wife before the entire economy flat-lined. So, after less than a fortnight in a pampered, prima donna prison, Suexliegh was, thankfully, heading home.

"I'm a free man, Quincy, a free man," Suexliegh turned on the air conditioning and breathed deeply. "Free air never smelled so good."

"It's wonderful to have you back in society, sir," Quincy said sweetly. "We have missed you."

"Is that the royal we, or are you speaking for everyone?" Suexliegh rolled down the window and stuck his head out to survey the world as if for the first time.

Quincy giggled with delight, "Both, sir. I've taken the liberty of getting you back in the public's eye and fulfilling the duties of your parole all in the same evening."

"Do tell," Suexliegh glanced at all the buildings in town that he didn't own… yet.

"A charity art gala at the Piedmonte Piazza thrown by Verena Terena. She's Persian, and exquisitely beautiful."

Suexliegh raised his eyebrows, "Persian, you say? Like the cat?"

"Yes indeed," said Quincy excitedly, "but she's a human."

"Are you trying to set me up for an arranged marriage? I'm too young to settle down."

"I would say you're of the prime marrying age and any woman would be lucky to have you," Quincy turned off the highway and wove through the towering gates of Acropolis Heights. "I'm not saying you need to marry the girl, but a night under the wiles of a female wouldn't be the worst thing. When was the last time you were on a date?"

"Recently," Suexliegh said as he tried to cover his story. "There was that girl that one time, you remember her right? The girl with the hair? I do. We went on so many dates together."

"Oh right, yes yes, the girl with the hair, I remember her now," Quincy looked into the rear view mirror and saw how uncomfortable Suexliegh had become. "Well this girl is even better, she's from a very old and noble family. Their money is in oil. Olive oil to be more precise. Her father controlled the largest olive field this side of the Caspian and makes a king's ransom in profit every year. Sadly, upon choking on a pit from the fruit, he passed away not too long ago leaving the entire inheritance to Verena making her, for all intents and purposes, the richest woman in the world."

Suexliegh's eyebrows raised higher, almost onto his forehead. Now this, more than her beauty, or her family's good name, or the fact that she was a woman, her being comparable to him in terms of monetary status, floated his proverbial yacht.

"Sounds like my kind of girl."

Chapter The Twenty-First
Quincy's Two Cents

"QUINCY, what should I do? I know nothing about women except that they can vote. They *can* vote, yes?"

"Yes."

"Of course, of course. Separate but equal and all that. They're such an enigma to me, what with their long hair and all. Quincy, how do you make your wife happy?"

"Well, when she was still alive, she loved flowers. I still bring them to her."

"But you just said she was dead. How do you do that? Are you a clairvoyant? Can you see ghosts?"

"Certainly not, sir, there is no such thing as ghosts."

"Good good, you had me worried for a moment. So I should bring her flowers? Do women like other plants too? Perhaps I should have a garden installed or one of those glass houses!"

"Calm down, sir, you're making too big a deal of this. You just need to find the way to her heart."

"Through her chest?"

"Not quite."

"Speak plainly for landsakes! I'm not a poet!"

"Just look at all you have to offer. The Suexliegh name is not something to be taken lightly. If I do say so, you're wealthy, you're handsome, and you're modest."

"That's an understatement if I've ever heard one! But can't I just buy her something impressive and be done with it?"

"A gift, that's a wonderful idea. It shows you care, that you're thinking about her. What did you have in mind?"

"I need something giant and majestic."

"Not too overwhelming, mind you, you don't want to appear as if you're trying too hard."

"What about the moon?"

"You're going to buy her the moon?"

"Not enough? Fine then, I'll buy her all three: the big circular one, the half one and the crescent one. That's all of them right? That should suffice."

"Um, quite so, sir, but perhaps you should take her out to dinner, someplace fancy, but not too fancy. You don't want her to think you'll open your wallet at the drop of a hat for just anyone."

"Oh, that's a brilliant idea. Food! Everyone likes food! And I'm having the taste for French cuisine come to think of it."

"Splendid choice."

"Yes yes, I do so love that little place on the Seine."

"Well, perhaps something more local to begin with."

"You mean London?"

"No, a French restaurant."

"A French restaurant in London? Why not just go to France? It's just a puddle hop away!"

"No, a French restaurant in town."

"London is a town."

"No, this town. Which you are currently living in. At this moment. Where I am talking to you. Here."

"Ah, good, very good. I forgot about those dastardly time zones, we'd never make it by supper!"

"I'll hail a taxi."

"Yes, taxi the plane out front, I'll be dressed and ready shortly."

"No, a taxicab."

"Which will take us to the plane?"

Chapter The Twenty-Second
The Gal & The Gallery

"IT'S PERFECT, just like it was five minutes ago, and five minutes before that. I used enough hairspray to make you flammable from a distance of two meters, so please, use caution around candles."

Quincy slowed the Bugatti out front of the museum which had burgundy drapes flowing from the roof like a cascading river, flanking a sign which read, "Art of Darkness: A Charitable Evening Hosted by Verena Terena."

There she stood, Verena herself, like an armed Winged Victory, atop the stairway greeting guests with smiles. She was as beautiful as Quincy promised, with dark features that drew his eyes straight to her. Suexliegh ducked out of sight, cramped low in his chair.

"There she is!" whispered Suexliegh. "Go around the block."

"Pardon me, sir?" Quincy turned to see his master scrunched pathetically under the window.

"I'm not ready, I haven't thought of a good entrance yet. Just once around the block."

"As you wish," Quincy went from brake to gas and continued on, causing the valet who was just reaching out to open the door to tumble to the ground, bystanders to turn up their noses in confusion, and Verena to furrow her brow. The Bugatti cruised right past everyone and just kept going.

"Think, you old dog, think!" Suexliegh tapped his temple with the force of a pile driver, but before he could, they were out front again, this time the valet made sure to keep his distance. Suexliegh sat up just enough to see where they were before turning to Quincy.

"Just one more time around."

So again they went around. Right turn, right turn, right turn, right turn, before a devilish Grinch smile appeared on Suexliegh's face.

"By Jove I've got it! Hurry up Quincy, all this circling is making me ill."

As always, all eyes were on Suexliegh when the car finally did stop, mostly out of pure curiosity about who would perform such a stunt. The suicide doors opened and Suexliegh stepped out, squinting his eyes in preparation for the onslaught of flashbulbs. Being Suexliegh's first public appearance since his release from prison, every photographer within shooting distance pounced like a flock of predators chasing their prey as they channeled him up the stairs straight past Verena without him ever catching her eye.

Who was this man trying to upstage her? she thought, and how can I destroy him for making me look bad?

Suexliegh turned in an attempt to make a formal introduction, but the rip-tide of reporters swept him further inside the museum. Questions about his time in prison, his release, and the food he ate streamed out of the reporters' mouths in an overlapping cacophony, but for once Suexliegh wasn't thinking about himself, he was still hoping to salvage this most important of first impressions. Swimming against the tide soon wore him out, and if he hadn't found sanctuary on a cushioned seat, he would have surely drowned. The sea of reporters was parted as a red-faced Verena stormed towards him.

He flashed his pearliest of whites as she came into view and was she ever a sight to behold: more curves than the Nile from head to toe in a classy, yet voluptuous, evening gown that showed all the right parts, and hid all the rest.

"You must be Verena," Suexliegh began as he reached to kiss her hand, "I've heard so much about you."

Before Suexliegh could get another word out Verena lifted her foot and stamped squarely on his big toe with the spiked heel of her shoe.

Chapter The Twenty-Third
Verena Versus Suexliegh

ONE MUST ALWAYS behave like a gentleman, even in the most adverse conditions. And these were very adverse conditions. Suexliegh clamped his mouth shut and concentrated on not breaking into a fit of hysterics, profanity, and blaspheming as shooting pain streaked up his leg. If steam could have shot out of his ears, it would have. Suexliegh mustered all his strength as he reached out his shaking hand.

"How-"

"Do you do," said Verena, cutting him off. "My name is Verena Terena and I will be your host tonight. Are you a patron of the arts?"

"All of them, but in particular, the flat rectangular kind that you can hang on your wall," Suexliegh struggled to not sound too pained.

The crowd ate it up, laughing to themselves and their neighbors at the joke. *What a cad.* Suexliegh managed a meager smile, but realized his mistake too late as Verena drove her heel further into his toe, twisting it as she went.

"Ow-ow-how about you show me your favorite painting here? I would love to have someone as well-educated on the subject as you show me the ropes," puffed Suexliegh in one long strained breath.

"Fine," Verena turned on her heel and marched away as Suexliegh gasped a lungful of air and recomposed himself. He looked down at the scuff mark on his imported Italian loafers with dismay.

"It's into the fire for you," Suexliegh shook his head at the besmirched shoes.

By now, the opening theatrics had subsided and the guests were perusing the hanging rectangles around the room, pausing at each just long enough to give the impression that they knew what they were looking at and gave a damn. Verena stood alone next to a landscape of a rolling Celtic countryside spotted here and there with sheep draped in a dreary color palette. Suexliegh sauntered over with a slight limp that he tried to hide by only walking on his heels which created the most unsettling clacking sound. Verena did not even bother to turn her head as Suexliegh positioned himself close enough that she could smell his impressive musk. He culled the image with his eyes.

"Ah, it's positively striking! The subtle olive hue, the cross-hatched dappling of the clouds, nimbostratus I believe, and the brushstrokes feel like a young Botticelli if I'm not mistaken," rattled off Suexliegh.

Verena's eyes lingered on the painting for a few moments more as Suexliegh eagerly anticipated her response.

"I think it's shit," she spat.

"Pardon me?" Suexliegh gasped.

"It's garbage. It's not worth the gum off the sole of my shoe. I wish someone would burn this piece and the artist along with it."

Verena marched off without another word, leaving Suexliegh speechless. Now, Suexliegh had never taken much interest in women, he believed he didn't have time or money for them and was content with the life he had made for himself. A life of leisure and plenty, but without the tender caress of the fairer sex. On occasions more than once Quincy had hoped his master would find a lady to fill his heart with love and birdsong and that the two would have many grandchildren for Quincy and his grandchildren to take care of and everyone would live happily ever after. But, it was not to be, for Suexliegh was a picky, picky man with intentions solely outside the realm of husbandry.

Yet there was something about this woman. Something he couldn't quite put his finger on, but surely his heart grew several sizes that day, for Verena was vicious and wealthy, not to mention pretentious and without empathy, condescending to the level of cruelty, while at the same time proper, elegant, beautiful and perhaps the only person on Earth with whom Suexliegh might find love.

Chapter The Twenty-Fourth
Love is Patient

SUEXLIEGH was like a kid in a candy shop who had just gotten his braces off. He followed Verena around as she lasciviously denounced every single painting in the gallery to the status of, as she called it, "dentist waiting room artwork." Her increasingly negative critiques were only matched by Suexliegh's increasingly positive view of her. Verena's tone was so biting, her stare so seething, that he was often at a loss for words. This was a concept entirely foreign to him... the man with a golden tongue speechless? Even when he was struck mute with a bout of pneumonia, Suexliegh quickly learned sign language so that he wouldn't have to miss chin-wagging at a single cocktail party. And he didn't, though no one had any idea what he was saying. Verena was a combination of the two things he desired most: expensive and unattainable. When Suexliegh wanted something, he always got it.

Quincy watched with affection as his young master finally stretched his wings and went in for the kill. This was all he had ever wanted for his master, but at the same time Quincy's heart was beginning to ache, for what if when Suexliegh found a mate he no longer needed, or Heaven forbid, wanted, an elderly butler tending to his every need? He would have a wife for that. Quincy shuddered at the thought. No, his master would not forsake him. I was there at his birth, Quincy said to himself, and I will be there at his death too.

Suexliegh cracked a joke which made the corner of Verena's lip curl into the most imperceptible of smiles and at once Quincy knew he had her. Little Master Suexliegh, Quincy thought, all grown up. Quincy left the two in peace and made his way out into the crisp evening, slowly taking one step at a time down to the Bugatti. His aged bones creaking, he slid into the car and waited alone for his master to return.

As the night melted away, one by one the guests left until it was only Suexliegh and Verena. Neither had ever been in such a situation before and rightly had no idea what they were to do. A kiss was out of the question, on the lips at least. As was a handshake, too conventional. Neither of them had ever hugged another human being before so that was not even an option. They took a long moment staring into each other's eyes, which, to outside observers must have seemed romantic, but inside the two were racing to find a diplomatic solution to saying "goodbye." Suexliegh decided to combine the best two options, he took Verena's hand, and kissed it, with a twinkle in his eye. Verena was flattered, she had never had a man, or woman for that matter, behave in such a caring, intimate way before and it terrified her. She withdrew her hand, said not a word, and briskly marched down the stairs to her waiting car which soon slipped away into the city.

Suexliegh smiled and looked up at the few stars that were permitted to shine within the city's light-polluted limits. He breathed deeply and took each stair down to the street with great conviction. At the curb stood Quincy, beaming with pride, holding the door open as always. Suexliegh grabbed Quincy with both hands about the neck and pulled the old man towards him so that he could firmly plant a kiss on his forehead. He then slid into the backseat and laid down on the cushions, looking up through the skylight, his face shining brighter than the moon.

Quincy touched a hand to his forehead and chuckled to himself. Oh, to be young and in love! He hobbled around to the driver's seat and started the car like he had done so many times before.

"Where to, sir?"

"Wherever you like."

Chapter The Twenty-Fifth
Quincy Jr. and the Wonderful World of Dating

THE FOLLOWING MORNING Suexliegh woke to the gentle chirping of birdsong. At first, he thought they were outside his window, but no, they seemed to be coming from somewhere inside. Suexliegh shot upright in bed and looked around only to see the most peculiar sight: Quincy Jr. chirping like a bird.

"Quincy Jr.!"

Quincy Jr. finished whistling a beautiful warbler tune then rushed over to Suexliegh's bedside with a breakfast tray in hand. He was grinning with overwhelming delight.

"Good morning, sir! I brought you breakfast exactly as my father told me you prefer it: blood-orange juice, ostrich eggs sunny side up, just like today's beautiful weather, and a snifter of snake oil. Always good for what ails ya, as they say," Quincy Jr. beamed.

"Quincy Jr.!" Suexliegh said again.

"Yes, sir?" Quincy Jr. stood at attention, one gloved hand folded neatly in the small of his back, the other still holding the serving tray under Suexliegh's nose.

"What are you doing here? I thought I told you to go out into the world and find a woman!" Suexliegh fired back.

"I did find a woman," said Quincy Jr., "in fact I found many."

"And? And!? Don't make me wait all day," Suexliegh scooted back against the headboard and picked up the snifter.

"And it wasn't to be," Quincy Jr. whispered, downtrodden. "Perhaps I'm not cut out for the birds and the bees. Besides, I've found my love in life and that's serving you."

Suexliegh choked on the snake oil.

"Wasn't to be? What kind of attitude is that?" Suexliegh jumped out of bed. "Love is a wily beast and when it rears its ugly head you must grab it by the teeth, shake with much vigor and say, 'You listen here Love, you listen to me damn well and good and do as I say!"

Quincy Jr. blinked several times, hoping every time he opened his eyes he would somehow understand.

"Sir, I don't quite understand what you're getting at."

"You don't have to understand, you just have to do it! Take a page from me. Why, just last night I shook that love beast right in its teeth and now I'm halfway on the road to being made an honest man."

"My father told me, sir, congratulations! I hear she is quite the catch. Should we expect the pitter patter of little feet anytime soon?"

"Her feet are normal sized and don't let your father tell you otherwise!" Suexliegh roared as he plucked a tuxedo out of his closet. Like a flash, Quincy Jr. was there attempting to wrestle it away so he could dress him, but Suexliegh resisted.

"I can do it myself," Suexliegh quipped and stood up on one foot, aiming his other at the pant leg. "Easy does it, one at a time."

On the first attempt, Suexliegh put his pants on backwards, and the second, inside out, but the third time, they went on like a charm and were soon zipped and buttoned. A three-year-old couldn't have done better.

"See? And they say prison doesn't work. I can put on my own two pants now without any help. You saw it, didn't you?"

Quincy Jr., feeling left out, was on the verge of tears.

"I did, sir, well done," Quincy Jr. sniffled.

"You know what? Maybe you should stay at the manor for a bit longer so you can learn a thing or two from me about dating. I am, after all, an expert," said Suexliegh, full of piss and snake oil. "I plan to have my lady love over for dinner this very evening so you can see exactly what happens when love rears its ugly head."

II.
Venus

Chapter The Twenty-Sixth
That Very Evening

IT WAS a week for firsts. Suexliegh traipsed down the long, curling staircase into the foyer, picked up the phone, used his own fingers to dial, and attempted to call Verena using an old-fashioned candlestick telephone. Quincy, always at least one step ahead of his master, had thoughtfully taped her number to the rotary dial.

"Quincy! What are these numbers for?" Suexliegh said.

"It's Verena's telephone address. I'm positive she's awaiting your call," Quincy's voice echoed through the mansion, it could have come from anywhere.

With confidence, Suexliegh picked up the receiver, spun the number dial in the correct order, and waited for Verena to pick up. One ring. Then another. Then ten more, but no answer. Suexliegh hung up.

"Quincy! It just kept ringing!" Suexliegh shouted.

"Perhaps she's in the shower."

"I very much like the thought of that."

"Try her again in just a moment. She wouldn't be away from her phone for too long as she knows you will be calling her to arrange a proper date," said the disembodied voice of Quincy.

Suexliegh sat and waited, watching the littlest hand on his watch make several laps around the track, until he couldn't wait any longer.

"I can't wait any longer, I'm trying her."

Once again, he dialed the numbers and once again the line just kept ringing. Suexliegh's smile, which he had conjured up in order to sound frisky and alert on the phone, slowly became flaccid as the ringing continued and didn't stop. He hung up.

"Quincy... I don't understand," Suexliegh sighed sadly.

A moment later, Quincy whisked down the stairs to his master's side having heard the sigh from the other side of the mansion. It was a rare event when Suexliegh sighed as Quincy worked diligently to keep him satisfied at all points in time. In fact, the only other time Quincy could remember it happening was at his yacht's christening when Suexliegh realized he would have to waste a perfectly good bottle of champagne in order to send his boat off properly. Quincy, the quick thinker that he was, floated in a dinghy below the bow and caught the bubbly champagne, and shards of glass, as it fell, into a container for his master to enjoy later. Crisis averted.

"Where is she?" Suexliegh whimpered.

"She... she must be traveling, yes, that's it, she must be out of the country and unreachable. There really is no other explanation for this. You know, I believe I heard her mentioning she was going home overseas to oversee the placement of a few new olive groves, yes, I know I heard it so that's where she must be and shame on her for not letting you know," Quincy wheezed in one long rambling breath. It was a lie, yes, but sometimes lying is the only way to save someone's feelings. 'My, don't you look pretty in that dress' is much more considerate than 'My, if that dress could talk it would say, "Get this fat woman out of me!"'

"Maybe she just has no interest in me," Suexliegh stood up and melancholically walked away.

"Not interested!?" Quincy leapt to his feet. "Come now you're the most desired man in the world. Just look at you."

Quincy spun him towards a mirror revealing his statuesque bust in the reflection. Suexliegh didn't know the meaning of the expression "bed head." He slowly began to smile as he ogled his own visage.

"I am rather attractive."

"And rich. So you're one step up from being a deity. And I know just the thing to make you feel better: let's go buy you a new suit."

<u>Chapter The Twenty-Seventh</u>

James Henry Stuart Francis Sawyer Plantagenet Fitzgerald-Cavendish

Or, the Man With Eight Names

JAMES HENRY Stuart Francis Sawyer Plantagenet Fitzgerald-Cavendish, the twenty-seventh titular Baron Charles Und Gotha: if there was ever a man to buy a suit from, it was him. For short, he went by Dylan, but Suexliegh liked to use his full name whenever possible, or whenever it wasn't, simply the more regal "James Henry." With the soft, gentle facial features of a prince, and a rectanguloid body shape, James Henry was in a class of his own both in upbringing and style.

Due to years of royal intermarriage, he was cursed with the notorious "Habsburg Jaw," a form of prognathism which left him with a rearward sloping chin and overall weak-looking mandible. Thankfully, due to the invention of modern orthodontia, his malady was corrected with numerous painful surgeries, and replaced with a proud, jutting chin more fitting his royal heritage. James Henry sported a coiffed, waving brown mane and pale complexion (he always carried an umbrella to block both the rain and shine) which was made more striking by his dark hand-tailored suits, built with a brilliant blue lining, which he had to receive special permission from the Lord of Skye in Scotland to use, and a secret rear pouch where he could stuff dead quail were he to wear the jacket out hunting. Like all good gentlemen, he was never without two things: his pipe and his gun.

James Henry worked downtown in the financial district at a store called Trolley Car Clothier, a throwback to the popular turn-of-the-century conveyance. The name was very fitting for a store that sold only high-end suits, hats, britches, belts, cuff links, hosiery, suspenders, pipes, canes, monocles, and all forms of accoutrements for the discerning patron. As many of these forms of attire had long since gone out of fashion it would appear to the average bystander that the store made no sales at all because hardly anyone ever went in, or perhaps that it was a front for a well-dressed mafia. Suexliegh's need for such fine things was the only reason Trolley Car Clothier was in business at all so every time he opened the front door it was like the second coming of a rich Christ.

James Henry was trusted with keeping Suexliegh in only the best and most fashionable garments indefinitely. Last year it was a woolen worsten cheviot vested suit in a very handsome medium grey Donegal tweed with multicolor flecks, for formal occasions, complete with an applewood shaft walking stick which was a real hit at the one and only gala he wore it to. As it was springtime, James Henry had a selection of lighter vests and britches to be worn in the heat, along with an imported ivory comb whittled from the tusk of an extinct Wooly Mammoth.

The two met when they were paired up at a charity golfing tournament in Edinburgh on a blustery autumn morning which was far more suited for sitting oneself in front of a roaring fire with a shot of Islay scotch than anything outdoors. After the first hole, it quickly came to Suexliegh's attention that he was a much better player than poor James Henry. Not one for losing, Suexliegh found a loophole: he would hit his ball, far and true down the fairway, while James Henry would purposefully (and sometimes not) drive his ball into a nearby thicket. Suexliegh then followed James Henry to help "retrieve" the ball, but in reality would actually be the one to drive it out right onto the green when no one was watching. The pair won and James Henry was nicknamed "Lucky Strike" within the links community for his seemingly miraculous sophomore shots. James Henry considered himself forever in Suexliegh's debt for his face-saving swing and swore an oath to do whatever he could to repay him. In his case, that meant becoming his personal tailor.

Chapter The Twenty-Eighth
Well Suited

"IT'S GOOD to see you again, you old hand," James Henry said lightly as Suexliegh walked through the front of the shop, arms wide and smile even wider. Quincy held the door open then followed him in like a silent shadow on the wind.

"James Henry," Suexliegh started as he picked out a walking stick from a nearby bin and began twirling it, "you haven't aged a day! You must tell me your secret."

"If you promise not to tell another soul," James Henry, who squeezed himself out from behind the display counter, suddenly became very serious.

"Quincy, shut your ears," Suexliegh commanded, using his cane to reach up and pluck a deerstalker hat, popularized by the Sherlock Holmes novels, from a hanging rack. Ever since he was a child, Suexliegh had been fascinated by Sherlock's crime solving prowess and fancied himself an apt gumshoe as well. For years he would yell "Watson!" and Quincy would come running.

"Yes sir," Quincy said as he plugged his ears and turned around so as not to be tempted to read lips. James Henry held up three fingers.

"There are three things in descending order of quantity," James Henry began, "one glass of red wine, one tablespoon of olive oil, and one drop of-"

"Snake oil?" Suexliegh grinned.

James Henry's eyes grew wide.

"Why yes? How did you know?" James Henry said with an ounce of skepticism.

"I use the very same to give me youth and vigor, an ancient secret from my one-hundred-plus-year Oriental acquaintance Vi-Yee Huang. Perhaps you know him?" Suexliegh raised an eyebrow but continued speaking without giving James Henry a moment to respond. "For me, it's one glass of the blackest stout, one tablespoon of snake oil, 'dLagon oiR' as ol' Vi-Yee would say, and a nibble of dark chocolate."

"But enough about me," Suexliegh exclaimed as he tossed the deerstalker onto an umbrella stand which spun around and around. "A female who shall not be named did not answer when a gentleman caller called, and that gentleman caller who called was me. So I'm hoping to take my mind off her by putting my mind on me."

James Henry shook his head with a knowing sigh.

"Women: can't live with them, can't continue your family's lineage without them. Follow me, I think I know just the one."

James Henry led the way through the tiny indoor labyrinth which, as per usual, had no other patrons. Walls lined with tweed coats and waistcoats, untouched. Rotating displays of neckwear and knitwear, un-rotated. Rows and rows of caps, unworn. At least the place looked nice.

A flickering, fire-lit back room doubled as James Henry's office and was where he kept all of Suexliegh's pre-tailored articles of clothing. After years of hemming the same lengths over and over again, James Henry had memorized Suexliegh's measurements which were all in handy whole numbers, no quarters or halves for old Suex, making it easy to have everything ready the moment he walked in. Hanging from an armoire like the clothing of a deflated ghost was a crimson coat with bone buttons, bowler cap, and plaid wool pants. Suexliegh's eyes lit up with joy.

"I've been keeping this for a special occasion," James Henry said proudly as Suexliegh rushed over, stripped nearly naked, and put on the suit. Being the second time he had dressed himself, it was far less catastrophic.

"You're going to need this too."

James Henry held out a double-barreled shotgun.

Chapter The Twenty-Ninth
Fowl Play

"PULL!"

Bang!

"Pull!"

Bang!

"Stop yelling that, you'll startle the birds!" whispered James Henry as he crept low through the underbrush, his shotgun resting in the crook of his arm. "And stop shooting the tree trunks!"

Suexliegh unloaded both barrels into a nearby tree, splintering the trunk in an explosion of wooden shrapnel which teetered then toppled onto the forest floor. A plume of leaves and dust whirled up around them as a family of quail, frightened by the noise, leapt into the air and flew away.

"Down!" James Henry whirled around and pointed the gun straight at Suexliegh's head who ducked with a yelp. Bang! But the family of quail kept flying, unscathed.

"Damn!" James Henry threw his hat angrily on the ground, then quickly picked it up, dusted it off, and placed it on his head. Suexliegh chuckled to himself.

"What a terrible miss! Maybe you'd hit them if they were the size of a zeppelin! Haha!" Suexliegh slapped his knee and caused his shotgun to go off into the dirt. James Henry jumped back in alarm as Suexliegh continued laughing feverishly.

"That was a close one! Aren't we having fun?" Suexliegh wiped a tear away from his eye, and in doing so, accidentally lifted up his shotgun so it was pointed precariously towards James Henry. From then on, he decided to stand behind Suexliegh. "*I am.* I've completely forgotten about what's-her-name and I won't mention her again. Being out here in the wild with a fellow red-blooded male doing manly things, why, I never realized the only way to truly feel alive was to make something else dead! Verena would die if she could see me now!"

The two stalked in silence through the mountain forest as low hanging mist collected into dew and formed droplets that pitter-pattered onto the leaves below. Sniffing around at their feet was James Henry's basset hound, Seymour, whose belly and ears swept the ground as he trotted. He might not have looked it, but the dog was demonically bloodthirsty and often known to eat birds whole instead of retrieving them for his master.

Suexliegh began to whistle a favorite sea shanty when suddenly James Henry placed a hand on his shoulder, silencing him. A low cooing sound echoed somewhere in the fog. James Henry's head snapped towards it. He cupped his hands around his mouth and made the most peculiar chortling noise, his eyes bugged out in concentration. A branch snapped. Like a flash, a lone quail burst from the bushes and belted for the sky. James Henry, not wanting to miss again, pushed Suexliegh aside and crouched for better accuracy. He squeezed his non-aiming eye shut, peered down the barrel, sighted the fowl, and pulled the trigger.

The bird stopped flapping but continued its aerial arc until it thudded into a nearby field. Seymour galloped after it, leaping through the thicket before pouncing on the wounded bird which he proceeded to clamp in his canines and shake vigorously before happily trotting back to his master.

Suexliegh knew they were out hunting but he didn't think they would actually *kill* anything. The only thing he had ever killed was a clay pigeon and even then he felt a tinge of remorse.

"Good shot, old chum," blubbered Suexliegh, holding back tears, "well hunted. She will look beautiful above your mantel."

"Mantel?" bellowed James Henry. "Surely you're joking, we're going to eat it!"

Chapter The Thirtieth
Dining With A Dynasty

PLINK. Plink. Plink.

The sound of bouncing metal on porcelain became the musical accompaniment for the evening. With nearly every mouthful, diners would painfully crunch down on hidden pieces of birdshot lodged in the tender quail breast. One of the drawbacks to James Henry being a perfect marksman was that the bird was peppered with shot. A wager had started that whomsoever had the most pellets at the end of the night got to keep the head.

Earlier that day, as Suexliegh was still in the throes of shock due to witnessing his first death, James Henry proceeded to root out and massacre what might well have been the entire quail population in the area. After their pouches were loaded full, the two were forced to pack the birds wherever they could for the long walk back to camp: into their belts, down their shirts, and in their hats. At one point, James Henry contemplated leaving the rest behind, but Suexliegh insisted that they be given a proper burial in his stomach. It was the very least they could do.

As was customary after the first successful hunt of the season, James Henry would throw an elaborate dinner party for high society gentlemen and women who he acquainted, and subsequently tailored, over the years. One diner in attendance, Royland Hogarth, the slovenly son of a wealthy railroad tycoon, was a man Suexliegh despised instantly. No, not because railroads were hemorrhaging money left, right and center to more modern means of transportation and Royland was quickly losing the legacy his father had made for him, it was because he was a clumsy eater.

When Suexliegh ate he made sure to give every course its due attention and in the correct order as designed by the chef. Tonight, it was a French onion soup to start, a Beluga caviar salad on the side, followed by quail with wild mushrooms and truffle risotto, and a fresh strawberry cheesecake for dessert. A perfectly balanced meal blending savory and sweet and worth a good sniff to get the olfactory going before eating. Suexliegh consumed the correct way: he cracked through the golden brown cheese and scooped spoonfuls of the soup until the entire bowl was drained, he washed the first course down with a light Chardonnay, then he turned his attention to the salad, making sure to get each flavor with every forking, alternatively smelling and eating his food to obtain maximum satisfaction, he then washed down this with a sultry Merlot, turning next his attention to the quail which he dissected like a skilled surgeon saving just enough room for the triangular prism that was the cheesecake. Perfection.

Royland was not. He gorged on his cheesecake *first*, shaving off the strawberries so as not to get anything remotely healthy with his dessert. Ate caviar off his *butter knife*. Drank his wine with a *straw*. Dipped his quail in the soup using his chilled *salad fork*. Not to mention *skipping* the salad entirely! All the courses blurred together on the plate like a Pollock, no no, a *child's* finger painting.

Suexliegh had never been so disgusted in his life, and if he had a glove to wear he would surely have backhanded Royland, but the thought of touching the glutton's face sans protection seemed deleterious to his well-being. So instead he let his words speak louder than his actions, spinning whimsical stories about his wealth, influence, and virility growing his aura ever larger as his fellow diners cheered and smiled along with him, all the while Royland sunk further and further into his seat, into his failing empire, spooning the mush he created into his mouth, bite by bite, until it was all gone.

Chapter The Thirty-First
The Unfairer Sex

IT IS A TRUTH universally acknowledged, that a single man in possession of a good fortune must be in want of a woman.

"Perhaps I'll just wait near the telephone, she could have been trying to call this entire time!" announced Suexliegh excitedly as he plopped down next to the telephone. He did not believe in answering machines, one either spoke directly to him or not at all, so he had to make sure he was present at all times if someone was trying to reach him.

"Of course that is what happened. There really can be no other explanation. She is most enamored with you, you know," said Quincy as he placed an assortment of fine cheeses, olives, nuts and crackers onto the table just in case his master might get hungry while waiting. The olives were from Verena's orchard and Quincy had been serving them to his master ever since he made up his mind to arrange the two. He thought of them as tiny, oblong, love potions.

"I'll just keep myself entertained right here on this seat until the telephone ring-a-lings," said Suexliegh as he munched on some cave-aged emmenthaler. "Yes-siree, any minute now I'll be hearing her lovely voice magically teleported from her luscious lips to my hungry ear like the sweet chorus of a mother quail."

Suexliegh rocked back and forth in his chair, "Any minute now."

But time ticked on and Quincy became nervous. He first considered calling from a separate line and attempting to mimic Verena's voice claiming the reason she sounded so gravely was due to "mild bronchitis," but even with love blinding him, Suexliegh was no fool.

"Quincy, I've never asked anyone this before," whispered Suexliegh, his eyes searching for answers, "but did I do something… wrong?"

Quincy leapt to the defense; the "W" word was strictly off limits.

"Right and wrong is tricky business with the fairer sex," Quincy began as Suexliegh lethargically got up and trudged down the grand master hallway of the estate past numerous painted portraits of himself, one for every year of his life. "What you perceive to be right is often what they perceive to be wrong, and sometimes doing what you think they think is right is also wrong, but when you alert them to one of their own wrong doings, even though you are in the right, you feel as if you've done wrong too, even when you were right in the first place! Am I not making any sense at all?"

"No, you're making perfect sense," Suexliegh paced, arms folded, tapping his chin in careful contemplation. "So... I should do the opposite of what I think is right?"

"Yes and no. But not always," offered Quincy, trying to justify his thoughts with an uncertain wave of his hand.

"Well then... I shouldn't do anything at all and let her make the decision?" proclaimed Suexliegh.

Quincy nodded, "As often as possible."

"But what if I am right?"

"You're not."

"But what if I am?"

"It does not matter."

Their soft footsteps echoed in the hallway as the two walked side by side in silence.

"Quincy, I'm beginning to think I know nothing about women."

"No one ever will."

Then, like the flash of a mighty surprise, the doorbell rang.

"It's her!" Suexliegh shouted and was halfway back down the hallway in the blink of an eye, his long arm outstretched with a smile as he opened the door.

"Verena!"

Chapter The Thirty-Second
The Man Who Lived One Hundred Lives

IT WAS NOT Verena at all, but a solid, leathery, sun-aged man with a bulbous red nose and striking blue eyes that could kill an ox at one hundred paces, who hung two paint buckets from his work-worn hands and grinned from ear to ear. Dimitri the Painter, he was called. No, not Dimitri whose occupation was painting, he was "Dimitri the Painter" as if "the" were his middle name and "Painter" his last, and he always referred to himself as such regardless of circumstance or familiarity with whomever he was speaking.

There are few men with more myth surrounding them than Dimitri the Painter, and rightfully so: it was as if he were dripped straight out of Homer's pen. Legend had it he met his wife while performing a dance on top of a wine glass, which was on top of a wine bottle, which was on top of a chair. Rumors circulated that he had Poseidon-like proficiency with a trident having killed over one hundred and fifty octopi during an annual Aegean festival. He kick-boxed a kangaroo and won. He died twice, once on the field of battle, and again during an unexplained event in Egypt, both times giving death the finger. He never went to the dentist yet had flawless teeth. However, his having put a lion in a headlock has been disputed, but when Dimitri twinkled his eyes, you knew he was telling the truth, even when he wasn't.

"Hello Mr. Big-Shot, how are you?" spouted Dimitri in an accent so thick one might swear he was still speaking Greek. Though he was fluent in seven languages and had been in the States for several decades, he still had not mastered the American accent. If he was sober, you could perhaps understand him. If he was drunk, there wasn't a chance in Hell. If you were both drunk, it all made perfect sense, even when it didn't.

"My wife call you... say come over, eat, have some wine, relax, but

I hear nothing. Kaput. If you no like my wife's cooking, okay fine, no problem for me, all I'm saying is you disappear, man!" Dimitri locked eyes with Suexliegh who slowly turned his smile into a straight line.

"Sorry old chap, I've been busy with matters most difficult," Suexliegh shot his collars and peered over his property hoping to see Verena's car rounding the bend.

Dimitri squinted at him, "A woman?"

"Why yes, however did you know?" exclaimed Suexliegh, flabbergasted. Adding to his list of fables, apparently Dimitri could read minds as well.

"Some things I just know," Dimitri dusted off his hands. "So who is she? Why she not here? You think she afraid of me?"

Dimitri playfully began jogging in place like a boxer and pretending to punch Suexliegh on the shoulder. A jab, a cross, an uppercut. At first the hits were light, but soon he was striking with unnecessarily strong force. Not wanting to lose face, Suexliegh put up his dukes and began fisticuffing. Dimitri's eyes lit with excitement and he let out a loud belly laugh at the sight.

"Come on then! Put them up! Put them up, you scallywag!" said Suexliegh as he hopped about with mesmerizingly fast and fancy footwork, pecking away at Dimitri with quick, bird-like jabs that landed light as a feather. All the while, Dimitri kept laughing which only served to provoke Suexliegh, "Oh-ho, take your best shot, boss! The only thing that can kill me is explosion."

Suexliegh planted and swung full force and landed a fist straight on his nose. Quincy gasped. A small trickle of blood dribbled onto Dimitri's lip. He sniffed, sucking it back up, and resumed his laughing. After the adrenaline and shock wore off, Suexliegh joined in with a hearty laugh as well. Quincy, not wanting to be rude, chuckled too.

"She's just a girl," Suexliegh finally said as a lone Rolls Royce rolled up the driveway. "Just a girl."

Chapter The Thirty-Third
A Very Important Date

PICK ME UP at eight.

That's all the letter said, not to anyone, or from anyone, but Suexliegh knew. Maybe it was because the chauffeur who handed it to him said, "This is from Ms. Terena," but he would have known anyway.

"Does she mean eight o'clock tonight? As in this evening?" asked Suexliegh, an edge of panic in his voice.

"I believe so, sir," said the chauffeur who twitched his manicured mustache back and forth like a mouse. Suexliegh immediately turned on his heel and marched straight back into the house.

"Quincy, hurry, we haven't a moment to lose!" The last thing Dimitri and the chauffeur saw was Suexliegh and Quincy clamoring up the stairs on all fours like a pair of wild apes.

"Have fun, bay-bee!" called Dimitri after them as he popped open a fresh bucket of white paint and began delicately applying a new coat to the front banister. "Come up some time and don't disappear on me, man!"

The chauffeur tipped his hat to no one in particular and walked back to the car all the while listening in on the terrible cacophony of Suexliegh yelling from within the manor. Inside was even worse as both Quincy and Quincy Jr. circled around Suexliegh mixing and matching nearly every piece of clothing he had. Most people believe in the power of first impressions, but Suexliegh knew the importance of second impressions. On first appearance, anyone can be Prince Charming, but being able to sustain that image to a second, third, fourth, and even fifth impression is how you win the game of life. Over time everyone's façade shows cracks or flaws as their actual, unkempt self breaks through the chiseled exterior. The teeth not so white. The hair not so thick. The wallet not so green. But like a true warrior, Suexliegh was ready for battle: shoes polished, pants cuffed, belt oiled, shirt tucked, coat cuff-linked, and smile bright.

"May I?" said Quincy Jr. as he raised a tooth brush and paste.

Suexliegh extended his mouth into an oversized smile and Quincy Jr. got to work immediately. Previously a job his father had been in charge of, Junior relished the privilege of brushing his master's teeth for the first time. Yes, he thought, they were as smooth, aligned and plaque-free as he always imagined.

"Now just remember, a woman most likes a man to be himself. Since you are yourself that shouldn't be very hard," counseled Quincy.

"But what if she doesn't like who I am?"

"Then it wasn't meant to be."

"That's not making me feel any better," huffed Suexliegh. "I suppose I'll have to bring out the big guns tonight."

He stood on tip-toes and reached above his dresser, pulling out a small wooden cask from a hidden recess. He unscrewed the cask's top and slid out a finger-sized vial filled with an iridescent liquid. Carefully, he pulled out the dropper and placed one drop on either side of his neck. The vial contained musk from when Suexliegh was eighteen years old and the most sexually virulent he would ever be. Luckily, even at that age, he had the forethought to secrete and bottle his pheromones into a private essence which he could use to olfactorily intoxicate potential mates. After securing his hair into a rock-solid swoop and placing a handkerchief into his breast pocket, Suexliegh was ready for the night of his life.

"Good luck, sir. Though I know you don't need it," chimed Junior.

"Thank you, my good young man, and good luck to yourself!"

"Me? What for?" laughed Quincy Jr. hesitantly as Suexliegh tossed him the keys.

"You're driving."

Chapter The Thirty-Fourth
Gondolas on the Pond

QUINCY JR., nervous though he was, made it all the way to Verena's abode in downtown without so much as a missed turn signal or striking a pedestrian. They slowed to a stop outside a towering downtown skyscraper precisely at eight. Suexliegh had to press his face against the glass just so he could peer up to the topmost penthouse condo where his ladylove lived. Her light clicking off was his cue. He exited the car and tried out a variety of poses that he thought might impress her until falling back on the default: relaxed, leaning on car, smiling. As she lived on the top floor, and the elevator not as quick as he hoped, Suexliegh was forced to hold his dashing pose for several minutes as pedestrians passed by staring at him in confusion. Soon, the click-click-click of Verena's high heels heralded her arrival. She was dressed in a slinky black dress that sparkled like a supernova every time the light hit.

"Verena… you look dazzling," he said, extending his arm to help her into the car, "and you smell even better."

Verena scoffed but quickly covered it with a polite, "thank you" as Quincy Jr. drove the two off into the night.

Ever since Suexliegh met Verena, he had been planning this romantic evening, one that would make anyone with even half a heart fall in love with him. *Cortona Osteria* was an exclusive Italian restaurant built on the docks of a beautiful inland lake in the heart of downtown that had an exclusive, multi-year waiting list. Luckily for Suexliegh, he owned the restaurant and always had a private table on reserve.

A slick, wax-mustachioed maître d' awaited them at the door with a *buona sera*. Suexliegh replied with a wink and the man knew just what to do. Inside, the restaurant had the charm of old Tuscany, and rightfully so, when Suexliegh had eaten at the very same restaurant in Italy, he purchased it on the spot and had it brick by brick transported back to the States lakeside. On the walls hung paintings by famous Florentinian artists accompanied by musicians playing nothing but traditional Italian instruments. As they walked through the restaurant, nearly all the diners had their eyes caught by him and the murmuring began. Is that *Suexliegh*? Since when was *he* let out? Who *is* she? I wonder if he met *her* in prison?

"I decided Italy was too far away," began Suexliegh as he led her outside onto the docks, "we'd never make it by supper time, so this is the next best thing."

Suexliegh gestured towards an actual Venetian gondola bobbing peacefully against the wharf with a lantern hanging above a small table for two.

"You can't be serious," Verena monotoned with more than an ounce of reservation.

"I most certainly can," replied Suexliegh, already heading down the wooden walkway.

"But I get... seasick," Verena shouldered her shawl against a cool blowing breeze.

"I don't know about you but I've never heard about 'lake-sickness' so I'm sure you'll be quite alright," Suexliegh's eyes twinkled. "Trust me."

Verena stepped uneasily onto the wobbly gondola and fell into her seat as Suexliegh hopped in after her.

"And if you feel the urge to vomit you can easily do so over the side," Suexliegh added.

Their gondolier, a bright-eyed young man festooned with traditional black and white striped shirt and red-ribboned hat, pushed them off from the docks and out into open water where they drifted beneath city lights shimmering on the peaceful lake.

Chapter The Thirty-Fifth
Antipasto

"I HOPE you like pasta," chime Suexliegh excitedly as the gondolier rowed them deeper into the lake.

"It would be a little late now if I didn't," Verena quipped.

Suexliegh burst into laughter loud enough for the land-dwelling eaters to hear and be jealous of their good times.

"Have you ever been," asked Suexliegh as he dipped a piece of bread into a rocking dish of olive oil and balsamic vinegar, "to *Italia* I mean?"

"Many times, yes," said Verena, lightening up as she got her lake-legs. "The downfall of my Papa's waistline was due to gelato."

Suexliegh grabbed his stomach with both hands.

"Him and me both!"

"WHEN THE MOON HITS YOUR EYE LIKE A BIG PIZZA PIE THAT'S AMORE!" crowed the gondolier majestically as he suddenly began singing so loudly he drowned out everything Suexliegh was saying. Suexliegh turned around and tried to get the gondolier's attention, but, his eyes closed in concentration of singing so passionately, he did not stop.

"Excuse me, sir. My good man! If you could please keep your singing voice to a minimum the lady and I are attempting to converse!" shouted Suexliegh, his hands cupped around his mouth for maximum throw.

TWEET!

A loud whistle snapped both men to attention. Verena removed two fingers from her mouth and smiled cutely, "Sorry."

The gondolier looked at them with puppy dog eyes, "Did I-a do somethin' wrung?"

Suexliegh cleared his throat.

"I was attempting to court this lady here," Suexliegh gestured over his shoulder to Verena who shook her head in embarrassment, "so if you could please keep it down that would be most appreciated. *Grazie.*"

Suexliegh turned back to Verena and took her hands in his.

"I'm so sorry for that," he cocked his head towards the gondolier and said loud enough for him to hear, "some people have no decency. Would you care for wine?"

"Please."

Suexliegh snapped his fingers and, emerging from the darkness, another gondola sporting a waiter proudly perched on the bow, holding an opened bottle of wine and two glasses sidled broadside. Without stopping, the server placed both glasses in front of the guests, poured a fine Chianti, and floated away into the ether.

"So tell me, Verena-"

"*When the moon hits your eye like a big pizza pie that's amore,*" whispered the gondolier in a most unsettling way.

"Mr. Gondolier!" Suexliegh seethed, nearly at his breaking point. "What you are doing is most annoying."

"First I sing-a too loud, now I sing-a too quiet, eh? What can I do?" the gondolier pouted.

"Why don't you hum?" said Suexliegh.

"Hum? Hum is not romantic. You want a big, bold, bravado *DOPO UN GIORNO COSI COME E DOLCE LA SERA STARE QUI CON TE!*" he gestured broadly and sang towards the lonely moon before removing his cap and waving it around with every inflection.

"Humming will do just fine."

The gondolier gestured rudely, spouting indiscernible profanities in Suexliegh's direction before humming, beautifully it might be added, a romantic love song as the first course was gondola'd up to them.

Chapter The Thirty-Sixth
Primo

THE FLAPPING of restless wings echoed from a dodecahedral metal cage, an aviary, which housed birds of plethoric origins on an island out in the middle of the lake. To nocturnal caws, Suexliegh and Verena were served their main course: thick, homemade pasta noodles in a vodka cream sauce peppered with bits of bacon. Much like the German scientists who were annexed by the United States' scientific programs after World War II, Suexliegh's kitchen was stocked full of Italianos who each had a culinary secret weapon which would be dropped on the guests' plates every evening.

"So why did you come to my art show?" asked Verena suddenly. "I have never seen you around before."

Suexliegh licked his lips as the red pepper burned at his tongue, "Fate."

"Surely a man in a position such as yourself doesn't believe in fate?"

"You don't find the notion romantic?" Suexliegh leaned in, batted his eyelashes, and noisily sucked up a noodle.

"I find the notion quite preposterous; if you obtain something notable in life it should come at great personal strain and based on decisions you made of your own free will. That's like a person winning the Nobel Prize and thanking God for it. No, *you* achieved that, not God, it was you. Don't shortchange yourself."

"No matter how good you are at something, there is always chance involved," Suexliegh countered, dabbing his lips with a napkin. "You can't control it, but you hope the scale always tips in your favor. Some people call it fate, others, luck, I suppose the rest call it God. All I know is I'm loving this Pici Al Fumo aren't you?"

It was a poor choice for a first date dinner, pasta, as there is nothing less romantic than struggling to wrap a multitude of slippery strands around a fork without whipping pungent sauce onto yourself or your date. Supposedly, it's the thought that counts, but Suexliegh did not think very hard about that one.

"What about God?" she said.

"What about him? Suexliegh said back.

"Or her?"

Suexliegh smiled, taken off guard, "I suppose you're right. Then again I suppose God could be both a man and a woman. Maybe God's a hermaphrodite."

Verena caught herself mid-laugh and struggled to swallow her tangle of pasta before choking. The gondolier halted rowing momentarily and swooped down into a Heimlich maneuver.

"Sir! Take your hands off my lady!" Suexliegh vaulted to his feet briskly causing the boat to rock.

"I'm-a trying to help!"

"Well you could start by bringing your hands to the equator, you're traveling a bit too close to the Arctic if you understand me."

Verena coughed, her color returning to normal, and held up a hand to stop them.

"I'm fine. Why don't you both settle down and stop rocking this boat before you make me sick!"

Suexliegh calmed down and took a seat, as the gondolier, splashing the oar, angrily rowed them back towards the dock.

"Are you alright?" Suexliegh said softly, concerned.

"She is now that I-a saved her," snapped the gondolier.

Suexliegh was not a rude man by any means, he rarely engaged in confrontations, verbal or physical, but this man, no, this gondolier was threatening to ruin his most precious of nights so he stood, rolled up his sleeves, and shoved him into the water.

Chapter The Thirty-Seventh
Dolce

"THIS IS a mutiny! I'm taking control of this sea-vessel and you'll have no say in the matter! Had I been a less caring man I would have made you walk the plank," Suexliegh straightened his tie and hopped up onto the back of the gondola where he took control of the oar. Verena's shock turned to laughter as the two rowed away from the dock where horrified diners had come rushing outside to watched the commotion.

"Please I beg you, come back! I cannot swim!" shouted the sputtering man who flapped about helplessly.

"You should have thought of that before getting yourself into this predicament!" shouted Suexliegh. Though he was trying to prove a point, he did not want a man to die outside his restaurant so he picked up a lifesaver and tossed it to the gondolier, striking him in the head and knocking him unconscious. Within moments, the man slipped under the surface. Several waiters, well acquainted with Suexliegh's antics, were ready and had already jumped in the water for a rescue.

"Sorry!" Suexliegh called back.

The gondolier revived and sat, dazed, on the dock as he watched Suexliegh steal his boat.

"Well I never!" chuckled Verena as she smacked Suexliegh on the leg with her purse, "Dinner was fine, but dessert is turning out to be a real treat."

"We do have a real dessert waiting for us back at the restaurant... gelato," Suexliegh put a hand on his stomach and smiled, "but perhaps we should find safer harbor for the time being."

They drifted around the edge of the lake, lined with towering trees on one side, and light-spotted buildings on the other. Suexliegh had taken the gondola out on his own many nights when he wanted to be alone and had become expertly proficient at the craft, deftly weaving between the water fountains that cascaded out of the lake. Not to be outdone, Suexliegh cleared his throat and began to sing "That's Amore" in perfect pitch. He made sure to sing extra loud and clear so the gondolier could hear him. As the song ended, Suexliegh stopped rowing and let them just drift on the currents and wind, letting fate decide where they should end up. The boat rotated gently in place, creating a slow kaleidoscope of the city's lights around them. It was a perfect moment, a Hallmark card.

Verena shifted her gaze from the enchanting night to Suexliegh who was looking up at the moon. She studied him, this most peculiar of men, who had so much joy for life, was powerful beyond anyone's dreams, wealthier than anyone she had ever met, but when it came right down to it was hardly able to tie his own shoes. Yet he was different, he was not like the other men she had met, for better or for worse.

"Why do you like me?" Verena looked suddenly up into his eyes.

"Why?" the question caught Suexliegh off guard.

"Yes, why? And don't say it's because I'm beautiful… or smart, or rich. Those don't count. In fact, no adjectives at all. I want a thesis," Verena smiled astutely.

Suexliegh stopped and thought, something he rarely did. He considered himself a man of action and instinct, he spoke first and asked questions never.

"I don't know why I like you," said Suexliegh softly, taking his time to think through every word, "but I do."

Maybe it was the way the moonlight drifted on the fog, or the pearl necklace of lights strung around the shore glimmering beside the boat, or the lonely violin from the restaurant that wafted in on the evening breeze, but to Verena's knowledge, that was the nicest thing anyone had ever said to her.

Suexliegh did not come home that night.

Chapter The Thirty-Eighth
Around the World in Eighty Dates

AND SO it began.

A Chateaubriand overlooking the Golden Gate Bridge.

A night of sushi and sake in Beverly Hills.

A tandem bike ride through the rainy streets of Seattle.

A skiing escapade to the snowy peaks of Park City.

A canoe for two down the Grand Canyon.

A deep-dish pizza in the windy city.

A spicy gumbo on Bourbon Street.

A weekend retreat in the Hamptons.

A cupcake in New York City.

A land-flanked catamaran down the coast.

A cross-country ski trip in Labrador.

A view of geysers in Iceland.

A midnight salsa in the Dominican.

A view of the sun from Teotihuacán.

A stroll up wispy Machu Picchu.

A zip-line through the trees in Ecuador.

A full equatorial tan in Rio.

A plate of spiced rice in Chile.

A hike through the jungle in Patagonia.

A sighting of whales off the Antarctic.

A safari in Botswana.

A view of the Atlantic shores from Casablanca.

A dusk-lit waltz in the crooked streets of Barcelona.

A wine-and-cheese picnic in the vineyards of Couyssel.

A plate of Pici Al Fumo in Cortona.

A gondola tour of the Venice canals (no singing this time).

A bowl of risotto (and a caviar tasting) at Lake Como.

A diamond strung, jewel encrusted necklace in London.

A fine shot of Laphroaig in Edinburgh.

A pint of stout in Kenmare.

A Danish in Denmark.

A museum of art in Frankfurt.

A fireworks show over the fjords in the land of the midnight sun.

A hotel of ice in Jukkasjarvi.

A coat-and-tails operatic soiree in Prague.

A cold stroll over frozen roads in St. Petersburg.

A taste of olives in Kalamata (Verena did not approve).

A gifted pair of earrings that belonged to Cleopatra.

A night in King Tut's tomb in the Valley of the Kings.

A five-star resort nestled in the canopy over Victoria Falls.

A samosa in New Delhi.

A taste of olives in Tehran (Verena did approve).

A second Taj Mahal built just for Verena.

A heli-ski drop onto the summit of Mt. Everest.

A designer dress in Kathmandu.

A Thai massage in Thailand.

A spa of ancient Chinese healing medicines in Hong Kong.

A his-and-hers geisha in Tokyo.

A submarined tour of the Great Barrier Reef.

A hang gliding panorama in Wellington.

A bed perched on stilts above the clear blue bay in Bora Bora.

A torch-lined Fijian luau under a sky of palm fronds.

A celebration of Easter on Easter Island.

A fine day to dive with turtles in Kona.

And so it ended, where it began, with the two in love.

Chapter The Thirty-Ninth
White Tuesday

EVERYTHING was made right again. The crippling stumble Suexliegh had sunk the world's economy into with his wanton disregard for that government agency with three little letters (I, R, and S), was just as easily re-animated with three little words (Love, you, and I {Not necessarily in that order}). All that and more while doing what every good gentleman should: spending money on his lady. The flights, boats, trains, cars, hotel rooms, condos, resorts, spas, pools, gifts, treats, breakfasts, brunches, lunches, suppers, dinners, midnight snacks, room service, shots, pints, glasses, decanters, carafes, barrels, pearls, rubies, emeralds, diamonds, and all manner of purchases infused so much currency into every country they visited that the IRS deemed Suexliegh's literal debt to society absolved, nullified, and wiped permanently off of his permanent record. Clean as a whistle. Free as a bird. As with everything in his life, Suexliegh had skipped, with effervescent glee, like a rock on a pond over the murky depths and onto the waiting shore, unscathed, and unstoppable.

It was just fine for everyone, everyone except for Quincy who was left nervously pondering where on God's green Earth his master disappeared to. Like a worried parent, he didn't sleep the first night when Suexliegh failed to come home. That wasn't the first time it had happened, why, when Suexliegh was a young post-collegiate lad he had often stayed out all night with the Scoundrels before chasing the sun up in the morning and arriving back on his doorstep to an anxious (and graying) Quincy. Yet never more than one night in a row was this done, for Quincy surely would have died of fright. So when the second night came around with no tell of Suexliegh, Quincy became panic stricken and disagreeable, calling local law enforcement from Child Protective Services all the way up to the

FBI. They asked if it was a missing person's case to which Quincy replied, "He is not missing, he is simply someplace where I am not."

Suexliegh Missing? Suexliegh Kidnapped? Suexliegh Dead? Tired of the spotlight? Gave up all his money and became a monk? Fly fishing in Montana? Starting a hotel chain on the dark side of the moon? The headlines grew more and more ridiculous as time tick-tocked forward, but the moment Suexliegh made landfall in his first city, myriad cameras turned towards him, snapped up his likeness, and spread it to every outlet that had a front page. It was a silly notion that Suexliegh was trying to attempt a cloak-and-dagger, Houdini-esque, Where's Waldo? vaporization from the public's all-seeing eye for it was a bonafide impossibility. He was more well known than Jesus. There were even countless incidents of Suexliegh sightings in jam jars, carpet stains and MRI images over the course of his oh-so-brief disappearance.

Once people had gotten over the buoyant jubilee that Suexliegh was indeed still alive, they noticed there was another figure in the photograph, and that figure was a woman. *Who was that woman? What was she doing with Suexliegh? Where were they going next? When did they get together? Why were they being so secretive? And how did Suexliegh manage to look so sprightly and vivacious in every single photo that was taken of him?* A fervent furor of new found intrigue had infected the public with mass Suexliegh hysteria. Before, the world adored him because of his playboy lifestyle, but now that a missus was attached to the equation they all wondered if he would finally settle down. Not two steps onto the tarmac after arriving home from his whirlwind trip, Suexliegh was coaxed, coddled, and finally convinced to appear before a live studio audience for a one-in-a-lifetime interview concerning the man, myth, and fortunes of the once and future socialite.

Chapter The Fortieth
Impatient Patient

AS WAS mandated by the studio's contract, Suexliegh had to undergo his most dreaded of all encounters, a yearly physical with his general practitioner. The interview was to be conducted live and if anything were to happen the cameras wouldn't have time to stop rolling so he had to be checked out to make sure his heart wasn't a ticking time bomb set to go off mid-broadcast. If Suexliegh made a guffaw-able off-the-cuff remark, all of America would see it. If Suexliegh died suddenly of spontaneous human combustion, all of America would see it. Either way, it would make for great television.

Quincy, having witnessed Suexliegh's tirades over the years, had developed a cunning sympathy to the situation and often attempted to bribe his master with treats if he would go see the doctor, or when he was less fortunate, tried to mislead him that they were going to a themed park. Try as he might, sometimes Suexliegh caught wind of Quincy's efforts and called in sick to the appointment, a tactic he didn't realize was missing the point. He loathed the chipper/sterile nature of the doctor's office, like a clown with a smile painted over its non-smiling face. It wasn't the endless waits or the tedious forms, he despised these "Doctor Days" because at any moment for any reason any number of things could be wrong with him and he wouldn't have the slightest idea. One number on a chart too high. Another too low. One right where it should be, but for a man half his height. All of it completely outside of one's control it seemed.

In his youthful years, Suexliegh had become something of a hypochondriac believing every headache to be a brain-eating parasite, every sneeze the Black Lung. Why some might even argue a hypochondriac knows just as much about health as a doctor. Perhaps even more because he or she feels the symptoms of every disease, virus, and pox known to man. Something a doctor never does. An avid sporting fan who has never played the sport.

"What is it this time, Doc? Shingles? The whooping cough? Lemon-lime disease? For the love of God man tell me!" shouted Suexliegh.

"I haven't found anything wrong with you yet," said Dr. Wright, a sea-salt and pepper haired, middle-aged Bostonian holding a clipboard.

"Yet?" Suexliegh spun around with eyes the size of the moon. "What do you mean *yet*? Where haven't you checked?"

Dr. Wright squinted up at the buzzing fluorescents and cursed his childhood self for his influential love of *Doogie Howser, M.D.*

"We've gone through this same routine for years now and it never seems to get any easier," started Dr. Wright. "You're still wearing all your clothes for starters."

It was true, Suexliegh stood awkwardly in his pressed suit looking sheepish (and like a million bucks).

"I don't want to lie prostrate on that butcher paper like some poor animal about to be diced into cold cuts! I'm a human man!" exclaimed Suexliegh, pounding his fists against his chest.

"Of course you are," Dr. Wright clicked on his pen. "Now, we can either do this the correct way and I'll check you for any potentially life-threatening conditions so that I can properly treat you and prolong your time on this earth. Or we can do it the wrong way."

"If we do it the wrong way do I get to remain clothed and leave right now?" Suexliegh petitioned curiously.

Dr. Wright rubbed his eyes, knowing the answer already, then began to sign the release form.

"Yes."

"The wrong way."

"I'll see you next year."

Chapter The Forty-First
Interview with Mr. Suexliegh, Part 1

SNAP. Crackle. Pop. Lights all around struck brightly onto Suexliegh who was so used to the blinding glare of paparazzi he hardly batted an eyelash. He sat, reclined in his chair, right leg over left, with a casual posture only someone worth more than every person in the building could muster. Even before the red light blinked, telling Suexliegh that millions of pairs of eyes around the world were looking directly at him, he set his gaze to smile.

Tilda Leavenheart, the interviewer, sat clutching her ruffle of notes like a giddy schoolgirl about to ask the star football player for a lock of his hair. Her body was all circles in the most pleasing and cloud-like way, her clothes, layered and muted pastels, her hair, curls, golden curls, her cheeks rosy. Tilda was a favorite amongst the middle-America middle-aged demographic who looked up to her non-threatening figure and down-home, living room wisdom. Though every news agency in town wanted the interview her network literally had the luck of the draw. Suexliegh decided to write down all the contenders onto slips of paper and put them into his finest top hat. His divining rod fingers did the rest, finding their way to portly old Tilda. Suexliegh's luxury aircraft, the High Class, was being doubled in length, not by purchasing a new larger vehicle twice the size, instead by cutting it clean in half and adding a new midsection to it, so he decided to have the soundstage recreated near the outlying hedgerows on his property. Besides, Quincy simply wouldn't stand for his master to be away another day.

The red light turned on and people began clapping fanatically.

"Family and friends, do we got a show for you tonight! I'm talkin' dreamy seaside getaways, I'm talkin' fancy shmancy diamond necklaces, I'm talkin' spending cheddar up the wazoo! Ladies, what piece of jewelry is missing from this equation: earrings, necklaces, and bracelets?" coaxed Tilda, her head bobbing towards the predominantly female (plus a few catatonic husbands) audience.

"A ring!" they all chanted back.

"That's right," said Tilda, leaning in to Suexliegh. "So tell us Mr. Suexliegh... do you hear wedding bells ringing?"

Suexliegh stopped, cocked his head, and listened.

"No," said Suexliegh as the audience gasped. "No wait... I hear some buzzing lights, your rumbling stomach, and, yes, maybe a mouth breather or two, but definitely no wedding bells."

"You silly goose! We're talkin' about marriage! Gettin' hitched! Nuptials! Some holy matrimony here!"

The audience erupted like a well-oiled laugh machine.

"So tell us, cause that's really what we wanna know: when are you and Verena getting married?" said Tilda, the overbearing mother.

"Married?" spurted Suexliegh sitting up stiff as a board.

"Yes, married! When a girl meets a guy she thinks about three things: is he nice, does he have money, and am I gonna get married before my friends?" Tilda smiled, the women in the audience nodding their agreement.

"That logic is most peculiar, from a man's perspective of course. We think: is she nice, does she have money, and I wonder if her mother is still attractive."

All the men in the audience erupted into voluminous laughter as the women made disapproving "humpfs" and "haws."

"Certainly you must understand our reasoning," started Suexliegh. "In most cases, when a man gets married he has around five, ten years tops before his wife more resembles a potato on a hot day than the vigorous, supple cherub he fell in love with. I'm simply attempting to protect my genetic lineage. It's really a rather romantic notion if you think of it that way."

Tilda's jaw dropped, "We're gonna take a quick commercial break."

Chapter The Forty-Second
Interview with Mr. Suexliegh, Part 2

"I THINK that went quite well don't you?" mused Suexliegh as the crowd's hushed, angry whispers drifted through the darkness.

"Good not great," grumbled Tilda, though it was quite obvious she meant "terrible." Entire pages of questions were ripped out, mostly ones she feared Suexliegh might have an objectionable answer to, and based on their previous conversation, that could be anything.

"Not great?" no one had ever said that to Suexliegh about his performance in anything so hearing it was most unsettling.

"Let me give you some advice," Tilda scooted closer to Suexliegh who leaned in, turning a kind ear to listen, "you see those people out there?" Tilda pointed to the studio audience, which, due to the blinding stage lights, were un-see-able.

"No," Suexliegh squinted.

"Well they're out there, and they don't wanna hear about all your big, great accomplishments."

"But why not? I love talking about them," said Suexliegh, concerned.

"You know the secret to my success?" Tilda unclipped her microphone. "Pandering. Before I started this show, I was a respected businesswoman and a size zero. Now… look at me. All I do is talk about humdrum housewife gossip. And I'm fat. God, I'm fat. But I'm just like the rest of them. In fact, worse than most, and that's why they love me. I'm the ugly friend who they drag to parties just to make everyone else look better. They need me, because without me they have no comparison to their own lives. But you, you're a rich, powerful man with everything going for him and what do you think these women want to do with you?"

Suexliegh fumbled, and in a high-pitched voice, the voice of someone who has no idea what the questioner is asking, squeaked,

"Lunch?"

"Sex."

"Sex?"

"Sex," snapped Tilda. "Bring it up somehow, I guarantee you'll have everyone's attention, but you gotta be subtle about it because this is being broadcast to all of America. Not to mention my parents!"

Suexliegh nodded in understanding, "I understand."

The cameraman counted down, an applause light blinked on, the automated audience reacted as told, and Tilda flipped her frown upside down just as the cameras rolled.

"And we're back again with the lovely Mr. Suexliegh," she said with the pep returning to her voice, "but first, I'd like to take a moment to thank our sponsors at HouseHelp, makers of fine kitchen products, for sending us this *Effortless Eggs* poaching kit, guaranteed to save the hurried cook work before they have to go to work! So tell us Mr. Suexliegh, how does the richest man in the world start his day?"

The audience held its collective breath. Would he say cereal or toast? Perhaps he was a waffle man.

"Sex," stated Suexliegh.

Tilda let out a gasp that rippled through the entire crowd.

"Oh my!" she chuckled, trying to play it off as a joke, "TMI! TMI! I meant for breakfast silly!"

Suexliegh, not understanding, continued with much vigor.

"Yes, every morning, and throughout the better part of the day, and now and again come evening, I engage in exercises of a sexual nature. Why, the person who said, 'The best things in life are free,' undoubtedly must have recently copulated."

Within seconds, they were off the air. Cameras cut, plugs pulled.

It was the shortest broadcast in the network's history.

And the most successful.

Chapter The Forty-Third
The Horse's Mouth

"DID I EVER tell you about the time Edward lost his shoe a minute before the big race?"

"No! Do go on. I so love these sporting stories."

"I tell you, we were in le Midi."

"Edward was Randall's son was he not? Big nose, short brown hair?"

"Closer to chestnut, but yes, the very same. Anyways, where was I... oh yes, Edward was such a pure athlete, swift like the wind and he had the biggest heart. He loved to compete, rising with the sun to train. Well now just moments before the race while warming up he lost a shoe, went sailing clear over the fence!"

"Oh my stars!"

"I've never heard of such a thing!"

"No!"

"Yes! But you know Edward, stubborn as a mule, he ran the race anyways and won! Can you believe it?"

"That's positively sublime! I wish I had been there to see it."

"It was his shining achievement. If only he had his shoe on he never would have tripped and broken his leg walking off the track. The doctors had to kill him right there on the ground. A dreadful shame."

Suexliegh and Verena, having just arrived to the Annual Wild Goose Chase dinner, were horrified by the conversation. A man being murdered for having a broken leg? Surely medicine had advanced beyond the Dark Ages; Verena's cousin once broke his arm and they didn't stick his neck through a guillotine. Before they had a moment to question, the mess of a woman who told the story, sniffling through her tears, muttered, "Poor horse." The rest bowed their heads in silence.

The table to which Suexliegh and Verena were placed consisted entirely of show jumpers, equestrianeers, "horse people," and former colleagues of Dingle Steed's until he laced their horses' feed with a strong laxative to give himself an advantage at the Grand Prix. Every single horse, and one handler who occasionally took a free nibble of horse chow to calm his appetite, lost nearly one fifth of their body weight and began hallucinating wildly due to the purging effects of the drug. One horse started running towards the horizon and never stopped, another began eating all the leather in the stable, another merged into west-bound traffic and caused a four lane pile up, another just stood in his stall, staring blankly, and never blinked again. Needless to say, Dingle won.

The Annual Wild Goose Chase was a fundraiser collectively thrown by the city's elite to combat a growing threat amongst their ranks: baldness. Every day thousands, nay, millions of follicles died on the tops of these men's heads and no one could seem to stop it. "Mane Murder" they called it, and adopted a bald eagle as the mascot on their crest. Suexliegh, gifted with gracious Samsonite locks, never had such a problem but gave generously to the cause for he felt sorry for such men who were without hair or without a top hat to cover their shame. Suexliegh and Verena were last minute invites as they had been unavailable due to their perpetual globe trotting but everyone was so desperate to welcome the new couple back to society that two unfortunate (and now very surly) ex-invitees were axed from the list.

An actual goose chase occurred that very morning on a nearby polo field which lasted much shorter than anyone anticipated when the winner, James Henry Stuart Francis, simply shot the bird with his rifle and walked over to pick it up. To honor the bird's noble death, a five course meal consisting of every part of the goose, was prepared and currently enjoyed by the attendees. Suexliegh, already witness to the death and dinner of a bird shot by James Henry not too long ago, opted for just wine instead.

Chapter The Forty-Fourth
Pistols at Dawn

AFTER ALL the forks and knives were put down for the last time, couples and hopefuls paired up on the ballroom floor as the orchestra broke into favorite lettered sonatas such as "Canon in D" and "Air on the G String." Dancing was more a formal show of tradition rather than a physical example of one's prowess in the bedroom; all the time-honored steps had been drilled into their feet since their first cotillion.

Suexliegh's attempts to spice up the night by doing every dance in reverse, and trying a move called the "Goose Step," in honor of tonight's event, drew nary a smile. Verena became increasingly frustrated with Suexliegh who wasn't going to be content until every last person in the room paid attention to him.

"May I cut in?" came a nasally voice which could only emanate from a man who held his nose too high. A man named Dingle.

"No," Suexliegh didn't even look over as he twirled Verena away forcing Dingle to awkwardly sidestep past another couple, ducking under their clasped hands.

"You're being quite rude and a poor sport at that," spat Dingle as he crisped the front of his tuxedo. "All I'm asking for is the honor of spending one song in the arms of your lady fair."

"And all I am saying is no."

"Come now, darling, it's just one dance," whispered Verena, trying to be polite while keeping the two out of fist's range. "I think it could be a laugh, and perhaps the jealousy will make you love me even more."

Suexliegh instantly dropped his grip as if she were a leper.

"Fine! But don't come crying to me if you get hand cancer from touching him!" Suexliegh huffed, pointing to Dingle angrily. "And as for you, Heaven help us if they play a waltz."

He marched off between the oscillating couples to wait in the wings with a glass of scotch cooling his fingers.

"Why thank you," called Dingle after him. "Give that old ticker of yours a rest before it pops! We shan't be long."

Dingle, who was much shorter than Verena, groped her stiffly and sent the two spinning into the crowd like a whirling dervish. They made a spectacle of themselves as Dingle tossed Verena around in an overly compensative routine which knocked many other dancers off kilter with "how rude!" and "some people!" replies. All the while Suexliegh paced, a caged lion whose lioness was dancing with a hyena. Every time the strings dipped, Suexliegh assumed the song was over and headed back through the crowd, only to be disappointed as the melodies soared up again. He cursed every classical composer he knew and vowed to use their records as target practice when he returned home.

At long last, the song ended, and Suexliegh pushed through the sea of couples just in time to see Dingle dip Verena and, ungentlemanly, sneak a peak of her cleaved breasts.

"You dastardly bastard!" cursed Suexliegh, his face volcanic. "Unhand my woman!"

"I was just about to compliment Verena's fine form," smiled Dingle. "You're a lucky man to have a woman as sweet as her."

Suexliegh cocked back an arm and clocked Dingle straight in the nose. Onlookers shouted in fright as Dingle's eyes began to water and his nose to swell.

"How dare you!" shrieked Dingle.

"How dare *you* get in the way of my fist!" Suexliegh shouted back.

"Darling no! It was just a misunderstanding," Verena rushed to his side and looked out at the crowd's contemptuous glares.

"Poor form, Suexliegh, poor form," Dingle disappeared into the hushed crowd who stared disgustedly at Suexliegh. His smile slowly faded as Verena let go of his arm.

Chapter The Forty-Fifth
The Long Drive Home

SUEXLIEGH was an honest man with nothing up his sleeve but his arm, and an affront on his lady was too much for him to retain all common dignity; it turned him into a primal beast of rage. Even gentlemen must defend themselves if such a situation arises.

"Dingle… DINGLE!" seethed Suexliegh as the limo rocked gently back and forth. "That vagabond… has he no manners? No principles? I'd like to dance with his mother to return the favor! God rest her soul."

Verena sat in silence, arms crossed, looking out the window as the city slipped past. Suexliegh unbuttoned his cuffs and leaned over to her.

"He didn't hurt you, Honeycakes, did he?" coddled Suexliegh, popping a bottle of champagne and drinking it straight. Verena sat in silence, feigning aloofness.

"Did he?" Suexliegh said with a hint of fear in his voice.

"No, but you did," Verena turned away from him.

"Me? He was the one who offended my honor!" Suexliegh's violent reaction scared even him and caused the champagne to bubble over. He rolled down the window and let the fizz blow off into the night.

"Of course, it's always about your honor, your business, your everything," Verena fired back sharply. "Well what about me? How could you embarrass *me* like that… in front of all those people? Next time they invite us back, if they ever invite us back, they'll all see me as the woman whose boyfriend throws temper tantrums."

"That wasn't a tantrum!" Suexliegh folded his arms indignantly, after draining the last few good drops of the bottle, the rest being wasted on foam.

"Dingle was right, it really didn't look good for you," said Verena contemptuously.

"He provoked me!"

"And you hit him!"

"Sticks and stones, I suppose. Oh well, the night is over and everyone will have forgotten about it by tomorrow," Suexliegh tapped on the glass dividing them from the driver. "Quincy! Hurry home on the double, I want to get the smell of Dingle off of my hand."

"Would you listen to yourself? You're worse than he is," Verena reached for the door handle. "Quincy, let me out."

Quincy leaned back over his shoulder, becoming alarmed at the rising blood pressure behind him, "We're moving much too fast, you'll injure yourself."

"Then slow down!" screamed Verena.

Quincy slammed on the brakes and Verena went sailing into Suexliegh's arms. She struggled to escape but he held tight.

"Apologize to Dingle or I'm leaving," she hissed.

"I can't do such a thing. He'll tell the whole world I'm a yellow! People can't think of me as a coward, how will I ever live that down?"

"Alone."

Verena reached for the door and stepped out, her high heels clicking as she walked into the night. Quincy blinked rapidly, not believing what he was seeing.

"Sir?" Quincy whispered, cautiously keeping his voice low, "Sir?"

Suexliegh stared out the window as Verena disappeared around the corner. He sighed, then picked up the car phone, "Follow her."

The limo pulled up beside Verena and coasted at her walking speed. From within the car, Suexliegh dialed.

"Yes, Dingle, it's Suexliegh. I'm calling to inform you that I'm sorry for punching your nose. I'll be sending you flowers, I hope you can smell them. Good night."

Verena stopped as he opened the door, and after a moment's hesitation, got in. The two drove in silence all the way home.

Chapter The Forty-Sixth
Deli Meet

VERENA had become a ghost, floating morosely through the manor and haunting Suexliegh with her silent distance. Quiet breakfasts, though Suexliegh tried to strike up many a conversation. Lunches apart, though Suexliegh tried to sit next to her. Dinner on opposite ends of the table, by which point in time Suexliegh just asked Quincy to pass the rolls instead. He needed a distraction, a reason to get out of the house and away from Verena's cold-shouldered war for a while, which the first rain of the year thankfully provided. No matter where they were or what was disposing them, the Burgundy Scoundrels had a long-standing tradition that they must find a way to meet the first day it rained or disband forever. This pact was taken with the utmost seriousness so as the first drops of rain began to fall, Suexliegh donned his most adventurous hat, which was tradition too, and went straight down to the prison to post Willard's bail. Still fresh from his humiliating encounter with Dingle, and the ensuing maelstrom of attacks on his honor, Suexliegh needed the company only a Scoundrel could provide.

Willard's newfound freedom was not of his own choosing, nor the court's, which turned out to be a double-edged sword as he now realized he had to fend for himself again in the big bad world filled with normal people. To sooth his culture shock, Suexliegh took him to see Genova, the local delicatesseneer, who was a whale in man form with thinning white hair raked tightly back against his scalp and the expression of a bored basset hound constantly stretched on his face. If he could howl his remorse at the moon, he would. Since as long as anyone could remember, Genova had been there, looking bored, making perfect sandwiches. Perhaps it was the years of customers yelling "pastrami on rye" or "the usual" but the moment anyone checked in an order, the old man checked out. Perhaps he was trying to concentrate so he could remember all the nuances of condiments, or perhaps he was thinking of retiring to a small house by the lake where he could fish his days away and never put meat between two slices of bread ever again. Regardless, the Scoundrels went to him for any and all of their sandwich needs.

The little corner deli was packed as it always was between breakfast and dinner; the aisles of imported pastas and handmade gnocchi gazed upon idly by the parishioners waiting for their number to be called. There are perks to being rich, one them is never having to wait in line for a sandwich; Suexliegh's number was always up.

"Genova!" grinned Suexliegh as he pushed his way through the obstinate crowd who checked Suexliegh's hands to see what number he held.

"Pepper turkey with Swiss cheese on Dutch crunch with lettuce, tomato, onions, pickles, pepperoncini, mustard, mayo, and balsamic vinegar," recited Genova from memory.

"The usual for me, thank you," said Suexliegh.

"Yeah I know," Genova went to work immediately and pointed to Willard with his knife. "He'll have his usual too."

Willard and Suexliegh spent their afternoon on a private steam train in a small grove of trees near the top of Suexliegh's property, eating, talking, and laughing which caused Willard to choke on his football-sized sandwich on more than one occasion.

"It's good to see you again, old friend," Suexliegh slapped Willard on the back as he coughed up a bite of pastrami. "I feel like I've gone ten rounds with life and I'm on the losing end these days. Women! Need I say more?"

"You know what I always say," began Willard, "when life's got you down, sometimes the best way to turn it around is bottoms up."

Chapter The Forty-Seventh
The Albatross

THE TROSS, as it was colloquially known, held a dear place in Suexliegh's heart for it was the first place he ever got drunk. One would think, "Why, a man such as he would never be caught dead in a lowly public house! Why isn't he snorting caviar off a supermodel's breasts and drinking Courvoisier out of a supermodel's bellybutton?" Suexliegh had tried, Lord had he tried, but Quincy had the mindset that alcohol led to salacious behavior unbecoming a social gentleman, so to his word, he kept Suexliegh sober. Or so he thought. Even before the Burgundy Scoundrels existed, Suexliegh was a scoundrel all on his own. His prodigious cunning and charm loosened the tap of every bouncer in town when he was young and every barista when he was older. Yes, Suexliegh and alcohol became very well acquainted. Very well acquainted indeed.

The Ally, another beloved moniker, was slow the night Suexliegh and Willard cozied into a fireside booth behind two tall pints of the blackest stouts on reserve.

"This is just what I needed, Willard, a night out of the house away from the balls and chains," Suexliegh drank the first foamy sip and wiped his mouth. "A night where I can feel like a man again. I want to shoot things, and then set them on fire. It's been too long since I've done that. I want to kick down doors and get into fights!"

Willard puffed his pipe, bringing a warm red glow to his face as he tried to keep the tobacco burn smoldering. He shook out the match, "Why don't we have a Scoundrel reunion? All four of us back together."

Suexliegh smacked a palm on the table, "Willard you're a genuine genius! I'll have Quincy organize it post haste. It's high time I dusted off my old prank book."

Quincy had once gifted a pocket-sized, leather-bound diary so

Suexliegh could collect his daily whims and happenings for use in a future memoir, but alas he instead filled the pages with every conceivable type of prank to bolster the Scoundrels' arsenal against the public.

"I say we pull a fast one like the world has never seen! To the Scoundrels!" puffed Willard through his pipe clenched teeth.

"The Scoundrels!" Suexliegh replied.

Willard clinked his glass against Suexliegh's and before they knew it they were both royally trousered. Suexliegh had a discerning palette, one that he had developed over many years of cocktail parties and courtesy drinks, and as such chose only "the richest" spirits for they reminded him of himself. On one of his many Scottish golf outings, he discovered that when you said the name of a Scotch, like *Laphraiog* or *Glenfarclas*, you already sounded drunk. Perhaps if you strung a few into a sentence it would sound like a rather trollied fellow trying to pick up on a beautiful bar-side woman: *Ardbeg glenrothes balvenie oban?*

Not only were the scotches difficult to pronounce, they were difficult to drink and made getting drunk a challenge, but Suexliegh wouldn't let any alcohol get in his way of a good time. So, sip by sip, he muscled past the peaty bite and learned to love the burn. An acquired taste it was, but he considered himself amongst the few who enjoyed it. For there are drinkers, and then there are scotch drinkers.

Willard on the other hand drank beer. In the spring it was lagers, the summer, ales, the fall, IPAs, and the winter, stouts. Throughout his college years, he and Suexliegh's dormitory reeked of hop plants and carbon dioxide as every closet was filled with a different bubbling cauldron of home-brewed beer. His theory being whomever had alcohol, had friends. The hobby even lead to the naming of the quartet as newcomers and oldcomers alike would walk past their room, take a sniff, and remark, "What are those scoundrels up to in there?"

Chapter The Forty-Eighth
The Naked Mansion

THE WITCHING HOUR dragged on and the two soon found themselves at the gates of Willard's former mansion. When Willard had been voluntarily incarcerated the previous autumn, the house went into instant foreclosure and the bank snatched it greedily up thinking such prized property would be worth a fortune. Unfortunately for them, as the economy face-planted, there were far fewer with fortunes who could afford such an abode so there it sat, for months, untouched. A diamond re-roughed.

Willard slipped through the once-imposing wrought iron front gate and walked leisurely up the driveway to the plantation-styled manor followed closely by Suexliegh whose half-closed eyes assured anyone who saw him that he was happily intoxicated. Months of lax attention left the grounds looking much like a post-apocalyptic garden with plants greedily retaking the land for Mother Nature. Grass grew thigh high, ivy crept to the chimney, and animals found refuge in the unintentional wildlife preserve. Ripping through the backlog of eviction and dereliction notices, Willard pushed open the door and entered into his grand foyer.

"My God," guffawed Willard, "I've been robbed!"

It was true, the entirety of his possessions, the great grand piano, the diamond chandeliers, the Etruscan artifacts, everything was gone, all gone. On the same day Willard left his house for the big house, the bank repossessed all of his valuable assets as collateral against his unpaid debt. All except the Easter Island stone head that could only be moved again by the force of God (or a small army of migrant workers). So there it sat in the drawing room, surrounded by nothing but thin air. The only sign anyone had ever lived there at all were white shadows surrounded by faded dust outlines on the wall where portraits, armoires, mirrors, fixtures, and other home décor had once existed. The ghosts of glory days passed.

"Those sneaks!" Suexliegh's shouts echoing through the empty mansion as he spoke. "We'll get it all back, by hook or by crook, I promise we'll get it all back."

"Meh," Willard waved his hand as he walked into the cavernous living room, "I never really liked the way it looked anyway."

Without any furniture in the rooms, anything at all for that matter, the space felt enormous; the vaulted ceilings and oversized fireplace gave the illusion a gathering of giants once lived there. Willard kneeled by a pile of priceless oil paintings which had been broken in the apparent feeding frenzy that had taken place during the federal heist. He scooped several into his arms, stacked them in the fireplace, and tossed on a match. The dry canvas and ancient oils instantly burst into flames and provided a soft glow to the cave-like dwelling. Willard warmed his hands and looked deep into the fire as the timeless strokes of art liquefied back into the ink from which they came, tinting the smoke brilliant hues as it curled away up the chimney. The two stood gazing at the flames, listening to the crackling pops of priceless artwork returning to carbon.

"Do you ever fear you've made the wrong decisions in life?" Willard said plainly, his eyes still fixed on the hearth.

Suexliegh slowly rotated his hands to evenly cook both sides, "Of course, everyone has, though at the time they felt correct. What kind of talk is this, Willard?"

"I sacrificed all this, everything I had, and for what?" Willard tipped another painting into the fire causing a swell of embers to float across the room.

"I think you've had too much to drink, you seem to have the fear in you now. Perhaps we should call it a night," replied Suexliegh.

Willard looked over, the glow from the masterpiece fire casting an amber glint in his eyes, "Have you ever heard of the Barrister's Curse?"

Chapter The Forty-Ninth
The Barrister's Curse

"AN OLD BARRISTER in England was infamous for his cruel cunning in the courtroom, always on the winning end whether it was for good or, more often than not, evil. His decisions were heartless and only inspired by the amount of gold it would put in his jingling pocket. The entire town turned against him after he forcibly closed an orphanage just so a profitable shop could open in its place.

"One blustery winter evening, the ghost of an orphaned girl came haunting to show the barrister the error of his ways but his soul was too black to see the pain and misery he had caused. It was not until his own daughter died due to his neglect that he finally realized his misdoings and set out to right his terrible wrongs. The Barrister was too late to save his daughter, but he still had time to save what was left of his soul," Willard finished the story and tapped the remaining leaves out of his pipe into the fire.

"That story wasn't very scary," huffed Suexliegh a bit disappointed. "You know I don't believe in ghosts."

"It's not the ghosts that scare me," Willard packed the pipe into his pocket and leaned back against the mantle, looking out into the empty room which flickered giant shadows of the two men on the walls, "it's the Barrister."

"Come now, the Barrister was just a wicked old man who got what was coming to him," Suexliegh quipped rather sternly. "It's a typical moral tragedy written to scare little children into being good for Christmas."

"I fear I am more like him than I care to admit. Everyone has their ups and their downs I suppose, but look around," Willard gestured to the empty mansion as he spoke with a heavy heart, "this used to be my home, now it's just four walls, a floor and a roof. Perhaps I should be more careful in the future. Perhaps I shouldn't take things for granted."

"What kind of talk is this?" Suexliegh scoffed. "That pipe-weed must have gone straight to your head."

"I don't know, I feel more trapped out here than I did in prison," Willard began pacing around the room, staring at the forgotten outlines on the walls. "Here I have money, I have responsibilities, I have a family name to uphold. A rose preserved in glass that's never allowed to wilt. There, all that mattered was being me, nothing else, but here, I feel a draft: air is slowly making its way through a crack and one by one the petals are falling away."

"And if you stayed in prison you would have had a grand old time day in and day out drinking tea and playing games of chance forevermore?" Suexliegh put his hands on his hips.

"Sounds just fine by me," interrupted Willard.

"I'm sure it would have been for a while, but you need to save a bit of living for yourself. Grab life by the horns and shake it, I always say! In there everything would have been handed to you until you were old and gray," Suexliegh became flustered as he walked over to windows which were covered in thick, dusty curtains. "Nothing would ever go wrong until, on your deathbed, you would realize that you did nothing right either. In fact, you did nothing at all."

Suexliegh tore open the curtains sending a plume of dust into the air. Outside, the world began to glow faintly as the sun rounded the bend of the Earth.

"You still have time, Mr. Barrister," said Suexliegh, looking to Willard whose sad eyes began to slowly lighten. A narrow slice of dawn crept through the window and up the walls. Day was breaking.

"See," Suexliegh added as he reached his hand into the swatch of light that cut across the dusty room, "the sun has come up. All the ghosts are gone now."

Chapter The Fiftieth
Not Even A Note

THOUGH WILLARD had decided it was high time he should indeed grab life, he was also a temporary homeless-man, something Suexliegh despised, so he invited him to stay at the manor until the banks opened on Monday and he could attempt to salvage what was left of his fortunes. Neither he nor Willard had driven a car in years, always supplanting that necessity with a chauffeur, so the return trip home was a bit bumpy. The two swung by the Bugatti dealership where Suexliegh put a brand new car on his tab and left everyone in eye and earshot squirming as the multi-million dollar beauty had its gears ground to bits as he rode the clutch, left the emergency brake locked, and kept his left turn signal on the whole way home. That they were both egregiously hung over didn't help the matter one bit.

"Quincy! Look sharp we have company!" Suexliegh burst through the front doors and strode right into the kitchen, kicking his shoes off into the wall as he went. "Willard here will have two eggs scrambled over jellied toast and a side of latkes."

There was no answer, no pitter-patter of feet, nothing. Suexliegh looked around suspiciously, "Quincy… where are you hiding?"

Quincy, who was previously face down asleep on the kitchen table, awoke with an "oh!" and tried to get his bearings by swiveling around in all directions and blinking rapidly.

"Master Suexliegh! Oh my stars! I tried to stay awake until you got home, you know how worried I get, but sleep must have gotten the better of me. I've been trying to get ahold of you all night!" Quincy chattered as he leapt to his feet and gave Suexliegh a looking-over to make sure nothing was broken.

"That's quite alright, Quincy, I had Willard here to protect me," Suexliegh grinned as he put his arm around his friend's shoulder. "He'll be staying with us for the time being. If I remember correctly you like to sleep in basements, is that still the case?"

Suexliegh sat down at the breakfast table, tucked a napkin into his shirt, and pulled out a knife and fork, ready for whatever food came his way. Quincy burst into a flurry of activity loading up a full armload of ingredients from the pantry and cooking at warp speed.

"Every man needs his cave," replied Willard who rubbed the lack of sleep out of his eyes.

"Then it's settled. Quincy, prepare the bottommost floor for our good guest. He'll need round the clock attention and care now that he's a free man and deserves all that is coming to him," Suexliegh snatched a ripe apple from the bowl and munched into it. "And bring Verena in here, it's about time she met my bestest of friends."

Quincy paused his preparations for breakfast, letting the potatoes sizzle in the oil. His face went sallow.

"I'd completely forgotten. That's why I was trying to get ahold of you," Quincy turned to Suexliegh, his eyes brimming with tears. "She's gone."

Suexliegh stopped chewing then raised an eyebrow, clearing room in his mouth to speak through the bits of apple, "When will she be back? We have a new guest and she's being rude by not introducing herself."

"I don't know, sir, she took all her things," tears trickled down between the crevasses in Quincy's cheeks. "I'm so sorry sir."

At this, a wave of dread washed over Suexliegh.

He checked their bedroom, she loved sleeping in, "Verena?"

He checked the library, she often read before breakfast, "Verena?"

He checked the garden, she always took morning walks, "Verena?"

He checked everywhere, she had to be somewhere, but he soon realized that it was not there.

III.
Zephyr

Chapter The Fifty-First
Mint Condition

SUEXLIEGH did what every man who has his heart broken does: he went to work. No, not finding some new trifling floozy to patch his shattered soul, but an actual occupation. For him, it was the Suexliegh Federal Mint and Reserve. The mint was one of the oldest buildings in the city which had sat for over a hundred years right on the edge of the Bay. Six massive stone columns outside the front door made all who enter cower under their magnificence. The building was kept under the strictest of security as literally an endless supply of bills coursed through its veins every day. Only a few men had access to it at all, and only one could be there without restrictions. Most of the money was, after all, his. After Verena disappeared without so much as a note, Suexliegh's life of leisure left him doing too much of what should have been doing very little: wondering. So that very night, Suexliegh lit his candles at both ends and went straight in to work, something he hadn't done in years.

"Quincy, I'm feeling restless, I think I should like to go into the office," Suexliegh tied a perfect single Windsor knot in the mirror as he spoke.

"Certainly, sir, I'll bring your loafers and some Earl Grey right away," chimed Quincy as he hobbled up the stairs.

"No no, not my office, the *office* office," Suexliegh buttoned his coat and laced up his shoes. Quincy stopped, hand on the banister for support, and turned back to him.

"If you don't mind me asking... what's an office office... sir?" said Quincy with a look of puzzlement on his face.

"The one at the mint!" Suexliegh could barely contain his delight.

"But sir, it's past midnight," cautioned Quincy who was hoping he could get to bed soon himself. "Perhaps you should get some rest, you've had too much for one day already. I'll drive you there in the morning and you can begin fresh."

"Pish posh and damnation. The day officially starts at twelve ante meridiem and I for one would like to take it up on that for once."

Suexliegh picked up his briefcase, which he had never used and still contained the receipt inside, and opened the front door. His footsteps were accompanied by the distant sound of crickets as he made his way down the front steps into the cold night.

"If you won't drive me, I'll just have to drive myself," said Suexliegh who tossed the keys up and caught them in his jacket pocket. Quincy, knowing Suexliegh would wake up the entire neighborhood if he started up the car, woefully put on his chauffeur cap and followed him outside. Suexliegh fiddled unsuccessfully with the seat adjustment, first cramming himself under the steering wheel then sitting so far back as to nearly be in the back seat. Quincy came around to the driver's side.

"Have a seat in the back, sir, I'll have you there in no time," chimed Quincy as he tried to get the keys from Suexliegh.

"No, I think I'd rather drive myself there this time," Suexliegh slammed the door on Quincy. "Why don't you have a seat next to me?"

Quincy blinked, dumbfounded.

"Well come on Quincy we don't have all night."

Quincy could hardly contain his surprise, and glee, as he jumped in next to Suexliegh.

"To the mint!" shouted Quincy excitedly, followed by coy embarrassment. "Sorry, sir, I've always wanted to do that."

"Right away, sir, I'll have you there in the blink of an eye," Suexliegh chuckled and made the motion of tipping his hat. He wrenched the car into gear and peeled out, blowing all the leaves off the driveway as Quincy was thrown forcibly back into his seat.

Chapter The Fifty-Second
The Many Faces of Money

BY THE TIME the car came to a screeching halt outside the mint, thankfully not due to a collision, Quincy had seen his life flash before his eyes more times than could be counted. Apparently Suexliegh had forgotten that red lights meant "stop," instead, he seemed to view the color like a bull would, charging the matador with a blinding instinct to gore. Suexliegh tossed Quincy the keys, who was trying to keep his knees from knocking together, as he trotted up the grand front steps to the mint and told him to, "Wait in the car." And Quincy did.

From outside, the mint had an air of Roman imposition: soaring columns, stone foundation, and solid bronze doors. From inside, the mint had an air of James Bond impregnability: biometric scanners, latticed laser trip wire, and a security guard named Boris. The man was a Russian expatriate who now lived the American dream by guarding U.S. currency all night while reading cheap romance novels. In lieu of anyone to converse with, as the bank was always deserted by five, Boris preferred these novels because he felt they were as close as he could come to hearing gossip from a fellow co-worker about their life and sexual indiscretions.

Boris' ears perked up at the sound of Suexliegh's sharp footsteps echoing off the marble-lined lobby as he trotted up to the security checkpoint. As soon as he realized it was the boss, he tossed the novel into the trash, buttoned his shirt, and stood at attention, sucking any remnant of vodka from his teeth. Had there not been portraits of Suexliegh all over the mint, he never would have recognized him for this was, apart from the ribbon cutting, the first time Suexliegh had ever been in the building.

"Good evening Mr. Suexliegh," stammered Boris, trying his hardest to make all his vowels sound American. "I did not expect it to be you coming in here tonight for to working."

He cursed in Russian as he let the last bit of foreignry slip past his mental buffer. Suexliegh worked his way through the metal detector, infrared scanner, and retinal verification systems.

"Good evening," Suexliegh glanced at the security guard's name tag, "Boris. I thought I would come in early to get a head start on the day. Carpe diem. You must seize the day before it seizes you!"

Suexliegh picked up his briefcase and made a beeline for a curving marble staircase to the second floor.

"Carpe diem... sir, I didn't know you spoke French!" Boris called after him as he disappeared up the first flight.

It took numerous attempts to find the right key for his office. Living in a house with one hundred rooms made things tricky enough, but when one factors in the planes, the cars, the *other* houses, one might imagine a key ring that looked like a porcupine. A bit of detective work lead him to the key that was still brand new and had never deflowered a lock. Inside, the office was an equally pristine time capsule showing photos, electronics and décor from several decades before. A bottle of champagne and a "Congratulations!" note from Quincy sat on the desk. Suexliegh paced the room, reveling in the fact that he had a place in this world, and an office.

On the wall hung a framed collection of every currency from George Washington on the one-dollar bill to Woodrow Wilson on the one hundred thousand dollar note. Their faces were the most famous on the planet; everyone in America had at least a few copies of their portraits on little green slips of paper in their pocket which had always made Suexliegh wonder, why couldn't he be one of them?

Chapter The Fifty-Third
Legal Tender

"I HAVE a proposition for you. Create the two hundred dollar bill and I'll allow you to use my likeness on it."

Suexliegh stood across from Mr. Green, a grizzled, bulldog-faced man who had, until Suexliegh showed up suddenly the previous night, been in charge of running the mint. Mr. Green was hired for a very important reason: Suexliegh liked that his name was Green which was the color of money. Oh yes, he had a strong list of references and previous work experience suitable for such a challenging position, but that his name was green and he dealt with money all day tipped the scale in his favor.

"Why do we need a two hundred dollar bill? Especially one with your face on it?" grumbled Mr. Green through grinding teeth. For decades he had run the mint without a single day off or an attack from the Illuminati and now suddenly Suexliegh came waltzing right through the front doors to upset everything. He had so much respect for the money they printed that he did not own a credit card and only carried cash by the thousands. It was a commonplace sight to see him counting bank notes for everything from groceries to a brand new car. Mr. Green's fingers were always covered in band-aids from all the paper cuts.

"The fact that my face happens to be perfectly symmetrical, which, as you know, is a strong indicator of genetic superiority and virility, is beside the point altogether," offered Suexliegh, clearing his throat. "With a new piece of currency in circulation people will be excited about money again, everyone will want one. People obtaining money will inevitably lead to people spending money which could very well fix our recession to an even greater degree."

He had a point, thought Mr. Green, but it really wasn't a very good one. Unfortunately, Suexliegh was his boss but even more unfortunately Mr. Green didn't get to where he was by being a "yes" man.

"And tell me you wouldn't want to open your wallet and see this mug staring back at you," Suexliegh attempted his best presidential pose which came off more menacing and confused than stately. Mr. Green stared right back into Suexliegh's eyes without a hint of emotion.

"I'm sorry, Mr. Suexliegh, but the answer is no. No now, and no always," Mr. Green stood up and tried to escort Suexliegh to the door but he didn't take the hint.

"Well why not? I have just as much right to be on legal tender as any of these old, dead men," Suexliegh began to pace around the room in pre-tantrum mode. "George may have been our first president but I was the first man to become a trillionaire! That counts for something, in fact, it counts for over a trillion… and counting! And Benjamin, don't get me started on him, all he ever did was play with kites in a lightning storm like a little girl. Sounds more like a man who belongs in an asylum than on the hundred dollar bill!"

Suexliegh had circled all the way around and plunked into Mr. Green's chair who now stood on the wrong side of his own desk. Mr. Green scrunched his eyes closed and looked up at the ceiling.

"Alright," exhaled Mr. Green in defeat as a smile broadened on Suexliegh's face, "I'll make some calls."

"Top bombing! That's what I like to hear," Suexliegh sprang out of the seat and made for the door. "I'll be waiting in my office, ring me the moment you have news. And remember, tell the President how symmetrical my features are."

Mr. Green breathed a sigh of relief. He had learned long ago that Suexliegh had a shorter attention span than the flap of a hummingbird's wing. One moment he was on fire about this or that, and the next he was somewhere else all together. By tomorrow morning, the whole event would be forgotten.

Chapter The Fifty-Fourth
The Miraculous Manifestation of Amon Huxley

SUEXLIEGH did not know what one did when they "worked" so he mostly spent his day stalking the hallways for straggling employees whom he could correct or congratulate on their present tasks. He had never filled out paperwork, or balanced spreadsheets, or even turned on a computer, someone else was always delegated that responsibility which made him utterly helpless when said person was not around. Give a man a fish, as it were.

Late that evening after everyone had already gone home, Suexliegh paced through the printing press contemplating which side of his face to use for the two hundred dollar bill, or more simply "the Suexliegh," or simpler still, "the Suex." An unnaturally sharp breeze gusted open a side door and caught the freshly-cut currency sitting on the mill in a swirling vortex which lofted the bills towards the factory's ceiling. Money began falling from the sky until it caught another draft and pirouetted skyward once more. All Suexliegh could do was watch as millions of dollars, enough money to satisfy anyone's hopes and dreams, danced, twirled, and glided every which way. The side door slammed shut with a final push of wind and the remaining notes lazily made their way Earthward. Suexliegh's ears perked up at the sound of footsteps followed by a soft creak. He squinted, trying to make out movement, but the green snowflakes obscured his vision.

"Hello?" he called. "Quincy, I thought I told you to wait in the car."

No answer. Suexliegh crept past the sleeping metal monster that was the printing press and poked his head around the corner. To his surprise, he was greeted by the sight of a man who was kneeling on the ground, feverishly stuffing handfuls of cash into his tattered jacket pockets. The man had the look of a fallen star: at one time his brilliantly tailored suit, top hat, monocle, and loafers must have shone bright, but now the suit was torn and dirty, the top hat ruffled and bent, the monocle glassless, the loafers scuffed.

"Who are you?" Suexliegh said as he approached without caution. The man's heart leapt right out of him in fright as he jumped back, crushing his fallen top hat and spilling money from every ripped seam.

"Who are *you*?" gasped the man who scurried crab-wise away.

"I asked first, lest we forget our manners," Suexliegh matched the man's every move as he retreated.

The man took a moment to regain his composure and pop out the flattened top hat, "The name's Amon, Amon Huxley. I found this in the door jamb when I was... breaking in."

Amon held up *Love Love*, a risqué romance novel about two tennis players, competitors on the court, courting each other in real life. Boris must have stuck it in the emergency exit door to stop it from locking when he stepped out for his afternoon smoke then simply forgotten about it. Amon's eyes lit up as he finally recognized Suexliegh.

"You," Amon's hissed, "you're the man who did this to me!"

"Me?" scoffed Suexliegh. "I've never met you in my life and I'll ask you kindly to empty your pockets and vacate the premises before this devolves into fisticuffs."

Suexliegh unbuttoned his cufflinks and rolled up his sleeves as Huxley tossed the money from his pockets, disgusted.

"I don't want *your* filthy money," he said as he polished his monocle, forgetting as always that there was no glass present. "I used to be like you, money coming out of my ears, then you just had ruin it for the rest of us. I lost everything when the economy tanked. Now look at me, not a million dollars, not even a million pennies to my name."

Suexliegh stopped himself short of launching into a tirade and softened as he remembered the Barrister's Curse.

"Perhaps I can help right this wrong," Suexliegh said, planning as he spoke, "what do you know about money?"

Chapter The Fifty-Fifth
Two-Faced

SUEXLIEGH felt a tinge of compassion for Huxley as it was due to his own indulges that lead to this man's demise. As Quincy, who at first was shocked by the disgruntled looking transient Suexliegh arrived at the car with, drove them back to the manor, Amon explained in depth that he had gone bankrupt in the ensuing collapse of the financial system and was now scrambling to make payments on his prized Aston Martin. How could he ever appear at an event again without such a showy means of conveyance? A taxi? He would rather be caught dead with a hooker, or caught with a dead hooker. Either would be much better than being looked at from behind an upturned nose. A wise man, though rather foolish, he decided his best chance for some quick money was to go straight to the source, the mint, and with the aid of some unintentional espionage from a Russian named Boris nearly made off with the heist of a lifetime. This intricately inexplicable series of events led to his current occupation at the mint which was met with stern opposition by Mr. Green who once again felt Suexliegh was attempting a bloodless coup.

"Don't take this the wrong way," started Mr. Green who spoke though clenched teeth, "but why the hell is a dirty vagrant in my office?"

Suexliegh brushed off the comment as he put a supportive hand on Amon's back and cleared his throat.

"This is Mr. Huxley, he's my coinage liaison," said Suexliegh, putting extra emphasis on Amon given title.

"Your what?" spat Mr. Green.

"I had an epiphany, it doesn't make any sense that my face should be on paper money," said Suexliegh pleasantly, Mr. Green sighed with relief, but when Suexliegh breathed in again thought, 'Oh no, there's more.' "My face should be on a coin. On both sides of a coin to be precise. I just couldn't decide if my left profile or right was stronger so I thought to myself, 'Why not both?' Then it dawned on me... a coin! The left half of my face on one side and the right half on another! Wouldn't that be something!?"

Mr. Green was dumbstruck, not only by the sheer preposterousness of Suexliegh's new proposal, but also that he remembered he wanted his face on money. It was unprecedented; a Suexliegh who remembered was a very dangerous notion indeed. Suexliegh had only been back in Mr. Green's life for two days and he was already contemplating his retirement, but the crippling fear that tingled up his spine at the thought of Suexliegh being left in charge of the nation's entire line of currency guaranteed that he would show up for work until the day he died.

"Huxley will take care of the whole thing, you won't have to lift a finger," Suexliegh expounded proudly as Mr. Green raised his finger to object. "Stop right there! Put it down! I want to make big picture changes here, re-organize the pyramid from square one, synergize our assets, and really do good. I know you don't want me here, and now that I've spent a full twenty-four hours on the job, I don't want to be here either. So you can either deal with Mr. Huxley or with me."

Mr. Green was at a crossroads, if he opened his mouth negatively the conversation would explode into a mushroom cloud of lost jobs and pensions, but if he kept his mouth shut, he just might be able to afford that pony his daughter so badly wanted for Christmas.

"You're right," breathed Mr. Green as evenly as he could. "Mr. Huxley can stay. It will be good to have a fresh perspective on the market, especially coming from someone who was on the inside as the walls came down. Welcome aboard."

Mr. Green shook Amon's hand briskly then left the room, left the building, left the city, went out to the nearest stable and bought that horse for his daughter.

Chapter The Fifty-Sixth
Second St. Patrick's Day

ONCE the board of directors caught wind of Suexliegh's proposal for a new coin, hiring of a hobo, and creating an ungodly mess of the mint that took days to clean up, they put an end to the whole ordeal right away. Though Suexliegh argued valiantly, he was forcibly coaxed into extremely early retirement which was deemed "best and necessary" for the future health and relations of the mint with the United States Government. As the board went over Mr. Green's head to make the decision, he was thankfully spared any repercussive action and allowed to keep the foal he had just purchased named Gatsby.

Quincy took the shortest route home from the meeting fearing any scenic route put them in jeopardy of too much interaction with the outside world. The more his master was allowed outside the gates of the manor, the more harm seemed to come his way: the loss of his freedom, the loss of his girlfriend, and the loss of his job. Within his property line, nothing could upset Suexliegh for Quincy had made it bullet proof. Hungry? Why the manor had a super-market sized pantry and triple Michelin starred restaurant. Bored? Why the manor had a library that rivaled Congress's and a court for every sport. Tired? NASA scientists had been brought in to engineer a perfect sleeping chamber that balanced temperature, light, sound and comfortability to guarantee a good nap. Suexliegh Manor was, for all intents and purposes, the happiest place on earth.

No, thought Quincy as they drove through the front gates, I won't let him leave the house again until the New Year so he has time to come around to his old self.

Suexliegh, heads in hands, peered woefully out the window as the manicured landscape rolled past. He sighed and fogged up the glass which had to be wiped clear again with his sleeve. Quincy had never seen his master like this. Not when the manor caught fire due to an unfortunate candle snuffing accident. Not even when his favorite slippers burned up in said fire. Drastic times caused for likewise measures so Quincy decided to revive a dormant event created by his master: Second St. Patrick's Day.

Suexliegh was keen on Ireland, believing it to be a nation of underdogs, like himself. His love of the little green men gave rise to a rousing St. Patrick's Day party every year filled with stout stouts, hearty stews, a jigging contest, and fiddles aplenty. The moment someone came through the front door they were either instantly brought to tears at the melancholy plucking of a harp or heaved into laughter by a foot-stomping ditty that shook the whole house. All guests were invited to stay the night and often such a request was made mandatory due to the rampant inebriation.

Every party left behind a year's worth of stories which kept all who attended chuckling nostalgically until the festivities came around again. Last year, Mrs. Obalong Hollows, Willard's former lover who made her first surprise appearance since they split, was so obsessed with the potatoes Quincy prepared that she attempted to steal away with some in her blouse for a midnight snack later. Unbeknownst to her, Mr. Gibbles, a guest's poodle, happened to be likewise infatuated with said potatoes and hungrily attacked the woman's bodice as she ran screaming out onto the lawn. People claim they can still hear the phantom laughter at Mrs. Hollows' unfortunate endeavor.

Some years The Second, as it was known, came before the actual St. Patrick's Day yet no one gave it a second thought. A mandate had been created that stated a Second St. Patrick's Day could take place whenever or wherever was deemed necessary and with Suexliegh's spirits lower than they had ever been, Quincy realized he had to pull out all the stops and finally re-unite all four Scoundrels.

Chapter The Fifty-Seventh
The Best Night of the Year

TO THE SOUNDS of feverish fiddles, sharp penny whistles, rousing bagpipes and much singing, guests filing in were swept up by the arm and spun dizzily around the manor. This was the first gala Suexliegh had thrown since leaving prison and as such acquaintances from the four corners of the globe arrived to welcome him back to high society. It seemed everyone who was anyone had decided to show; the This Family and the That Family of Heavens-Knows-Where were all there whether they were invited or not and soon the manor was bursting at the seams with socialites. Even Mrs. Hollows made an appearance but this time dressed in slinky, form fitting attire that told the world (and everyone at the party), "See my figure? I'm hiding nothing here. Not one potato." Yet Mr. Gibbles paced the poor woman like a shadow and refused to leave her alone the entire night.

Quincy worked without sleep for three days to get everything ready, cleaning, calling, even cooking a sumptuous, overflowing cornucopia of corned beef and cabbage, bread pudding, various game meats (supplied by James Henry of course) and boiled, mashed, and stewed potatoes of all origins. A special ring of garland consisting of only four-leafed clovers (supplied by a crack team of experienced midget clover-hunters, their natural stature giving them closer proximity to the ground thus increasing clover collecting prowess) draped the length of the mansion. The pool had been dyed a deep green and anyone brave enough to partake in a night dive was rewarded with an actual pot of gold sunk to the bottom.

In no time at all, the party's patrons were thoroughly intoxicated except for Quincy who rushed from room to room making sure the guests were having a fine time and not ruining the carpet. Suexliegh, who up until that point had been tasting every single spirit on tap found himself on the dance floor opposite Willard flanked by the other members of the Scoundrels, Nicholas Flynn, a reclusive vintner from up north who only spoke when he had a few drinks in him, and Liam Daniel, the man with two first names. Suexliegh pointed to Willard, calling him out. The two stared each other down with serious glares then proceeded into a firm handshake. Guests cleared the area and the fiddlers tightened their strings in preparation for the Jig Off.

Suexliegh clasped his hands behind his back, straightened his posture most erectly, and locked eyes with Willard who did all of the same. Drums began to pound followed by the shrill squeaking of rapid fiddles as the two quick-footedly jigged this way and that around the room, revolving with every beat like the Earth and Moon intertwined in geosynchronous orbit. Willard advanced suddenly to Suexliegh and caught him off guard. He stumbled and the crowd alternately cheered and booed. Suexliegh regained his composure and went on the offensive by striking up a high-stepped, hopping jig that Willard struggled to match with his long gangly legs. Just as Suexliegh's victory seemed close at hand, Willard reversed him with the most feared jig imaginable: the Double Dublin Doubloon, a move so dangerous and magical, it had to be seen to be believed. Suexliegh chuckled with delight at the dexterous footwork of his friend and bowed graciously to the victor. The crowd burst into applause and clinking drinks as Suexliegh put his arm around Willard in congratulations.

"Beat these feet!" shouted Suexliegh.

Without warning, Suexliegh pushed Willard away and attempted a feat of feet even more daring, the Triple-Toed-Fairy's-Folly. Yet one step away from a complete one-up-manship his luck failed him and Suexliegh tripped, twisting off balance and crashed into a plate of potatoes au gratin which soared through the air onto Mrs. Hollow's dress followed shortly by a hungry Mr. Gibbles.

Chapter The Fifty-Eighth
Enjoying A Good Sit

QUINCY was a disaster for days after. How could this have happened? His master didn't even leave the house and ill fortune befell him. The party was a success no doubt and with all the alcohol in his bloodstream Suexliegh didn't feel a thing when he broke his leg yet it still tore at Quincy's heart for now his master was no longer the shining perfection of humanity, his brass plate tarnished, as the doctors ordered he remain wheelchair-bound until further notice. People would look down on him, thought Quincy, he'll be so much shorter than they. For the briefest of moments, Quincy contemplated resigning his post as caregiver and subservient of Master Suexliegh due to his lamentable performance, but it was gone even quicker. No, he would remain steadfast and redouble his efforts to be the best butler the world had ever seen. His Master deserved it and Quincy had a sneaking suspicious Suexliegh might actually die without his help.

Suexliegh rather enjoyed being in a wheelchair as now Quincy had to push him everywhere he wanted to go. Yes, his arms were wholly undamaged but, unlike his legs for walking, felt that using them constituted "manual labor" and decided to refrain just to be on the safe side. Quincy rolled him to restaurants, to the opera, to the track so Suexliegh could do laps. The old butler often had Quincy Jr. take his place for "training" which was code for "I need a breather or my heart might implode." Oddly enough, even with his ambulatory handicap, Suexliegh became even more mobile and insisted they start every day by heading, on foot and wheel, down to the mint for his daily withdrawal.

He had always experienced a kind of respect that only a man worth more than everyone on this side of the equator could achieve, but with a wheelchair beneath his bottom became witness to nearly angelic reverence. Whenever people saw him, wearing his Sunday best, a broad smile across his face, being pushed down the boulevard by a charming young servant, they instantly felt sympathy due to the current use of their own legs. When they learned he was a trillionaire thought to themselves, "If a person can face adversity like that and go on to become successful, then I can do anything!" Without knowing it, Suexliegh had become a moral martyr, an inspiration, which all arose from a drunken jigging competition.

"Bless your heart, sir, you're a true hero," said a motherly mom who stopped her husband and two kids to greet Suexliegh as he and Quincy Jr. rolled past them down the sidewalk. The husband put his hands lovingly on his children's shoulders.

"You're an inspiration to us all, really," smiled the husband, secretly thanking the Lord for gracing him with strong, God-fearing legs.

"Do they hurt?" said the young boy.

"Not a bit," chuckled Suexliegh, leaning in for emphasis, "but due to my accident this knee can predict the weather."

"Really!?" piped the boy, his eyes lighting up. Suexliegh tapped his bad knee and closed his eyes in concentration.

"Yes, I do believe we'll have... thunderheads coming from... the west... this very evening!" Suexliegh winked. The little boy and girl exchanged excited looks and laughter.

"We should be going, but it was nice to meet you, sir," the husband stuck out his hand to shake and was positively dumbfounded when Suexliegh stood up on his own two feet to greet him. The mother let out a gasp and fainted on the spot, crumpling right to the ground. Suexliegh shook the husband's hand vigorously.

"It was certainly nice to meet you as well. Remember to pack an umbrella tonight!" Suexliegh plunked back into his wheelchair as he and Quincy Jr. rolled away.

The husband just stood there, hand still outstretched, blinking, as his kids cried over their fainted mother.

Chapter The Fifty-Ninth
Young Master

RING RING.

"Master Suexliegh's residence. How may I be of assistance?" answered Quincy as he lofted the phone to his ear, making sure to sound extra pleasant as the person on the other end couldn't see his smile.

"Good day sir, I hope this call finds you well," said the butlery sounding voice on the other end. "I am calling on behalf of Madam Victoria Petit on behalf of her son, Reynold, on behalf of a request. The Madam inquires if your Master would be so kind as to offer her son lessons in etiquette so as to be true and proper when escorting a fair damsel to her cotillion."

It was customary for butlers to call in their master's stead as they couldn't be bothered to use their own larynxes for such mundane tasks as operating a telephone. Butlers around the globe had become a living simulacra and, it could be argued, experienced life, mostly the rougher edges, for their masters. Doing dishes, folding laundry, cooking, cleaning, driving, setting up, taking down, arranging, canceling, just about everything that wasn't simply enjoying Earthly nectars was left up to them. Without butlers, people to take care of ninety-percent of one's life, one would have ninety-percent less life to live. All the greatest men and women who have ever existed were able to achieve such renown due to the unseen numbers who toiled beneath them.

"And whom might I ask is the young master escorting?" chimed Quincy.

"Deidre Van Every, daughter of Margeaux and Dagobert Van Every," said the voice with all pomposity.

Ah yes, recalled Quincy, the Skinny Skeleton who so injudiciously accosted Suexliegh at his birthing day party. I hope her daughter's braces are finally off.

"How does tomorrow morning sound? I'll drive Reynold over at eight o'clock sharp… if that isn't an inconvenience."

"Let me check," Quincy put a hand over the earpiece and peered down the hallway at Suexliegh who was carefully balancing himself in the "wheelie position" in his wheelchair.

"Mr. Suexliegh's schedule is *very* busy for the next month, but perhaps we can make a special arrangement."

"Hurray! Young Master Petit, and Mrs. Master Petit will be most pleased!" squealed the voice. "If only the late Master Petit were here to see this day."

Quincy politely sat and listened on the other end of the line as the voice sniffled and blew its sorrows into a tissue.

"But enough about that! Before I go, I thought I should ask, are you going to… The Conclave this year?" whispered the voice.

The Chamberlain's Conclave was a secret annual meeting amongst butlers the world over and took neurosurgical precision to execute as, for one day, every single powerful man, woman and child in the world would be without hired help. Excuses were hard to come by for a job that required three hundred and sixty five days of attendance. Long lost visiting family members, full-day errand runs to the shoe shiners, or twenty-four hour bouts of highly contagious insert-animal-name-here flu were the most often employed.

"Unfortunately, this year I will not," said Quincy, shifting the phone to the other ear and turning away so Suexliegh could not overhear, "but perhaps my son might."

"Then we shall welcome him with open arms! Until the morrow!" The line clicked dead.

Chapter The Sixtieth
Butlers' Bane

A LONG TIME AGO, butlering was considered a prestigious and noble career path that one would be honored to take part in. Kings, sultans, presidents, tycoons, wealthy businessmen and women of society were all in need of an attentive individual who would manage the daily flow of their life. One might think these butlers were signed into a life sentence of servitude, constantly on the clock, with no chance of upward mobility or improvement save for release due to the death of their master. Slaves in suits. Yet there was a silver lining often overlooked in this minor scheme of existence. A mouse in a King's kitchen is far better fed than one in a pauper's.

Every time a socialitic family would go on vacation to a tropical paradise or splurge on a top cheffed restaurant their butler would be in attendance. Doubtlessly he kept himself busy making sure the family was well taken care of, but in the minutes between he could enjoy the breeze under a hot equatorial sun or take his pick of the leftovers on their way back to the kitchen. Everywhere they went, he went. Everything they did, he did. In fact, he was paid to do all of this and in return all he had to do was a few chores here and there, which begs the question: who really was the dominant one in the relationship? It was living life in the margins, but that's often where the best crumbs collect.

However, a new breed of wealth was emerging unfettered and spreading like weeds: celebutantes. These were people who had turned their fifteen minutes of fame into fifteen million dollars seemingly instantly and without effort in most cases. They enjoyed all the luxuries money could afford, yet their overnight opulence kicked in the teeth of families who had passed down their name, and fortunes, from one generation to the next and taught their children, and their children's children how one must behave in high society.

Needless to say, many of these celebutante's lives ran off course and spiraled into a shattered wreck just as quickly as they had begun without such control. It was like giving a child who had just turned sixteen his own sports car without ever teaching them how to drive.

A butler did not accompany their master to the mall. A butler did not go to Cancun. A butler did not wait patiently in the limo while their master vomited that night's inebriants into the club-front gutter after a full evening of bar-hopping, top-dropping, and shoe-shopping. Nouveau nouveau riche, or Neo Nouveau Riche, or Neo-Nou-Riche (NNR) for short, they were called. Hillbillionaires, the Vieux Riche or Old Rich, often called them. These faux-lebrities were a disgrace to everything graceful about affluence so the Conclave, a collection of the best and brightest minds of the butlering world, had been called immediately to decide on the matter. In Quincy Jr.'s very first vote, having been able to sneak away from his duties for only half an afternoon as Suexliegh needed double attention in his current state, the Conclave had decided that they should impose a world-wide boycott for any Neo Nouveau Riche. Individuals deemed NNR were blacklisted by butlering factions far and wide and soon found themselves helpless.

The ploy had worked, for a time, and in its wake left crashed Escalades, lost cell phones, and ripped skirts. Then, evolution ran its course and the Neonouriche mutated their own adaptations to the natural environment. They rented lofts instead of buying mansions, they leased cars instead of owning, they tricked gullible friends, who falsely assumed their proximity to lucre increased their own worth, into joining their "entourage" and playing the role of an assistant.

And so, the two species diverged, one took the high road, the other, the low road, like the water buffalo and the regular buffalo, utterly different, yet from the same lineage, and learned to live in harmony.

Chapter The Sixty-First
Reynold Petit

AT EIGHT, on the button, two brisk doorbell buzzes rang out into the manor. Quincy rushed to the front door and whisked it open, bowing so low he was only able to see the guest's shoes. Weathered leather penny loafers with two copper coins head side up. The coins, and the shoes, socks, feet and rest of the body, belonged to Reynold Petit, an overdressed and overfed puber-teen, whose eyes darted around the interior of the mansion with an overwhelming sense of disgust.

"Our house is twice as big," stated Reynold as he swept into the room and picked up an ancient mammoth tusk from its wooden cradle. His name, Petit, literally meant "small" in French but you would never know it from looking at him. Though he could have anything with a price tag, he walked around looking like someone had just put a dead fish in his trousers.

"There's your first mistake," announced Suexliegh as he wheeled right in front of Reynold, stopping him just short of reaching a specimen cabinet filled with the remains of rare, extinct birds. "A gentleman must never, ever, be caught using his own fingers for anything except shaking hands, supporting a glass of champagne, or gently caressing a woman. As you're not of the drinking age, or the hand shaking age, I suppose you're here for the latter."

"Oh yeah? What do you know about women?" shot Reynold as he crossed his arms. "I don't see your wife anywhere... are you married?"

"I'm such a gentleman I couldn't possibly be so selfish as to lavish all my love on just one woman. I'm an equal opportunity lover."

Reynold "humph'd" defiantly as he sidestepped around Suexliegh so that he could look down on the rest of the house, "Does this place have a sauna? Our house does, probably bigger than your bedroom.

Does this place even have a bedroom? Our butler's house has more rooms than this."

Reynold strolled through the manor belittling every priceless Ming vase, every crystal chandelier, every doorframe all the while Suexliegh merely rolled along behind him, studying the tiny fat man-boy. After exhausting every possible object in the house worthy of his indignation, Reynold stopped and shot back around.

"So how do you know my mother?" asked Reynold, posing the question like a statement.

"Prison," said Suexliegh causing Reynold to gasp. He turned morosely away only to find that he was looking at his sad form in a mirror. Reynold moved again, eager to hide his face so Suexliegh wouldn't see the budding tears in his eyes. After his father died, Reynold was left to be raised by his mother who, having not slept in forty years, often slipped into temper tornadoes that lasted days on end. Yet when she was taken away to prison, he was all alone. All alone except for his family's butler, Remus, who was forced to raise the boy through some of his most formative and difficult years. Reynold never went to visit her. He sometimes went to visit his father.

"She's a fine croquet player," added Suexliegh trying to lighten the mood after the poorly struck chord, "and her bouquets are to die for."

Reynold stood in silence, his leather shoes creaking.

"So... your first cotillion I take it? I've met the young lady and I say she's cute as a bug! You should count yourself lucky."

"I'm only doing it cause my mom wants me to marry a girl from a rich family and she thinks this will somehow make that happen."

"Well if it's the girl you want, I can help in that department."

"How are you gonna help me you can't even walk!" Reynold fired back. Suexliegh leaned forward, put his hands on the armrests, and stood up. Reynold stared at him in reverent shock. Suexliegh smiled.

"It's a miracle."

Chapter The Sixty-Second
Good Graces

"THERE ARE three D's of being a Gentlemen: dining, dancing and drinking. We shall cover each in thorough and complete detail to make sure you are well equipped to handle any situation this cotillion might throw at you. Before we begin, you should be made aware that there are also three D's of being a Dastard as well, or a knave or cad, if you will. They are debauchery, danger, and delusion and should never be confused with the former three.

"The basic human necessity is sustenance so that we may continue living on this Earth. As such, one of the most important lessons a man of society can learn is how to behave at the dinner table."

Suexliegh sat at the far end of an immaculately prepared dining room table which was covered with pure white cloth, sparkling fine China and silverware, and an imposing floral centerpiece. At the other end, sat Reynold, stomach grumbling, who wanted nothing more than to dig, face first, into a bowl of Mac & Cheese while his hands stuffed chocolate truffles in between breaths. He kept picturing the hydrangeas were giant scoops of ice cream ripe for the licking, when in reality their poisonous buds would put him in a coma before the sugar ever hit his stomach.

"First, unfold the napkin onto your lap. Do not shake it open like a pit bull with a chew toy! It may only be used to clean the corners of your mouth should you be so haphazard with your eating abilities. Second, a standard dining arrangement from left to right consists of the aforementioned napkin, salad fork, dinner fork, dessert fork, dinner plate with optional soup bowl, dinner knife, teaspoon and soup spoon. Above this one might find a bread and butter plate with butter spread followed by a water goblet, red wine glass, and finally white wine glass. The correct etiquette stands to 'work from the outside in.'"

"Alright, alright already, so how do I eat?" huffed Reynold, banging his fists down as he suspiciously eyed the empty table.

"That is one step you could probably do without a bit more often!"

Reynold glowered and made a mental note to tell his mother.

"Thirdly, in these United States, we eat thusly," began Suexliegh as he picked up his utensils. "Your right hand is for your knife, your left is for your fork. After cutting your food into mouth-sized portions, place the knife on the plate's edge with the blade facing inwards. Switch the fork to your right hand, unless you are left handed, and begin mastication. Once used, utensils, including the handles, must not touch the table again or so help you God. Rest them on the edge of your plate or within the bowl. When you're sufficiently stuffed, place your fork, tines up, knife blade in, with the handles resting at five o'clock and tips pointing to ten o'clock on your plate. Unused silverware is left on the table in its virginal position.

"Food shall be passed the same direction as English reading, left to right. Move the salt and pepper together, even if only one is requested so that no orphaned shakers are created. Should a carafe of wine or bowl of salad be passed before you on its way to another guest, do not interfere with its arrival. This is not American football, interceptions are not allowed! Eat with your mouth closed at all times even if a question is posed to you, the asker will simply have to wait until you have finished to hear your response. Always breath deeply when drinking wine to achieve maximum olfactory satisfaction. Toothpicks are for cowboys and martinis not cleaning your teeth. Oh, and one more thing, if you are so unlucky as to choke on your dinner you must allow it to happen as coughing is not permitted. Another guest will come to your aid and become a hero for an evening. Any questions?" Suexliegh allowed himself his first breath of air since he began the rant.

"So..." said Reynold, unimpressed, "what's for dinner?"

"Nothing until you can recite every single word I've just said back to me verbatim... in Latin."

Chapter The Sixty-Third
The Russian Rose

"DANCING. Nothing says you're physically fit and sexually competent like being a good dancer. It's a litmus test for genetic virility."

Suexliegh led Reynold into the mansion's gigantic ballroom which was flanked by bay windows, vaulted ceilings, and a standing stage for a full orchestra. The room had hosted more galas than all the houses on the block put together, yet not a single scuff mark could be found on the floor. Cleanliness was Quincy's forte; when Suexliegh was soundly snoozing he could often be found with a toothbrush and vinegar removing the previous night's wear and tear from all corners of the house.

Suexliegh had changed into an elegant evening tuxedo with flowing tails that trailed behind him as he performed a series of solo dance moves and kinesthetics to warm up his muscles.

"I'm only eighteen I don't want a wife," Reynold made sure to stay on the perimeter of the dance floor and far away from Suexliegh who was awkwardly attempting to touch his toes.

"Someday you might and wouldn't it be a shame then if you found out you had two left feet? Hmm?" grunted Suexliegh as he performed trunk twists. Reynold peered down at his feet to reassure himself that Suexliegh was wrong. He was.

"Look, dancing is as simple as counting. One step per beat. You can count right?"

"Of course I can count," Reynold began backing out of the room, "but you can count me out. I'm not dancing with another man."

"Then you may watch," Suexliegh quipped. Reynold raised his eyebrows, perplexed as Suexliegh turned away and called out, "Anechka, will you please come in here for a moment."

Reynold turned to witness the most beautiful sight his eyes had ever beheld. She was the epitome of grace and beauty, soft in all the right places, hard in all the others, and to a blossoming young man of just eighteen her physique aroused more than just his interest in dancing. The fair Anechka. Suexliegh held out his arms and she briskly stepped into position like a trained professional. An ebbing waltz began to play as the two circled around the room in perfect metronome time. Suexliegh's tails flying, Anechka's dress twirling. They whirled past Reynold allowing him to feel the speed of the dance and smell a waft of her heavenly perfume. He watched them spin in exacting circles for what seemed like an eternity or for only a moment. Sooner than he would have liked, the dance ended, Anechka kissed Suexliegh on both cheeks and curtsied.

Reynold stared in an hypnotic state as he stammered a response, "M-m-my turn?"

"Your turn," coached Suexliegh with a twinkle in his eye. Reynold approached Anechka with caution.

"The first rule of ballroom dancing doesn't have to do with dancing at all," Suexliegh reached into his pocket and tossed a small white object to Reynold who fumblingly caught it then shot a nervous smile to Anechka.

"Keep your breath minty fresh. Women don't want to dance with someone who smells like a wild boar," Suexliegh laughed as Reynold quickly popped the mint into his mouth and chewed away feverishly.

"When asking a woman to dance the proper call-sign is 'May I have this dance?'" Suexliegh positioned the needle of the gramophone back to the beginning of the waltz.

"If the woman says 'yes,' nods, walks towards you, does anything at all besides say "no" outright, then you're golden. Now, take her in your arms," Suexliegh swooped right next to the young pair with a big grin on his face. "What do you say, Reynold?"

"May... may I have this dance?"

Chapter The Sixty-Fourth
The First Dance

REYNOLD gulped and hoped his palms weren't too sweaty or cold, but had just the right amount of pleasing heat. Anechka raised her arms into the correct position and allowed Reynold to struggle his way into the human puzzle piece. Suexliegh poked and prodded Reynold, molding him towards a standard waltz configuration with much difficulty as a small smile appeared in the corner of Anechka's mouth at the effort. When all was properly aligned, Suexliegh backed away as if he had just created a teetering house of cards on the verge of collapse.

"Don't be afraid to get close," coaxed Suexliegh as the music picked up. "Feel her fiery passion."

"What do I do?" asked Reynold who began to perspire.

"Lead me," Anechka whispered.

"What?"

"Move your feet, like this," Anechka pulled them into a turn and before Reynold knew it, he was dancing. Time slowed down, the room spun around them, the music softened, and all the while he kept his eyes on her. Those green pools shimmering brightly from the light streaming in all around. A voice somewhere far off and faint called out.

"Keep those feet parallel... lean to tell her where you want to go... don't step on her toes... counter-clockwise, move counter-clockwise we're not in Britain!"

All too soon the needle wandered into the run out groove but the pair continued to dance in silence. Suexliegh disarmed the gramophone and applauded them vigorously as he rushed over. The two stopped suddenly, embarrassed by the foolish tug of young romance.

"Can we do that again?" Reynold squeaked eagerly, his voice

cracking which he covered with a cough.

Suexliegh checked his watch, "If we leave now we'll be ten minutes early, which is five minutes late. There will be time for lessons later. Come along."

Suexliegh marched out of the room as Reynold sadly released Anechka's hand, trying to keep his fingers lingering as long as his outstretched arm would allow. Anechka blew him a kiss which he caught with a smile on his rosy red cheeks before disappearing out of the ballroom.

Reynold stumbled down the front stairway in a trance as Quincy held the door to the limo open for him. He slid into his seat and sighed heavily.

"I feel as if I don't quite have the dancing part down yet," Reynold said shyly, "could I perhaps come over for a lesson again… with Anechka?"

He looked up at Suexliegh with love-struck eyes.

"If you do well at the cotillion, you can come back whenever you want," Suexliegh winked knowingly, "for a lesson, of course."

Reynold's whole face lit up as he bounced excitedly in his seat.

"Yes, yes please!" he nearly shouted. "What next, please teach me!"

Suexliegh chuckled and put his hands up, "Drinking is the easy part, and although you cannot partake in said libations for a further three years, you should know how to be friendly with them."

"Drinking, libations, friendly, got it," chanted Reynold. "What else?"

"A true gentleman only drinks red wine and scotch, don't ask why that's just how it is," Suexliegh said as he checked his teeth in the car's window. "Should you happen to encounter any other spirits, here they are by percentage of alcohol in descending order: cognac, scotch, whiskey, rum, brandy, gin, port, vermouth, sherry, burgundy, champagne, bordeaux, cider, ale, porter, lager. Just don't get this list reversed or you're in for one hell of a night."

Chapter The Sixty-Fifth
Atlas Vanguard

SIR, Madam, Mister, Missus, Miss, Doctor, Esquire. Reynold kept repeating these titles over and over again in his head so he did not forget them when addressing the sure to be illustrious crowd. Tonight, he would be perfect. Reynold was going to prove to his mother that he could stand on his own two feet, prove to his father he was worthy of his family name and, most importantly, prove to Suexliegh that he learned proper, gentlemanly etiquette so that he could again waltz with the fair Anechka. He had been pricked by a Russian Rose, her poison now ran deep in his veins.

"Waltz, Tango, Foxtrot, Viennese Waltz, Cha Cha, Rumba, East Coast Swing, Bolero and Mambo," Suexliegh counted the dances off one by one on his fingers. "Each has their own style, but as long as you stick with what you know and pretend to be having the best night of your life you'll be the talk of the party. And should you have to ask a girl to dance apart from your date behave like a lone wolf. Never attack a pack, instead pick off a weak, wounded baby mammal and strike when she least suspects it. Got it?"

"Got it."

"Good," grinned Suexliegh. "Oh, and Magellan, keep your hands above the Equator, understood?"

Suexliegh watched with pride as Reynold trotted off to find Deidre amidst the mingling crowd which had already begun to fill the ballroom. The Atlas Vanguard Hotel was the last of its kind in the city having survived earthquakes, fires, storms and anything else Mother Nature could throw at it. Built during the boom of the roaring 1920s, the architecture screamed chichi art deco from floor to ceiling; a golden, sunburst patterned arch sparkled above the entranceway flanked by mighty sky-blue pillars with detailed striations running their length. The extravagant building seemed almost otherworldly, as if it had been pulled from the depths of Atlantis itself.

The Van Every's had spared no expense with their one and only daughter's cotillion. Those few with good fortune, or great fortunes, were invited, especially if they had a son similar in age to Deidre. It was no secret that prosperous families employed age-old tactics to force their offspring to marry not often for love, but for dowry. One family might need new connections to the gold reserves, another to land in New South Wales, another to a prominent name that was worth more than any dollar value. Black market marriages. The Van Every's future had been blown off course by an ill wind; their family enterprise, *Chien Haute Couture*, high-end designer garments for dogs, had begun slipping profit-wise since a rival foreign firm, *Der Sit Und Stay*, a German company, started catering in high volume and low cost to the middle class. Their last best hope for a quick turnaround was in their daughter, braces freshly removed, Deidre.

Throughout the night Deidre's mother whisked her from bachelor to bachelor, of greatly varying ages and physical appearances, hoping to catch their interest. For once, Suexliegh did not attend the party for enjoyment; he spent the evening shadowing Reynold as he introduced himself to sirs, madams, misters, missuses, misses, doctors, and esquires all correctly. Reynold used all of his utensils in the proper order and even had the good sense to decline himself a second piece of cake so he wouldn't have to loosen his belt. He even gave a courtesy laugh to a joke not worthy of any humor. The young charmer became the talk of the party and everyone wanted to know where he had learned to be such an upstanding gentleman. Reynold, happy to be the center of attention, excitedly pointed to Suexliegh who pretended to be wiping detritus off his coat sleeve. A gathering of socialites looked over and chattered to themselves, impressed, especially Verena.

Chapter The Sixty-Sixth
Significant Bother

"YOU look well."

"And you," Verena wafted towards him as if on a gentle breeze. This was the first time he had seen, heard, smelled, touched or tasted Verena since her abrupt disappearance and his nerves of steel were beginning to rust. One always hopes when they encounter a former flame he or she will have become fat, ugly or unhappy. One would be nice, all three even better. Unfortunately, Verena had become quite the opposite. Maybe it was the champagne or the lighting or perhaps a low-grade fever, but tonight she seemed effervescent.

"I didn't know you had a son," Verena gestured to Reynold who was in the midst of twirling Deidre around the ballroom floor with all the other couples. His date was smiling, perfectly straight, with small, off-colored squares in the center of every tooth leaving hints of a previously awkward period in life.

"They grow up so fast, don't they," Suexliegh let slip a knowing smile. A long silence ensued, filled with unspoken questions and hesitant answers, until Suexliegh gingerly put out his hand.

"May I have this dance?"

Verena recoiled slightly at the sudden invitation.

"Actually," Verena looked around as if afraid she was being watched, "I'm here with someone."

"Yes, she most certainly is here with someone. Me," said a voice.

Suexliegh's heart dropped into his stomach. Two stubby hands pried apart a dancing couple who hollered back an "Excuse me!" and "I never!" The hands rested on Verena's hips.

"You look well."

"And you, Dingle," hissed Suexliegh through his teeth. Dingle cleared his throat as he pulled Verena closer, smashing the two together.

"This is my *girlfriend*, Verena," Dingle's fake smile turned into a look of fake horror, "Oh no! Oh that's right! You two used to be... involved with each other. What a faux pas I've committed! I didn't meant to make this situation any more awkward than it already is."

"No, not at all," Suexliegh replied without an ounce of malice. "Time and tide heal all wounds."

"Good good!" Dingle chuckled as he spun Verena around into an exaggerated dance pose. "Then you won't mind if we have this dance. See you on the floor!"

Verena gave Suexliegh a furtive glance before she and Dingle joined the throng of tuxedo and gown clad waltzers. Fleeting glimpses was all he caught of her as she slipped in and out of view between the other pairs. Soon, all the guests had partnered up leaving Suexliegh the only player left on the sideline through the long waltz.

"Darling, you were magnificent on your feet," Dingle stumbled off the dance floor in a fit of jubilant hysterics trailing Verena closely behind him, "and I can't wait to get you off your feet next. Mrahwr!"

"I'm going to get a drink," Verena spotted a flash of anger in Suexliegh's look as she made her way to the bar. "A very stiff drink."

"Women, aren't they just the light of our lives?" Dingle wiped a laugh-tear from his eyes.

"Yes, and also the blackest of nights. Now if you'll excuse me, I believe this is where I say 'good evening,'" Suexliegh excused himself and parted through the guests on his way to the door.

"But we've only just begun! Surely, you'll stay a while longer? I think it's time we turn over a new leaf," Dingle gleamed, knowing every second near Verena was a knife in Suexliegh's heart.

"You know, you're right," Suexliegh said, turning back around, a glimmer of mischief in his eyes. "Why don't you come by tomorrow, say just after dawn, and we'll catch up properly."

Chapter The Sixty-Seventh
An Old Bet

"WHAT AM I supposed to do with these?"

Suexliegh held a bucket and mop outstretched, leaving Dingle in a state of utter confusion.

"What are those contraptions? I've never seen them before in my life!" Dingle peered at the cleaning utensils like they were from another planet.

"I've made a mess and I need you to clean it up," Suexliegh pushed the mop into Dingle's chest but he quickly batted it away.

"Clean up after you... never!" Dingle turned on his heel and began trotting down the steps to his waiting chauffeur. "I'd rather mouth-kiss my own mother first."

"That decision is up to you, but need I remind you of our wager," Dingle stopped and waited for Suexliegh to finish. "Pennywinkle won fair and square, and if I'm not mistaken-"

"You're not mistaken, sir, I have it all written down in the records," Quincy piped in, pulling out a ledger as he did. Suexliegh had made more bets than anyone could possibly remember, so Quincy was tasked with denoting the particulars. One time Suexliegh had bet a wealthy brasserie merchant that a certain drop of water would make its way to the bottom of a rainy window first. The man agreed to said bet and was soon several bank notes poorer.

"Then as we agreed you must never race your horses again and you must be my servant for a fortnight," Suexliegh took his revenge with a smile as he let it sink in.

"But... but... this is preposterous! These hands, look at my hands!" Dingle raced up the steps and showed Suexliegh his hermetically perfect hands. "They're not meant for manual labor, the flesh will rub right off. These are the hands of a god! All my years of moisturizing and manicures will be for naught. I beg of you, anything but that!"

"A deal's a deal. Unless," Suexliegh put the mop and bucket down, "you wish to renege."

Dingle gasped. Reneging was a fate worse than death, and Dingle knew it. If anyone found out that he wasn't a man of his word his entire existence in the upper echelon would be in jeopardy. No one would make gentlemanly bets with him anymore for he was no longer a gentleman. Dingle shuddered at the thought. He attempted to regain his composure and displayed an air of dignity as he shot out his hands.

"Hand me the stick and bucket," Dingle muttered indignantly.

"Aren't you forgetting something?"

Dingle looked up into Suexliegh's expectant face, "No."

"Ah ah ah, you didn't say the magic word!"

"Abracadabra?"

"*Please.*"

Dingle shook his head and suppressed his urge to return the favor of Suexliegh's earlier punch to the nose.

"Hand me the stick and bucket... *please,*" Dingle muttered the last word under his breath. "Now where is this mess?"

As he reached out, Suexliegh kicked the bucket so that it tumbled down the steps and splattered soapy water everywhere.

"You can start by cleaning up all this water. When that's done the chimney needs to be swept, the lake needs to be groomed, and the attic needs to be de-pigeoned," Suexliegh peeked at his watch. "That shouldn't take you more than one revolution of the big hand and if it does you'll have to answer to me. Chop chop!"

Suexliegh clapped twice as he headed back into the manor leaving Dingle fuming on the front steps. He had his nemesis by the scruff and he was going to hang him high.

"Quincy, you have the day off."

Chapter The Sixty-Eighth
Chore House

AFTER the chimney, lake and attic, there was trimming the hedge maze, all ten miles of it, scrubbing the yacht's rumpus room, categorizing shirts in rainbow order, and flossing the statue's teeth.

"I think I'll take lunch in the library," Suexliegh yawned. "I'm low on blood sugar right now and if you don't get some food in me I'm liable to go into shock!"

Dingle begrudgingly trudged over to Suexliegh who lounged on the bed still wearing his morning robe.

"And bring me my slippers. Warm them with your breath but try not to get any of your awful horse smell on them."

Dingle robotically picked up the slippers, puffed on them, and slid them onto Suexliegh's dangling feet.

"Now carry me."

"What?" Dingle snorted.

"I said carry me down to the library. Quincy does it every morning and he's a decrepit octogenarian! Don't tell me *you* can't do the same."

"Of course I can! I could carry you with both hands tied behind my back!"

"That would be uncomfortable for the both of us. Let's just do it the normal way, shall we?"

What normal way he was referring to, Dingle didn't know, as he awkwardly scooped up Suexliegh, who played the part of a passive resistor too well, and hobbled his way down to the library. Every step down the stairs was nearly the end for both of them, but Dingle conjured all the gusto he could muster before collapsing in a heap next to the chair into which he dropped Suexliegh. Dingle flopped onto his back, huffing and puffing, as he struggled to catch his breath.

"Hmm, no, there's not enough sunlight in here. The atrium seems more fitting. Up up! I haven't got all day."

Dingle heaved raggedly as he staggered to his feet and hoisted Suexliegh back into his arms.

"Oh wait my tea!"

Dingle stopped short, leaned his momentum the opposite way, and headed back to the side table where Suexliegh carefully balanced the green tea on its plate.

"Okay, you may carry on."

Sweat poured down Dingle's face as Suexliegh calmly sipped at his tea and flipped open his book without a care in the world. Steps from the atrium door, Suexliegh slowly slipped through Dingle's grip.

"Careful you knave, I almost spilled this scaldingly hot tea all over you!"

Dingle used the last of his energy to lean Suexliegh against an indoor willow tree before collapsing into a catatonic lump on the ground.

"This will do for now," yawned Suexliegh as he idly scrolled through the pages of his book. He snapped his fingers, "Oh devils! I forgot my spoon. We have to go back for it."

Dingle only managed to get single words out between his labored breaths, "We... why... don't... I... just... get... it...?"

"You won't know which one is my favorite," Suexliegh clapped his book shut and readied himself into leaping position, "besides, this is much more fun."

"Alley-oop!" he exclaimed, jumping onto Dingle's back who wasn't ready for the sudden weight in the least bit causing him to slam his knees onto the ground. Dingle cried out in pain.

"Sweet mother of God!"

"How dare you take the Lord's mother's name in vain! On your feet, blasphemer!" cried Suexliegh. "The sooner we get this done the sooner I can degrade you more."

Chapter The Sixty-Ninth
Revenge

DINGLE had had enough. Worse than having to perform menial and monotonous tasks for his sworn enemy stood the fact that Suexliegh was right there watching every single second with supreme satisfaction. He relished overly in Dingle's misery and had a perpetual list of odd jobs at his disposal the moment a spare instant emerged so the torturous humiliation could continue indefinitely. *Two can play at this game*, thought Dingle as he polished the codpiece on a suit of armor.

"Verena's a great kisser. Her lips always taste like honey," Dingle nonchalantly moved to the knight's helmet and began polishing the protruding visor. Suexliegh pretended not to hear and went back to his Sudoku with mock concentration.

"The way she smells too, like... olive oil. I would never have thought such a scent would be so... intoxicating. So... arousing, but believe you me it is," huffed Dingle breathlessly as Suexliegh cleared his throat loudly and rattled the paper in an attempt to cover up the pointed remarks. "And how she moves her hips when she walks, my goodness, it's hypnotizing. Any man would count himself lucky to walk in time with that metronome am I right, Suexliegh?"

Suexliegh shrugged indifferently, saying, "How's that armature coming? You can get to work straightening the lances next."

Dingle saw right through him. His fingers had the paper in a death grip, slowly choking the life out of the pages as his eyes bored holes right through the floor. The veins on his neck pulsed. It was working. Dingle had him. Time for the coupe de grâce.

"I have a secret, and I haven't told anyone yet but I think you would be keen to hear it," Dingle stopped dusting and theatrically waved a hand in the arm with a sharp intake of breath. "I'm going to ask Verena to marry me."

The pencil Suexliegh was holding snapped in two and the paper crumpled into a ball as both of his hands balled tightly into fists.

"It's almost tea time and I think you've paid back your bet in full," Suexliegh whisked past Dingle and wrenched open the door. "Now if you'll excuse me, I'd like you to leave so that I can go shoot something."

Dingle feigned concern, dropping the feather duster and rushing over to Suexliegh who backed himself away into the corner.

"I haven't upset you in any way have I? I know you and Verena had a… thing, but I thought you would want to hear how she's doing. If you truly loved her you would be glad to know that she is happy. With me."

"I never loved her!" roared Suexliegh, breathing heavily through clenched teeth. His whole body had become lobster red as his temper threatened to boil over and pop every button, cuff link, and collar. Dingle cowered at the display of rage, fearing physical retribution for his remarks. The term, "crime of passion" came to mind. Like a storm, Suexliegh's wrath slowly blew away as the color drained from his face. He looked around frantically, hoping no one else saw his momentary fall from grace, then quickly put himself back together. Straightening his tie, dusting off his jacket, slicking back his hair.

"Let me be the first to congratulate you," Suexliegh managed after a long moment. His voice was ragged at first, but gained clarity as he spoke until it was back to its usual luster, "and wish you… good luck. Verena is truly a remarkable woman who deserves nothing but the best, wherever and with whomever she finds it. I know the two of you will have a wonderful life together."

Suexliegh's wandering, tear-filled eyes finally fell on Dingle who was overcome with the show of compassion put on by his nemesis. The two looked at each other for the first time, not as enemies, not as friends, not even as acquaintances, but just as two men who were in love with the same woman.

Chapter The Seventieth
Quincy's Day Off

WITHOUT SOMEONE to answer to for the first time in his life Quincy felt the full weight of time on his shoulders. He could do anything he wanted for a whole twelve hours and it terrified him. What if Master wants his water iced or needs an impromptu back scratch, thought Quincy. The notion of Suexliegh unable to have what he sorely desired nearly made Quincy turn heel and rush home quick. No, Quincy mused, as he walked down the dirt pathway, through the towering iron gates, and out into the world, Master gave me the day off, in fact, he made a direct order of it, so I will obey his wishes.

"Father! Father, wait up!" a honking horn startled Quincy who spun around to see Quincy Jr. come barreling down the driveway in the Bugatti waving out the window like a maniac. He screeched to a stop kicking up a huge cloud of dirt around them. Quincy Jr. leaped out of the car, coughing and trying to waft the dust away.

"I have such terrible news! Mr. Suexliegh gave me the day off too so now he's all alone in that big house with Mr. Steeds and no one to attend to them! I'm worried about him," Quincy Jr. was nearly hysterical and began hyperventilating. "What if he wants his eggs deviled?"

"I see you've learned well," Quincy put a calming hand on his son's shoulder then brushed away some dust that had settled on him. "Always thinking of your master's wants and needs comes above everything else in life. You live to serve."

"I do very much indeed, yes," the young butler bristled at the compliment. "Thank you, father, I learned everything I know from you."

Quincy hobbled around to the passenger's seat and sidled in, "And you still have very much to learn. I shan't be around forever."

"Please don't say such a thing of course you will."

"Of course I will not!" Quincy rattled, raising the chair-back to make himself sit more vertically. "I'm a mortal man of flesh and blood; time will take me as it does everything else on this Earth. All I can do is make sure I use the time given to me with kindness and virtue in the service of a better man than I."

"I hope one day to find someone like Mr. Suexliegh whom I can serve, though I fear I will not ever encounter another quite the same," Quincy Jr. sighed at the realization. "How will I know if I've met the right one?"

"Like love, when everything is right, you will just know," Quincy stared out the window at the rows upon rows of mansions slipping past, each complete with their imposing front gate, manicured gardens, adorned architecture and butler who was at this very moment attending graciously to his master's needs. "There's a special bond between butler and master that cannot be defined in any practical way and sometimes just does not work out. You know, I was, for a short while, in the employ of a different master."

Quincy Jr. balked at the remark, nearly swerving into oncoming traffic, "You were!? But you always told me you had been with Mr. Suexliegh since before he was born."

"I have been, but I'm also a great deal older than the good sir and needed proper employed before he ever existed. If the fates hadn't brought the two of us together, I shudder to think where I would be now," Quincy rolled down the window to get a fresh breath of air and wipe clean the memories of a time before Suexliegh.

"Please tell me the story, if you don't mind too greatly, I think it will make me feel better knowing that we all, even you, go through a period of vast uncertainty before we find our way."

Quincy chuckled to himself as his eyes glazed over in remembrance, "It was the autumn before I met the Master, the leaves were starting to turn, and I still had a full head of hair."

Chapter The Seventy-First
The Inventor

"THOUGH THE MYSTICAL profession of 'inventor' had fallen by the wayside around the turn of the century in name, there were still many who followed its craft under different, less grandiose, titles. Isabelle Potrero, for one, was known as a 'New Projects Manager for Research & Design of Applicable Materials,' which does not really have the same ring to it, and would never go down in the history books amongst the likes of Benjamin Franklin or Nikola Tesla who designed marvelous creations that captured the imagination of the entire nation.

"In fact, many of her inventions seemed far too inconsequential to be of any value at all, but little did anyone know that the tiny cap that clicks so satisfyingly as one closes a tube of tooth paste created a multi-million dollar industry. The twisting lock contained within the door knob, that was her. The dimmer slide next to a light switch, that was her too. The hook that holds a wall mounted phone on the receiver, yes, Isabelle as well. Things you use every day but never give a second thought to, that was her specialty. Her ability to envision what was needed on products that already existed kept her in high demand throughout her long career as an 'Improver,' a term of endearment more to her liking.

"All the while, acquaintances of mine had been trying to set me up with dignitaries and captains of industry for years, but after no luck I was becoming desperate; I needed to find someone to serve and settle down with. As with every year, those of age and in need of employment are paired with those in need of a servant during the annual Conclave. Call it speed dating for butlers. At long last I was matched with Madam Potrero and could finally start as a real servant: living in the mansion and waiting on her hand and foot.

"So with a spring in my step I moved out to the city and soon found myself walking up the driveway to her manor with my entire life in a suitcase, but when I arrived I was startled to find moving trucks out front. The entire estate was being packed up and relocated to a condominium in downtown. 'This house is far too big for me alone,' Isabelle had said, 'I would like something that requires a little less work.' Day one and I was already being downsized.

"All that week we moved her to the penthouse condo overlooking the lake and I gained first hand knowledge of every single item she owned and learned exactly where she liked everything to be. Anything she told me I jotted down in a notebook which I memorized at night so I would be the absolute best butler anyone in the world ever had seen. I would be perfect. Seven days later, we were all moved in, and everything was where it should be. It was not quite what I expected for my first foray as a professional butler, but I was eager and willing to do what was expected of me. Yet that night when Isabelle went to sleep in her 13th century Romanesque four-post bed, immaculately prepared and tucked by my own hands for the first time, she never woke up again. And so, before it hardly began, it ended. I watched as the beneficiaries of her will piece by piece dismantled everything I had put together until there was nothing left but the empty room and me.

"Those were the darkest days of my life. One step forward, one step back and nothing to show for it except a broken heart. Then like a sudden storm, fate intervened on my behalf. A young master was due to be born, a boy, and the parents wanted to make sure he always had someone watching over him when they were not around.

"I was there when Suexliegh was born. I was there when they took him home. I knew him before he knew himself. I've lost a hair on my head every single day worrying about him. It has been a very long and wonderful journey working for Mr. Suexliegh, but he is the reason I am as bald as an eagle."

Chapter The Seventy-Second
Father Knows Best

QUINCY AND QUINCY JR. spent the better part of the day driving aimlessly around the city for they had no where else to be. Junior, as his father had taken to calling him lately, kept coming a steady stream of questions hoping to glean as much wisdom from the old man as possible. Though he had followed in his father's footsteps by learning the art of butlering, even attending the Royal Butlering Academy in Oxford, the etiquette capitol of the world, he still did not feel as if he were ready to be relied upon. As if reviewing for an entrance exam, Quincy Jr. went over all the areas he thought he should know: staff management, house administration, table and cutlery organization, laundry superintendence, cooking governance and even the oft overlooked valet supervision. Quincy explained how to hand tailor a suit, how to deal with a guest who was uninvited (or stealing), how to care for a proper pantry, and even the execution of a perfect Christmas day.

"Check your drain tonight, if you find a stray hair then you're well on your way," Quincy's smile cracked the lines in his face. The two were finally headed home as the sun raced beneath the horizon painting the buildings in an auburn glow for their arrival.

"I most certainly will," Quincy Jr. gave a soft tug on his hair, hoping to be rewarded with a few strands to lift his spirits.

"All in good time, son, all in good time," Quincy laughed. "You don't want to go bald too soon, you've got your whole life ahead of you for that!"

"Mister Suexliegh, we're returned!" Quincy creaked open the aged oak door into the main foyer and was met with stark darkness. All the lights were off save for a faint amber hue emanating from deep within the manor. "I hope you managed alright with your temporary 'help.' Junior and I are here now if anything is troubling you."

BANG! A short, sharp shot rang out making them drop instinctively to the floor as echoing laughter floated through the house. The two exchanged puzzled looks.

"You fool! What'd you have to go and do that for? It's already dead!" the eerily muffled voice of Suexliegh exclaimed. Quincy got up his nerve and cautiously peeked his head into the living room only to find the most peculiar sight: Suexliegh perched precariously on top of a chair, prodding a stuffed moose's head that hung on the wall with a freshly smoldering gunshot wound through its temple, and Willard blowing smoke out of the barrel of a rifle as he lay, intoxicated, on the couch. The smell of gunpowder and peat hung in the air.

"You never know," slurred Willard as he loaded another cartridge, "he might have been faking it."

"Is everything alright?" Quincy whispered as calmly as possible so as not to startle the two gun-wielding drunkards with questionably itchy trigger fingers.

"Quincy!" Suexliegh swung his rifle around so it was pointed straight at Quincy and his son who immediately reached for the sky.

"Don't shoot!"

"You're just time, we were on our way out the door," Suexliegh threw the rifle to Quincy, but Quincy Jr. stepped in front and caught it square in the chest knocking him back a step. Quincy Jr. carefully unloaded the gun and placed it back on the wall, making sure to stay out of Willard's line of sight as he did.

"But sir, you can't go out in your state, you're... you've had a few too many," Quincy petitioned kindly.

"All too true, my good man," Suexliegh reached above the roaring fireplace and pulled down an antique blunderbuss, "that's why you're driving."

Chapter The Seventy-Third
Stake Out

"I TAKE it things didn't go well today."

"Yes and no, but mostly yes."

"You're not thinking about murdering him are you, sir? I mean, I will help you do whatever you ask of me but please do not ask that of me!" Quincy began to hyperventilate at the thought. At least they would be in prison together.

"Calm your shiny little head," Suexliegh patted him on the baldest spot of his cranium, "we just want to give Dingle a little present from the Burgundy Scoundrels."

"I do so hope that present isn't a bullet," Quincy whispered to Junior as the Bugatti bumped and roared along a backcountry road miles outside of town. It had been a good long while since any streetlights had been seen and darkness was quickly falling all around them as they wound deeper into the countryside. For minutes on end they drove in silence, all the while Suexliegh scanned the horizon. On a distant pasture, a single home broke the rolling skyline growing ever larger as they hurried towards it.

"We're almost there," Suexliegh surveyed the land around them with a wicked gleam in his eyes. "Pull over here."

Quincy Jr. skidded them into the rocky ditch by the side of the road and turned off the car leaving them in a cricket-filled silence. Suexliegh pressed his nose up against the glass and squinted to get a better view of the ever darkening home.

"That's Dingle's place," Suexliegh tapped the glass alerting them to a top floor window which was lit. He shook his head and scoffed. "He must still be up chuckling, thinking he truly is a laugh-riot for making a fool of me in my own house! Who will be laughing soon? Not he but I, I tell you!"

Willard pulled out his flask and took a nip of liquid courage, "Does he have any dogs or other security measures we should know about?"

"Just horses."

"Guard horses?"

"No, just the regular kind."

Suexliegh opened the door and crept out of the car before closing it silently behind Willard. Quincy Jr. rolled down the window and poked his head out.

"What would you like us to do, sir?" Junior asked in a worried whisper.

"You two stay here. If all goes well, Willard and I will be back in a few minutes. If all doesn't go well, you'll need to come in and rescue us."

Quincy Jr. gulped at the prospect of having to be a hero, "How will we know if it isn't going well?"

"There will be a lot of screaming," Suexliegh winked.

"We'll keep our eyes peeled for the authorities," Quincy called after them as they crept over to the fence. "Godspeed, sir!"

A modest wooden gate with the initials "D.S." carved across the front gave outsiders the impression the occupant was a simple ranch owner who only supported himself with his livestock and made just meager enough a living to scrape by. Yet no one would have known the timber pieces used to build the gate and surrounding fence were priceless sideboards from the Titanic. Suexliegh craned his foot up on the fence in a heroic pose and pulled out the blunderbuss.

"Will one gun be enough?" Willard watched Suexliegh pour priming powder into the barrel, tamp down a lead ball and cock the blunderbuss before sticking it into his waistband.

"One will be plenty."

Chapter The Seventy-Fourth
The Blunderbuss Trap

SUEXLIEGH AND WILLARD landed with a soft thud on the other side of the fence into a grassy field where several dozen prized horses grazed idly in the moonlight. They crept, slowly, trying to make as little sound as possible in their tailored suits while keeping an eye on the lit window ahead of them.

"Try not to be afraid, Willard, horses can smell fear."

"Let's hope they can't smell scotch or else we're out of luck."

Like an invitation, a horse neighed then charged directly at them, its thick rippling legs churning up the turf with every stride. Suexliegh dove aside and tumbled down the berm into a shallow ravine but Willard wasn't so lucky, only managing to lie flat as a pancake before the horse galloped over him. Willard let out a muffled gasp and rolled over in pain.

"Willard? Willard, are you hurt?" Suexliegh dusted off his slacks and scampered back up the hill, thankful the finicky medieval weapon hadn't decided to misfire on his tumbling adventure. Willard moaned as he turned onto his back.

"That beast trampled my flask, but I think I'll be alright," a brown whiskey stain spread across his chest from the leaking flask as Suexliegh helped him to his feet.

"What do you think *that* horse smelled?" Willard asked, bewildered.

Suexliegh sniffed, "My guess would be scotch."

They continued without further incident through the pasture, making sure to give every horse that looked at them funny a wide berth. Just as they neared edge of the house, Willard ducked down and held up a hand to stop Suexliegh.

"Look!" Willard pointed to a silhouette that drifted around inside the lighted room, then stopped, and everything went dark. Suexliegh looked over at Willard with all seriousness.

"Willard, you don't have to do this, it's between Dingle and myself."

"When someone pains one Burgundy Scoundrel, they pain them all," Willard grinned. "Besides you can't keep all the fun for yourself."

Silent as shadows they made their way back to the horses, pulling out large handfuls of peppermints from their pockets. The horses' ears pricked as Suexliegh knickered softly, calling them over. One by one they tentatively padded up to them, sniffed the air, and licked the mints out of their hands. In only a few moments, the entire herd had surrounded them eager to get treats of their own. Suexliegh and Willard began slowly backing up the hill towards the house with their flock of horses in tow.

Running ahead, Suexliegh elbowed through the front window, shattering glass everywhere. He reached around the broken pane and felt the door click satisfyingly into the unlocked position. Suexliegh knew that Dingle would never hear the commotion due to his poor hearing from years of sport shooting. He used that same fact to deduce that Dingle would never hear as he and Willard led three-dozen horses through the house, up the staircase, and right into his bedroom. They heard him snoring peacefully, but he never heard them. Nor the band of peppermint smelling animals now occupying every free inch of his upper floor. The blunderbuss was rested delicately on the nightstand and the trap was finally set.

They dashed out of the house and down through the field to the Quincys who watched in silent amazement at their wildly grinning faces. The door slammed behind them as they caught their breath in the back of the car, huffing and puffing between excited giggles.

"Should we flee now?" Quincy asked hopefully. Suexliegh's eyes flicked from the house to the butler.

"No, now we wait."

Chapter The Seventy-Fifth
The Morning After

WHEN THE FIRST SLIVER of sunlight peeked over the hill, a rooster crowed and the trap was sprung. They eagerly watched and waited in impatient silence until an alarm buzzer jangled in the distance, followed by the crack of a gun. A horse whinnied and an earthquake erupted within the house. The entire building shook down to its foundation, windows fractured, chimneys crumbled, shingles skittered to the ground. Someone was screaming. Even the car itself wobbled on its shocks due to the trembling force. Quincy reached over and locked the doors. Everything went quiet. Quincy gave Suexliegh a look that said, "please let it be over" but the front door splintered off its hinges and a steady stream of horses trampled at full speed into the pasture, their manes billowing. Horses began jumping through windows, smashing open the front porch railing in their blind flight. The stampede seemed never ending until finally a lone horse, a baby, trotted out down the crushed steps and sneezed in the cloud of dust that had been kicked up by its big brothers. All that was left was a leaning structure and the sound of wood slowly splintering under the weight of a dead house. Suexliegh was as stunned as the rest of the group as he turned back to Quincy, "Now we flee."

What they knew was that the prank had been a resounding success, perhaps the most daring and destructive in the long history of the Burgundy Scoundrels. What they didn't know was that when the alarm sounded that morning and a lazy arm flopped over to turn it off, only to fire the cocked pistol instead, sending the swarm of horses into a frightened frenzy, that Dingle was not the bed's occupant. He wasn't at home, he wasn't in town, he wasn't even in the country, but poor Mrs. Pierce, the elderly housekeeper with a manly snore, was. She had been hired to watch over the estate while Dingle was away on a personal matter and awoke thinking the four horses of the Apocalypse had entered her bedroom as everything exploded into bucking hooves and horror. Mrs. Pierce ducked under the blankets hoping the nightmare would soon pass and she could wake up to a house that was perfectly kempt. Instead, not twenty four hours later, the building would have to be condemned.

"If only I could have seen his face!" Suexliegh had his head out the window and was screaming at the top of his lungs while Willard leaned through the other side yelling a war cry.

"His manor nearly toppled like straw shack! It was brilliant! I thought the horses would spook and maybe crack some of his fine China but we nearly killed him!" Willard slapped his knee and reached for his flask only to come to the disheartening realization that it was empty. If he were a lesser man he would have sucked the alcohol straight out of his shirt.

"You didn't kill him though, did you?" Quincy asked hesitantly. "I did hear a rather loud spot of gunfire."

"He's fine, Quincy, fine! Didn't you hear all that screaming? Dead men don't scream," Suexliegh laughed with glee at their triumph.

The celebration continued all the way back to the manor as the Scoundrels recalled the heist in vivid detail. Everything from the cragged mountainside Suexliegh careened down, to the ten-ton horse that nearly flattened Willard in a cavalry charge.

Suexliegh was the first out of the car and up the front steps, eager to call the other Scoundrels and tell them the news, where the morning paper sat leaning against the door. As he picked up the paper, his smile quickly faded. In the bottom corner, a small headline read:

Dingle Steeds and Verena Terena to Wed.

IV.
Roses

Chapter The Seventy-Sixth
The Octopus King

SWATHS OF WARM, coruscating light illuminated the rippled water down to the sea floor as the sun struggled lazily above the curve of the Earth, seemingly unwilling to rise for another day. Strong, weathered hands snapped off a bottle top and poured glugs of golden olive oil onto the frothy tide which spread across the surface, smoothing it out into a perfect window. Sea life flourished in numbers and patterns, darting too and fro with the ebb and flow of the morning current. A maroon blur morphed around the rocks and coral of the sandy bottom, staying visible just long enough to be a trick of the imagination. A slow tide rolled past creating a lull in the waves. The blur stopped to hold itself against the tug of the rip-current. A trident flashed through the water with hardly a splash and pinned the blur to the rock. The same strong hands hoisted the writhing mass of tentacles up into the air as it hissed and spattered ink.

"I've never been more terrified of any person in my entire life," Suexliegh shielded his eyes from the morning sun as he watched the silhouette of the octopus wind down until it hung limply from the three-forked spear. Dimitri pointed the trident to the sky.

"Octopus is very smart, see? Look at the shape, man, whole body is brain. You must strike where he is going, not where he has been. You attack the future or goodnight no food for you," Dimitri flung the cephalopod into a waiting bucket filled with the day's catch of octopi. Waves crashed against the jagged rocks overlooking a shallow cove where the two crouched, gazing intently through the water for signs of movement.

"Okay Mr. Big Shot, your turn," Dimitri tossed Suexliegh the trident which nearly sent him toppling over as he slipped on the slick outcropping. "If you don't kill right away, octopus will bite off his arm to escape. He has seven more, no? At least he won't be your meal today."

Suexliegh hefted the trident awkwardly into throwing position as he took aim. The tide crept in, splashing larger and heavier waves against the shore. Salty mist drifted into Suexliegh's eyes as the sea tried to protect its bounty.

"Quickly now," Dimitri coached, "octopus have busy lives so they can't wait around all day for you to kill them!"

Suexliegh's eyes locked on everything that moved, searching for the maroon blob to appear again but only colorful schools of fish flittered past. Dimitri turned his head slightly and peered over Suexliegh's shoulder into the water.

"There he is."

"Where? Where!? All I see are these goddamned minnows!"

"Look in the shadow, boss. Watch for his eyes."

Suexliegh took a step down into the ocean for a better view, his rolled up pant legs beginning to soak. In a flash, he saw them. Two black eyes glinted ever so slightly from beneath a large fan of coral.

"I see him! I see the bastard!" Suexliegh stabled his footing, raised the trident high above his head and thrust it downwards through the water where it lodged under the rock.

"Haha! I got him! That was dead on!"

"Collect your kill, Poseidon," Dimitri grinned with a dose of mischief in his voice. Suexliegh dove down to the bottom, grabbed the trident with both hands, and yanked it out. Instead of the squid, a voluminous plume of ink squirted out and enveloped him in the depths. He struggled to the surface kicking and sputtering as Dimitri fell to the ground laughing. Suexliegh crawled onto the shore covered in black ink stains from head to toe.

"I missed."

Dimitri wiped a tear of laughter from his eyes.

"But you killed the rock!"

Chapter The Seventy-Seventh
Scar Stories

ANTIKYTHERA was an old, white and blue striped, pot-bellied fishing vessel passed down through the generations of the Kouyias family to Captain Dimitri who was currently manning the helm. The ship required round-the-clock care as it had numerous persnickety leaks popping out of every bulkhead and a temperamental motor that was a game of Russian roulette to see if it worked. For two months of the year, every year, Dimitri and his family left America for the small village in Greece where he was born to do nothing but fish and enjoy the heat of the day.

Dimitri and Suexliegh had spent hours catching all the sea life they could find up and down the curving coast using poles, harpoons, and the occasional lucky trident strike. Their nets now wriggling and full, they decided to roast the first of their catch over a barrel barbecue fire on the back deck of the ship. Dimitri popped a fried tentacle from the grill and sucked it down like spaghetti, savoring every moment. He licked the grease off his fingers and went back for seconds, "This is life, yes? I am glad you come to visit. You make me a happy man."

"Thank you for having me, I needed to get out. Away from the city, away from work, the manor, from Quincy, though I know he's trying to find me right now," Suexliegh ground his teeth on an tentacle sucker but gave up and spit it overboard. "And especially away from women."

"Away from one woman yes, but here there are plenty more. Dark skin, long black hair, strong in arms. Stronger than you, my friend," Dimitri lifted one of Suexliegh's lithe arms and let it fall back down to his side. "Do you know what the Greeks say about a broken heart?"

Suexliegh shook his head as he chewed.

"More wine," chuckled Dimitri as he filled up Suexliegh's wine glass with a smile. "'One word frees us of all the weight and pain of life: that word is love.' Sophocles, you know him?"

"I know of him," Suexliegh took a sip and turned to Dimitri who was refilling his own cup for the fifth time. "Yet Socrates said, 'If you get a good wife you will be happy, and if you get a bad one you will become a philosopher.' Seems to me she must have been a real old crow then."

Dimitri laughed, spilling his wine all over the deck.

"You have scarred heart, baby. But that is on the inside, no one sees so no one knows you are hurt. This, you see this?" Dimitri twisted around, pushing up his hair to reveal a jagged scar along the back of his skull. "Goddamn bird try to steal my fish! Missed, got two talons in the neck instead. 'Cause of that stupid bird I have to keep my hair long! My head gets so damn hot!"

Suexliegh looked his arms over, then the rest of his body, but couldn't find a single scar. He shrugged.

Dimitri's eyes shot wide, "None?"

"Not a one."

"You and the world play nice, huh boss? Or you're just one lucky *Americano*," Dimitri dusted off his hands and put them in the air.

"A bit of both I suppose," Suexliegh glanced off towards the town where points of light began to blink on. Careful not to draw attention, Dimitri reached over and plucked a live octopus from the squirming bucket.

"Hey, boss?"

Suexliegh looked over just in time to see a tentacled creature fly and land on his arm which it quickly constricted around with its many limbs. Suexliegh let out a yelp of pain and shook the octopus with all his might, stumbling all over the deck. In a panic, he thrust his arm into the ocean and the beast instantly darted away. Suexliegh, breathing heavily, raised his arm and revealed a puncture wound that bled a red winding trail down to his elbow.

"What'd you do that for?" Suexliegh snapped in shock.

"Now you're just like the rest of us."

Chapter The Seventy-Eighth
A Night on the Town

THE TATTERED MOORING LINE tugged against its cleated restraint as Suexliegh hopped onto the dock and regained his land-legs. They had been out on the rocking water since before dawn and now every step felt as if the entire world were a massive seesaw. Dimitri swung a bag of the day's catch onto his back and jumped off, grunting with effort as he impacted hard with the wooden pier. He picked up two buckets filled with live fish, waving over his shoulder as they walked away into town, "See you tomorrow, boat."

Narrow, cobbled alleyways wound lazily through the town in a lattice spreading outwards from the church as if the architect had consumed one too many bottles on the job. There were no straights lines and several dead ends, but every stone felt as if it had survived hard years of weather and history. The white walled buildings with blue rooftops grabbed the sun's fading colors for its own as they slipped through orange to purple and finally to twilight. The day's scorching heat had faded and allowed families to emerge into the streets for a few moments of enjoyment in the relative cool of dusk.

Everywhere Dimitri went he was greeted with a familiar smile, a knowing wave and often a glass of wine which he gratefully accepted. If there was someone in town he did not know, surely they were a tourist, and even then it was a fair bet he would know them before the day was out. Dimitri hefted a bucket of fresh barbounia fish, still writhing in sea water over to a young boy who crumpled under the tremendous weight. The bucket toppled, spilling the flailing fish into the street.

"Oh no!" the boy cried out in horror as he struggled to toss the mass of flopping, slippery devils back into the bucket with little luck. Suexliegh chased a lone barbounia down the winding alley as it hopped its way back to the sea. "Mama will have my head!

"Just tell your mama they were already seasoned by the street and her work is done!" Dimitri called after the boy who was slinging what remained of the catch over his shoulder and hurrying off to his mother who stood, fists clenched against her hips, in the doorway. She yelled something in Greek and pointed emphatically to Dimitri which caused the boy to turn suddenly on his heels and run straight back to where he started.

"For you," the boy pulled a block of homemade feta cheese from his pocket and spun right around again back home. He stumbled through the front door as his mother shook her head and waved to Dimitri. He tossed the wedge of cheese up and down, feeling its weight.

"This is the best. I love her sheep."

"You seem to know everyone and love everything," said Suexliegh with childlike wonder as they passed an olive stand in the marketplace which was just closing up for the night.

"For Greeks, family is most important. No family, you've got nothing. I give food to friends, they give food to me, we're family too, yes? When you have family, what is there not to love in life?"

Suexliegh hesitated before answering, as if unsure how to proceed.

"I don't really have a family. Well, besides Quincy who is kind of like my father, and Quincy Jr. who is kind of like my son, but neither of them are related to me but they're related to each other so that is rather... odd come to think of it."

"Does not matter. You give to them, they give back to you," Dimitri ripped off a hunk of cheese and gave it a good sniff. "You are in Greece now, baby, you need to do like the Greeks! Live for this."

Dimitri tossed Suexliegh the cheese who smelled it as well then ate the whole piece in one bite. Immediately his face lit up with delight.

"You help give me fish, I give you cheese, you are family now."

Chapter The Seventy-Ninth
Family Dinner

THE SCENT of slowly cooked lamb and garlic potatoes wafted out through a cracked window as the two men dropped what was left of the fish into an ice chest and wiped their feet on the front mat. Though temperatures reached over one hundred degrees daily, when Suexliegh stepped into the house he felt an airy cushion of dragon's-breath even hotter. Doris, Dimitri's wife, kept the oven on at all times for she never knew when company might stop by and be hungry for an entire roasted chicken.

"Doris! It's too hot in here I hope you haven't cooked yourself!"

"Have a seat on the patio, it's almost ready. Natasha, bring your father and our guest something to drink," Doris called from the kitchen.

For Dimitri it was more wine, for Suexliegh it was a pitcher of ice water with an entire sliced lemon floating within. Not but a moment later, Doris backed through the door and revealed a platter of food fit for a Spartan army: spiced lamb, mashed potatoes, feta soaked in olive oil, Kalamata olives, rosemary bread, fresh-picked garden salad and several bottles of wine. The family members were very good eaters, professionals even, and put Suexliegh to great shame whenever they had meals together.

It was no small secret that Dimitri had recently become a septuagenarian, though in a match between himself and an ox he would be the sure victor. Years of carrying paint cans up and down ladders by hand had nearly torn his shoulders off the bone but he never complained once, only asking for a bit more wine each night to soften the pain. Suexliegh felt out of place eating with people who lived on less money a year than he spent every second.

"Doris, Natasha, Dimitri," Suexliegh looked at each in turn as he spoke, "thank you for taking me into your home. I hope one day soon you will all come stay with me in return. I can't possibly attempt to match your generous amount of sustenance, but you may stay in any room in the house that you like, for as long as you like."

"You first must ask me one hundred times like I did and then we'll be even. I ask you all the time, man, but you disappear! No call, just come over, my wife cook, you eat, okay? I think you forget about me," cried Dimitri.

Suexliegh held up his punctured arm which was already beginning to scar from the octopus's bite, "I can never forget now."

Instead of competing in a back and forth battle of telling the tallest tale that evening, Suexliegh was but a humble witness to the larger than life stories of Dimitri's strange and wonderful voyage that brought him to that dinner table. Listening intently to their host, the three gorged themselves on the cornucopia of food, as, after all, the refrigerator was full of fish; there was no room for leftovers whether they liked it or not.

"If I have another bite I'm likely to split at the seams," Suexliegh put down his napkin, pushed himself away from the table, and leaned onto the back legs of his chair feeling maximum contentness spreading through him. He rested a hand on his stomach and waved off Natasha who tried to offer another scoop of spanakopita. She took the heaping portion for herself and packed it away, putting Suexliegh to shame. Doris, who had disappeared minutes ago, re-emerged with a platter of home-made baklava hot from the oven. Suexliegh shook his head.

"There is always room for baklava," insisted Doris and offered the plate to Suexliegh. "Even if you don't think you can, it always finds a way to fit."

Not wanting to be rude, Suexliegh took the smallest piece he could find and tried a bite. The moment the treat hit his tongue he was miraculously hungry again and found his way through an entire row. Laughing, Dimitri drained the last drops of wine straight from the bottle.

"Looks like this is the end my friend. No wine, no reason to be awake. Off to sleep. We are leaving early tomorrow."

Chapter The Eightieth
The Island in the Shape of a Spearhead

ROUGH HANDS pulled Suexliegh from the gentle embrace of sleep, his dreams vanishing as the world morphed into dim focus. The sun was breaking dawn miles away but had yet to reach their shores leaving the house in night's cold clutches.

"Come," Dimitri boomed with no consideration for his slumbering guest, "it is time."

"Can't the octopi wait just a few more hours?" Suexliegh yawned as he rolled to the other side of the pillow and tried to find a warm spot under the covers. "If you interrupt my beauty sleep I'll be ugly for the rest of the day."

"No octopus today. Something much bigger."

Bags crashed and skidded across the deck of the *Antikythera* as Dimitri heaved them shipward without a second thought to the contents within. Knowing better, Doris and Natasha carried their own suitcases onboard. When you live with a bull, you learn not to wear red. The morning sun was still several degrees away but the Earth had revolved close enough that the inky darkness lightened to a deep cerulean. Suexliegh gingerly tip-toed up the gangplank, yawning as he went, and plunked himself down onto the aft life-raft for a quick nap. Just as he shut his eyes to drift back to sleep, Dimitri kicked him in the foot.

"You are captain today," Dimitri tossed his tattered old navy cap to Suexliegh which landed on his half-asleep face.

"Unless you want to re-live the Titanic perhaps you should man the helm," Suexliegh said, dusting off the cap and giving it back. "Yachts are the only sea-faring vessel I am friendly with."

Dimitri cranked full the throttle and the ship lurched away from the dock into open waters but he let the helm yew wherever it may.

"Aren't you going to..." Suexliegh trailed off as he nervously glanced back and forth from the spinning wheel to the panning horizon. Dimitri shrugged, pulled a persimmon from his pocket, and began to idly chew at it while watching for the sunrise. Doris and Natasha shook their heads and went below deck to save themselves the embarrassment and brace for possible impact. Suexliegh finally took the hint and grabbed the tiller before there was any loss of life or breakfast.

"See the light growing there?" Dimitri pointed far off towards the curving skyline where the sun was but minutes away from finally making its first appearance of the day. Suexliegh nodded. "That's our heading: into the sun."

They sailed easterly all day and night, winding through the slalom of Mediterranean islands stopping only to refuel or trade a fresh catch for local delicacies in port. After training Suexliegh in proper nautical navigational tactics which mostly consisted of "follow the sun in the morning, don't follow the sun in the afternoon, and yell loudly if you need help," Dimitri was free to cast out several lines and play angler with a pole in one hand and a glass of wine in the other.

"Land ho!" shouted Suexliegh with a large, childish grin on his face. It was amusing the first time, but after passing dozens of islands on their Aegean voyage the novelty wore off rather quickly. Dimitri reeled in his line and squinted at the tiny smudge of land ahead.

"We are here."

Suexliegh guided them through the busy thoroughfare towards the grand harbor inlet where numerous merchant and pleasure ships passed hurriedly to and from the bustling waterfront city.

"Look," Dimitri nodded upwards as they slipped between the harbor walls into the calm waters of the bay, "that is where he stood."

"Who?" Suexliegh craned his neck for a better look.

"The Colossus."

Chapter The Eighty-First
Rose of the Aegean

LONG AGO, before time itself existed, the island of Rhodes emerged fully-formed from the sea as a gifted offering to the sun god Helios who became its protector, blessing the land with never ending sunshine and the symbol of his sacred flower, the rose. In honor of their benevolent god, the people of Rhodes erected a colossal statue of Helios straddling the harbor's gates so that anyone who approached dare not attempt an invasion for fear of holy retribution. Or so the story goes.

The boat coasted into a slip along the horseshoe-shaped harbor allowing Suexliegh and the Kouyias family their first view of the ancient city. Beyond the bronze deer statues flanking the outer wall's minaret, pastel houses crammed together around a buzzing waterfront market. It seemed the entire populous of Rhodians had turned out in hustled preparation for a yearly celebration, the Medieval Rose Festival, which took place during the summer solstice and swept a transformation through the town reverting everything to its Dark Ages equivalent. Spice traders and cobblers. Alchemists and fairies. Knights and damsels. Suexliegh scoured the streets in rapt amazement with the feeling that the entire island had slipped backwards in time.

"We come every year," Dimitri flipped a coin to a merchant and picked a ripe pomegranate out of a wicker basket. He ripped the fruit in half and began to eat the seeds straight from the heart. "I come for the food. Doris for the clothes, and Natasha-"

"See you at dinner, Papa!" Natasha called back as she spotted a group of friends from the previous summer and ran over to join their pack. The swarm of giggling girls wove through the marketplace trying on hand-crafted jewelry and buying sweets.

"For her friends," finished Dimitri.

"Be back before sundown or you'll miss the opening!" Doris shouted over the din of the crowd into which Natasha disappeared.

"She does this every year!" Dimitri roared as he chewed through the tough seeds. "Natasha should be with family now!"

"She's been with us every day for a month, let her have some fun on her own for a once," Doris replied strongly as she examined a piece of vibrantly colored textile. Though of Greek descent, Doris grew up in America and carefully walked the line between old and new world and seemed to be the only person who actually understood what Dimitri was saying. He spit a mush of seeds into the gutter and wiped his hands clean as the three continued through the market place to the town center where preparations for the festival's events were being made. Everywhere Suexliegh looked hung the color red in flags, banners, and even painted on the walls giving the illusion the city was on fire. Considering the sweltering heat, it may as well have been.

As the last church bell ushered in the first signs of dusk, a loud horn rang out through the plaza which was met with turned heads and fevered chattering. People vacated the town center revealing a wide-open arena with two swords stuck in the cobblestone on either end. Standing behind the weapons were men dressed in knight's armor whose solemn waves aroused cheers from the townspeople.

"What's going on? Who are those shiny men?" asked Suexliegh who eagerly pushed aside the crowd for a better view of the action. A beautiful young woman with curling, hazel brown hair stood between the two men and lifted a handkerchief, embroidered with the silhouette of a dragon, above her head.

"The two men will fight for honor. I have money on the big one," Dimitri gestured towards the larger of the two knights who bowed to the damsel and nodded to his competitor before pulling a sword from the ground. A swell of cheering encouragement erupted.

"Whoever wins will get the woman."

Chapter The Eighty-Second
Knight Fall

SHING! A glancing blow off of the little knight's shield showered sparks and was met with gasps from the audience, if he had been a hair slower to react he would have been headless, but the little knight regained his composure and shouldered the shield with a grimace of pain, lifting the sword back into an attack position just as the big knight charged again, this time using his shield like a battering ram, yet the little knight was still quicker and sidestepped just in time to avoid being bulldozed only to return with a quick jab of the blade which was parried by the hilt of the big knight's sword and an elbow to the face-mask that knocked the little knight off balance as a mixture of cheers and boos rang out.

All eyes were on the fight and filled with ravenous bloodlust, fueled by their desire to see a glorious victory and double the cash in their pockets if they chose wisely, as the big knight stepped back and changed his angle of attack while the little knight tucked behind his shield with the point of his cutlass resting against the side in preparation for a quick stabbing blow, his only real chance to defeat the larger knight, whose saber fell like a hammer and nearly knocked his bones loose, was a well timed, accurate strike between the plates of armor, but his window was narrow as they both sparred, thrust, and blocked with supreme ability, swinging back and forth in a deadly pendulum that rose and fell with the heartbeat of the spectators.

The battle was to first blood, but the way these two men fought it felt to the death; the big knight let out a roar and started a flurry of attacks, slicing sideways off the breastplate, kicking with his metal pointed boots, then hacking downwards on his opponent's shield until it clattered to the ground off of a broken wrist and yelling from the crowd as the little knight let his injured arm dangle loosely by his side leaving his sword as his only defense against the impending onslaught, however, the big knight was honorific and cast his shield aside as well to put the two swordsmen back on equal grounds much to the chagrin of everyone, including Dimitri, who had money down and were hoping for a one-sided slaughter.

Shouting and Greek expletives heartened the big knight to end the match as he watched his adversary endeavor to stay on his feet through the pain of broken bones and bruising spreading throughout his body causing him to sway and dig his sword into the ground for stability at which the crowd heckled and taunted him further, but still he remained upright though his head hung dripping sweat out of the visor and the big knight knew it was time to deliver the finishing blow so he stormed forwards in a grandiose display of showmanship, his raised broadsword glistening in the sun, armor clanging in rhythm with his steps, ready to draw blood as the audience went dead silent when the weapon fell towards the little knight's neck arcing ever closer as time slowed to a stand still just before the impact allowing a quick turn of the heel and head making the big knight miss and splinter his sword off the cobblestone while the little knight twirled full around and nicked the thin leather guards on back of his challenger's knee cutting cleaning through the flesh in a well planned and executed feint.

A moment of stunned silence followed as the big knight toppled to the ground amidst a cry of pain before everyone in witness burst into overwhelming adulations. Dimitri looked on dumbstruck as the townspeople hoisted the little knight on their shoulders and paraded him around the square before depositing him in front of the damsel who wiped a tear from her eyes. The little knight removed his helmet, kneeled, and kissed the damsel's hand. She pulled him to his unsteady feet and presented an elbow with a smile. The two walked, arm in arm, down the street as trumpeting announced the official start of the festival.

And then, Suexliegh knew exactly what he needed to do.

Chapter The Eighty-Third
Demanding Satisfaction

A WHITE GLOVE whipped through the air and slapped the side of Dingle's face leaving a five-fingered mark on his cheek.

"I demand satisfaction!" Suexliegh announced as he stood in the doorway of Dingle's home brandishing a glove in his hand.

"What in the hell does that mean?" Dingle rubbed the increasingly red welt as he wiggled his jaw to make sure it was still attached. Several tears of pain began welling up in his eyes. "And what in the hell was that for!?"

SLAP! Another back-handed attack hit Dingle on the other side of his face causing him to yelp in pain.

"I insist that you stop immediately!" Dingle screeched as he massaged both cheeks in tandem. Suexliegh, disgusted that an article of his clothing had come in contact with Dingle, tossed the gloves in the trash and dusted off his hands.

"That first one was for Verena, but the second was for me," Suexliegh stalked around Dingle forcing him to turn awkwardly on the spot before stopping and staring his enemy in the face. "I challenge you to a duel."

Dingle marched over to a mounted display case and smashed through the glass revealing two dueling pistols, one of which was the blunderbuss Suexliegh had left at the scene of the crime.

"I believe this is yours," Dingle seethed with a smarmy grin as he handed over the ancient pistol. "I don't mind what you did, honestly, I was thinking about remodeling the place anyway and you gave me an apropos excuse. So what do you say, shall we have a go out back and end this once and forever?"

Suexliegh shook his head with a slight chuckle, "Pistols are too crass, don't you think? Besides, once I killed you I would be enemy-less and the rest of my life would be no fun at all."

Dingle ripped two shogun katanas off of the wall and brandished them with a wicked gleam in his eyes, "Swords then?"

"No no no… we're gentlemen are we not?"

Dingle had a hard time answering truthfully with three-foot long, razor-sharp blades in each hand, "Yes, of course we are!"

"Then let's settle this like gentlemen, in a gentlemanly sport: jumping," Suexliegh let the challenge sink in as Dingle slowly lowered the katanas. No, he was not referring to the, high, long or triple jump, but that of the equestrian discipline of show-jumping where riders must complete an obstacle course of elevated jumps whereupon whomsoever returns around to the finish in the shortest amount of time with the fewest toppled rails is declared the victor.

"While you may be the more accomplished rider, I own the better horse-"

"Debatable!" interrupted Dingle.

"I call this challenge even. A re-match if you will. Pennywinkle versus Winchester. You versus me."

"And the winner takes?"

"Only one prize, the most valuable in the world, the heart, body and mind of the woman we both fancy," Suexliegh said softly.

Dingle let the swords clatter to the ground, all the while keeping his eyes locked on his rival.

"Seven days," said Suexliegh.

"Six."

"Nine."

"Seven."

Suexliegh offered his hand to seal the deal, "Deal. May the best man win."

Dingle smirked as they shook, "You're shaking hands with him."

Chapter The Eighty-Fourth
Amor Vincit Omnia

"A DUEL? Have you gone mad!?"

"Not at all, in fact I believe this is the most sane I've ever been."

Quincy rushed over and wrapped Suexliegh in an arm-pinning embrace, "I apologize for my shortness, I don't know what came over me. It's wonderful to have you back, you had me so worried."

"There's absolutely nothing to fret over," Suexliegh wriggled out of the overly long hug and strode into the dining room where Quincy had set out a glistening pot roast dinner. He had prepared an equally appetizing meal every single night Suexliegh was gone and would have continued to do so until the end of his days, for there could be nothing worse in his mind than having his Master come home hungry to a cold, empty dinner table.

"Well what if Dingle wins?" Quincy said as he unfolded and dropped Suexliegh's napkin into his lap.

"Then he gets Verena, fair and square, and I will move on with my life and never think of her again."

"But he's a professional show jumper! You're quite skilled on horseback I admit but this is entirely different... have you ever even gone over a jump?"

"Penny and I have jumped a few streams and logs in our time, it's more or less the same thing," Suexliegh soaked a piece of bread in oil and vinegar as he scooted closer to the table.

"Streams and logs? There are over a dozen jumps taller than a grown man which you must clear at full gallop no less. You could be thrown to your death or worse! Not to mention you'll both be doing the course at the same time which I highly hope you reconsider."

"There's no spectacle if we went one at a time!" announced Suexliegh through a mouth full of food. "Maybe this way I can sneak in a few kicks to his ribs while I'm at it."

Quincy nervously paced back and forth which he tried to hide by constantly walking over to the other end of the table to grab more dinner rolls. Suexliegh watched him with amusement as, within minutes, a stack ten biscuits high toppled onto the floor and snapped Quincy out of his trance.

"I just don't know, sir, my heart is telling me one thing and my mind another," Quincy muttered, losing steam as he spoke.

"Don't keep that to yourself let me hear what they're saying," Suexliegh put down his knife and fork to give his full attention. Quincy paused, almost as if afraid of speaking how he truly felt.

"My mind says this is irrational, unnecessary, and dangerous, you have too much of a reputation at stake to risk it so publicly," Quincy finished picking up the dinner rolls and placed the tray back on the table, "but my heart says... do it."

Suexliegh double took at the unexpected reaction. Quincy peered at him with eyes filled to the brim with understanding sincerity.

"*Amor vincit omnia,*" Quincy whispered.

"Love conquers all."

"It is time to show her that you believe this," Quincy rushed over and grasped Suexliegh's hand in his with conviction. The two sat in silence, listening to the crackling embers in the fireplace and the light instrumental notes floating in from a far off record player. Suexliegh nodded curtly.

"I will. And I promise never to leave you again," Suexliegh said warmly. "Now I must go practice!"

Chapter The Eighty-Fifth
Jumping With James Henry

"PUT YOUR LEG on him! Block the outside shoulder or he'll run you into the wall! Keep a counter-bend in that turn you're wobbling all over the place! Get going out of the round more! Now sit back and make it fit!"

Pennywinkle rounded the turn galloping at full charge towards an imposing double oxer, a jump with two spread uneven bars, with Suexliegh flailing around on top and pulling at the reins like a maniac.

"Jump, Penny, jump!"

One stride from the jump, the horse did the opposite and planted her hooves in the ground while lowering her head creating a perfect catapult that sent Suexliegh topping cleanly over the jump. He crashed into a heap on the ground as a plume of dust scattered around the ring. Penny calmly walked over as if nothing had happened and began licking the mud off of Suexliegh's helmet.

"You know, this usually works better when you *and* the horse make it over the jump," James Henry stifled a laugh as he slowly sauntered over wearing knee high riding boots, stark white pants, and a black hunt coat. Today, he was all business.

"At least I didn't knock any of the rails down so that's an improvement," Suexliegh gestured to the start of the course where a half dozen jumps were lying bent and broken on the ground. The tell-tale sign of a tossed rider or two was also apparent.

"Dingle is a rider second to none, he will make it through the course clear and in record time too. You can't begin to compete with someone who has lived more of their life on four feet than two," James Henry hefted the rails back onto the jump and wiped off the dirt.

"There's less than a week to go! I'll never be able to catch him, unless… I could go back in time. They do say time is money but I do not believe that is something I can buy!"

James Henry tightened the straps on Pennywinkle's saddle and helped Suexliegh back onto the horse. Pennywinkle trotted sidewalks and snorted hot air. They had been running jumps all day long causing the veins across the horse's body to bulge under the stress. James Henry touched Penny's nose, calming her down as he leaned in towards Suexliegh.

"Again. We must do it again and again until you are as close to perfection as our time constraints will allow. Generally, men in these circumstances would advocate more drastic actions to ensure victory but they would be unsportsmanlike and unbecoming the current company," James Henry lead Pennywinkle out of the ring, "but for now, you need to rest for we are at the end of our rope."

Suexliegh spurred Pennywinkle's sides making her take off like a shot and nearly pulling James Henry's arm out of his socket as they blitzed around the outside of the ring. Faster and faster they hurtled back towards the jump. James Henry watched in horror as Suexliegh hit the horse's hindquarters with a crop picking up even more speed into the straight away. Penny dug in her hooves causing Suexliegh to squeeze tightly with his knees for fear of a repeated human lawn dart but instead they launched several strides too long. Horse and rider careened into the air scaling inches above the top rail before stamping down on all fours again safely on the other side. Suexliegh whooped with delight and stood up in the saddle whirling his crop in jubilation. His glee quickly came to an end when he failed to avoid the approaching wall which sent him spiraling out of the ring into a tuft of long grass. James Henry simply shook his head as Suexliegh feebly raised his hand to indicate he wasn't dead.

"We both made it over that time!"

Chapter The Eighty-Sixth
Back in the Saddle

NEWS of the gentleman's duel spread like wildfire through dry summer brush and had circled round the globe in a matter of hours. Telephones, telegrams (singing or otherwise), mail, typewriters, fax machines, and even carrier pigeons nearly burst with the outpouring of interest over the story. "Suexliegh Versus Dingle" was on everyone's tongues. Uppington Downs offered their venue for the event and within minutes had sold out bottom, middle and top rows with only standing room in the aisles. Not since the last time these two men raced the very same horses had the Downs been so thoroughly booked. Anyone who was anyone had to be there, by hook or by crook, and soon a black market of ticketing sprung up worth more than both horses combined. It was the show of the century, the greatest rivalry of the modern age. Chivalry was alive and well.

Suexliegh was oblivious to the hype as he spent sun up to sun down the entire week training at James Henry's private barn not even once returning home to eat, sleep or shower. He lived where Pennywinkle lived. He ate what Pennywinkle ate. As long as Suexliegh and Pennywinkle could stand on two and four legs respectively, they were out leaping jumps or riding at full wind through the meadow. James Henry watched with muted excitement as the two cleared higher rails, strode further, and turned sharper corners every single day. It would still take a miracle from on high, perhaps an errant lightning bolt or two thrown in Dingle's path to stop him, but Suexliegh's chance for success rose by bounds as the hands of the clock swept ever closer to the starting gunshot. Six revolutions of the Earth passed in a blink and James Henry decided there was no more training to be done. The board was set, it was up to the pieces now.

"This is for you."

In his hands, James Henry held a navy pinstriped hunt coat with three buttoned front and lined with the prestigious robin's egg blue of the Lord of Skye. There was only one coat like it in the world.

"It required a few modifications to suit your physique but I think you'll find the tailoring rather pleasant," James Henry helped Suexliegh into the lucky jacket. It fit perfectly, as always.

Suexliegh, who was covered in head to toe with mud after being thrown off of Pennywinkle one last time that afternoon, admired the clean new coat in the stable's mirror, "I don't know what to say."

"Say you'll give Dingle a royal trouncing and we'll call it even," James Henry gave a slight bow. "And should you so ever decide to go hunting for fowl, namely that of the Steeds family of bird mind you, I've left two buckshot shells in the pocket."

Quincy tried to contain an over-large grin as he drove an exhausted Suexliegh up the driveway to the waiting mansion.

"I feel like I've been beaten with a stick," Suexliegh winced painfully as he stretched out his sore muscles, cracking his back over the edge of the seat. "A very large, angry stick."

"We'll have you freshly shaven and shampooed in time for your big day tomorrow, but first it's off to bed after a sip of tea to warm your spirit."

"That sounds most good," Suexliegh yawned and picked stray straw out of his boots. "I've nearly forgotten the feeling of clean linens. Rolling in hay isn't as much fun as everyone says it is."

Quincy raced up the steps and eagerly flung open the door, unable to contain the surprise anymore, as he watched his master's frown invert into sheer delight at the company that awaited them.

Chapter The Eighty-Seventh
A Long Expected Party

"YOU VILE RAPSCALLIONS! How in the name of St. Crispen did you get out?" Suexliegh shook hands all around as he received friendly pats on the back from the Scoundrels and the old prison gang. Quincy quietly closed the door and motioned for Quincy Jr. to help him prepare for supper. Willard Austerio, Nicholas Flynn, Liam Daniel, James Henry, Verne Dempsey, Jules Reneau, Hans Haddinger, and Valerie Petit laughed at the sight of their mud-covered old friend.

"We would not be missing a chance to see you pummel Dingle with your horse," Hans Haddinger wheezed giddily. "So when they are asking if we are all better in the head, we said 'yes' and here we are."

Dempsey tossed a handful of Skittles into his mouth, "The place is practically deserted now. Once everyone heard we were leaving they tried the same trick and had their chauffeurs pick them up that very afternoon. The Warden must have thought we all suffered from an acute case of reformed guilt and changed our ways, but really I had eight figures down on your match and wanted to be there in person to collect. And to see you again, of course."

Verne inhaled a bad breath and sucked the candy down the wrong pipe causing him to choke. Within moments of the first gasp, Quincy appeared out of nowhere and performed a pin-point accurate Heimlich which made Verne shower the guests in rainbow spittle.

"Calm yourself man! The night has just begun and I cannot have one of my unexpected guests keeling over before we've even sat down to eat," Suexliegh escorted them down the hallway towards the dining room and put an arm around Verne. "Quincy! Get this man a glass of water with most haste and see that he has a pleasant, choke-free evening from here on out!"

ZACK KELLER

"Right this way, sirs and madames," Quincy made rapid little steps to the dining room as he pointed out some of the finer décor in the manor such as the original Edison light bulbs dangling from the wall sockets and the one-of-a-kind self-portrait of Abraham Lincoln. Valerie slowed until she walked in stride with Suexliegh.

"Thank you," Valerie whispered under her breath, "for Reynold."

Suexliegh noticed for the first time that Reynold was part of the throng of socialites winding through the maze of his manor, twirling and dipping one very rosy looking Anechka.

"I never taught him *those* moves," Suexliegh said plainly, until a slight dimpling revealed his amusement at the sight. The sadness in Valerie's tired eyes lifted momentarily and she allowed a minute simper to take hold of the corners of her mouth.

"Whatever you did… thank you. Reynold never really had a father, only some man who contributed half of his genetic code and lived in the same house with us," Valerie tucked a fallen strand of hair behind her ear and stifled a yawn as she watched her son sweep Anechka off her feet in a fit of giggles. "He seems happy."

"Young love, can you blame him?"

"I suppose not, we've all been there," Valerie gave a knowing look.

Quincy held up the party at the doorway and cleared his throat softly, "Gentlemen, ladies first if you please."

The men grumbled playfully as they allowed Valerie and Anechka, who curtsied delicately, to pass and take first pick of the seats. Once the women had sat, the rest of the party made their way into the dining room which was elaborately decorated in an equestrian manner. Suexliegh sat at the head of the table and placed a freshly creased napkin onto his lap just as Quincy revealed the contents of the silver platter: game hen brought in by James Henry that very afternoon. Quincy bowed his head.

"Dinner is served."

Chapter The Eighty-Eighth
The Upside Down Cake

QUINCY was pleased as a pickle to be throwing a dinner party in a house filled with laughter again as only once since Master Suexliegh's birthday nearly a year ago had they even entertained guests. Too long, he thought, we are putting our best foot forward this year and shall have smiles for three hundred and sixty five days straight. The old butler reveled in the night, going from one guest to the next making sure they always had brimming glasses of wine and clean plates whenever a new course was unveiled. He beamed with pride at his young son whose nervous hands steadied as the night wore on until he could toss a five course meal onto the table with his eyes closed. Like father like son. *If only Suexliegh would hurry up and have some children could my son have a son of his own to take care of*, Quincy thought. He abruptly pushed the notion from his mind and facilitated the entire duration of the meal from bisque to brisket.

Ding ding ding! Willard tapped the side of his empty wine glass (for at least the fifth time that night) and stood up from the table, wiping his mouth clean with a napkin. He cleared his throat. Quincy Jr. sped over with the carafe sloshing about and poured another glass. The rest of the guests turned their attention to Willard and raised their drinks in unison.

"A toast, to the greatest man in this room, if he were not here I would of course be referring to myself," the guests all gave courtesy laughs, "but he is here, and we must be very thankful for that. Now, I've been drinking and the words have begun to fall out of my head faster than I can get them through my mouth, so I should make this brief. I think everyone agrees with me when I say with much eloquence that tomorrow will be a momentous, gallant, brash, and romantic endeavor and we all want you to beat the piss out of that equine-loving ninny."

Cheers and clinked glasses all around as the guests drank deeply and applauded their man. "Speech!" they cried but Suexliegh brushed them off with a modest wave.

"Speech or we leave!" shouted Nicholas from the back of the room, spilling wine all over the tablecloth in his drunken fervor. Afraid the table would be upended if he didn't comply, Suexliegh jumped to his feet.

"Thank you all for being here tonight, it means more to me than you will ever know. Regardless if I win or lose, tomorrow it will be about how I play the game, as they say. With friends like you, I know I could never lose. To friends!"

"To friends!" they all cried.

"And family," Suexliegh raised his glass to a beaming Quincy.

Quincy Jr. backed through the kitchen door, supporting a hefty platter with both hands, "I hope you all saved room for dessert!"

He spun quickly around hoping to make a dramatic entrance, but the centripetal force slid the towering chocolate cake right off. Quincy Jr. watched in horror as the cake landed and stuck, perfectly upside down, onto the hardwood floor. Valerie gasped. The room went silent as Quincy Jr. lost all color. He felt as if spontaneous combustion was his best option out of the current situation.

"Ah!" Suexliegh's loud exclamation shattered the awkward silence. "Upside down cake... my favorite!"

Suexliegh snatched his dessert fork from the table and walked over to the sagging cake, scooping a heaping bite of peppermint frosting.

"Mmm... delectable! Peppermint and chocolate!" Suexliegh chewed as he looked up at the ghostly pale Quincy Jr. who still held the platter in a death grip. "Don't be shy, there's plenty to go around."

After a moment's hesitation, Willard grabbed his fork, followed soon thereafter by the others as they all gathered around the floor and picked away at the cake until there was nothing left. Suexliegh handed Quincy Jr. a fork with a sliver of cake stuck through the end.

"The last bite is for you."

Chapter The Eighty-Ninth
The Beast With Black Eyes

A QUICK pep-talk from Quincy about the time he accidentally dropped the Thanksgiving turkey into the fireplace lifted Quincy Jr.'s spirits and taught him a valuable lesson: always have a back-up plan. On that particular day in question Quincy had been thankful for James Henry's overzealous trigger finger which supplied an extra turkey from the morning hunt that he had put in the oven intending it to be used for left-overs. The flamed bird was tossed in the trash and the fresh one hastily garnished before being set out on the dining room table. Crisis averted and the guests were none the wiser, except for Suexliegh who was without a turkey and cranberry sandwich the next day.

Over packed pipes and a fine snifter of peaty scotch, Suexliegh regaled his friends with a modern legend from Greece about "The Beast with Black Eyes" when Dimitri was tasked with catching or killing, the latter preferable, a gigantic octopus that nightly crept from the ocean into the local village and devoured house pets whole. For weeks, animals had been disappearing without a trace until one unlucky owner awoke with a fright to see two dead black eyes staring back at her as the octopus forced the hind legs of a tiny Pomeranian down its throat. Her shrieks and a tossed lamp scared the monster back into the sea, but when it would return no one knew. Everyone feared that one day it would hunger for larger prey as it grew to even more savage proportions and they would wake to find their children missing. Something had to be done.

"The townspeople begged Dimitri for his help for they knew of no one with truer aim and colder blood than he," Suexliegh stalked around the room playing out the scene's dramatics before a roaring fire. "Brave Dimitri accepted the challenge without so much as an offered coin and asked if I would come along... as bait. So that evening I played the role of a foolhardy individual taking his bite-sized dog for a stroll while Dimitri trailed behind us, trident in hand, waiting for his moment to strike from the shadows. The minutes ticked tensely by without so much as a splash from the sea; the tide was far out and whisper quiet. Just as we were about to give up, long amber tentacles slapped into the light pulling the beast towards us with frightening speed, its black eyes staring right back. The dog broke for safety but the octopus kept right for me... he was interested in a bigger feast tonight. The beast leapt and my heart skipped a beat as I looked beyond its flesh-ripping suckers, disemboweling hooks, and jagged beak to the cavernous pit of its stomach that threatened to swallow me whole. As the first tentacle grabbed my neck, Dimitri vaulted from the darkness and hurled his trident which struck the beast clear through the eye, pinning the massive sea-demon into the local tavern's sign post. Blood and ink oozed into the gutter as Dimitri calmly walked over and offered me a hand, saying, 'I've seen bigger.'"

The guests laughed with delight and applauded the tale and the teller as they finished the last of their drinks. Knowing the hour was late, they wished Suexliegh good luck and retired for the evening. Their own butlers took them home for the first time in years, back to an old life they had abandoned long ago. Nicholas and Liam, as was often their tradition after a long night of drinking, went out for one last drink at the Albatross.

With an arm thrown over his shoulder, Suexliegh helped Willard down the stairs to bed so he could sleep off the whiskey in his veins and hopefully remember a bit of fun they'd had the night before.

"Good night, you scoundrel," Suexliegh whispered.

But Willard never heard it, for he was already asleep. Suexliegh made his way into the master bedroom as exhaustion finally took hold of his body from the long week when a loud crash of silverware rang out from somewhere in the manor.

Chapter The Ninetieth
Fell Wind

A TOPPLED POT of tea streamed Earl Grey onto the carpet as a dazed Quincy lay beside it, trying to place up-ended cups and crackers back onto the platter. He was pale and shaking from the effort.

"Quincy! My goodness are you alright?" Suexliegh rushed over to the top of the stairs in a panic and helped Quincy to a sitting position against the banister.

"Now look what I've done... I was just trying to bring you a cup of tea before bed. It's decaffeinated because I know you get the jitters," Quincy struggled as Suexliegh righted the teakettle and cups. Quincy Jr. quick stepped up the stairs and gasped at the sight of his downed father.

"Father!"

"Oh don't worry about me, I'm quite alright. My legs just decided to up and quit on me all of a sudden," Quincy tried to stand but it took a shoulder from Suexliegh and Quincy Jr. to get him there. "Bad legs! Very bag legs!"

Quincy Jr. put a hand to his father's forehead and looked over at Suexliegh, worried, as the two assisted Quincy into the master bedroom.

"He feels cold."

"No no, see? I can manage on my own," Quincy broke free from their grasp and tried to walk on his own wobbly legs only to lean precariously off balance. Suexliegh caught him before he fell again.

"We must get you into bed immediately," cautioned Suexliegh.

"You two are making such a fuss out of a little fall. I'm an old man, it happens all the time!"

Quincy Jr. looked at his father with concern, "It does?"

"No no, never! Must have been all that pipe smoke from earlier spinning around my head. Just set me down in bed and a warm night of sleep will make me right as rain."

Suexliegh and Quincy Jr. helped him under the covers and threw another log on the fire as they tried to warm up the room. Without another word, Quincy fell into a deep sleep.

"Will he be alright?"

"Yes of course he will, he has a stout heart," Suexliegh spoke softly as he clicked closed the door to the bedroom allowing Quincy time to sleep in silence. "Besides, he still has plenty of work to do for me and if he thinks a minor tumble will get him out of it he's quite mistaken!"

Suexliegh noticed that the light-hearted joke did little to assuage Quincy Jr.'s fears who was nervously biting at the skin of his thumbs.

"Your father will be just fine," Suexliegh added as he put a gentle hand on Junior's back.

"Would you mind if I stayed with him tonight?" Quincy Jr. choked back the tears in his voice. "I want to be there in case he wakes up and needs anything."

Suexliegh nodded and Junior crept back into the room without a sound. He sat by his father's side, not taking a moment's rest, all through the night.

Unable to sleep himself, Suexliegh did what all men do in times of trouble: find the highest possible place to think. He sneaked upstairs, careful to avoid all the creaks and cracks the aged house had hidden for him. The attic window's latch snapped free with much effort, allowing Suexliegh access to the rooftop where he shuffled over the shingles, grabbing onto a chimney to pull himself up. A cold current of air curled through the trees and caught him on the tallest point of the mansion's roof where he stood staring, and thinking, at the field of stars overhead, watching the infinite points of light drift ever further until the morning sun washed away the evening sky.

It was time.

Chapter The Ninety-First
A Stranger Comes To Town

FOR THE FIRST TIME in his life with absolutely no help, Suexliegh dressed himself. Toe to head. Socks slipped, pants pulled, boots tied, spurs knotted, belt fastened, shirt buttoned, jacket shouldered.

A gentleman going to war.

No one expected to see it, but when they saw it, they should have known. Suexliegh rode through town mounted on Pennywinkle, like a cowboy at dawn out to meet his maker, right down the street, where cars, bikes and people transited, heading straight for the racetrack as onlookers, some laughing, some confused, all in a state of sheer disbelief, watched. He took no mind to them, instead, staring straight ahead without any consideration for pedestrians crossing or red lights in his way which lead to more than a few pile-ups. Eventually, the traffic simply moved out of his way for everyone in town knew exactly where he was going. Following close behind with apologetic waves to the angry motorists was Junior who drove, with subdued satisfaction, the Bugatti with his ailing father in the backseat.

"You know, I've driven this car every day for I can't even recall how long and this is the first time I've ever sat in the back," Quincy coughs turned to a giddy chuckle as he lay comfortably extended across the rear seats. Gridlocked streets stretched for miles outside of Uppington Downs as lines and lines of chauffeured cars waited politely for what was sure to be the most talked about day of their entire lives.

The floor to ceiling oak paneling was dotted with golden trophies from Pennywinkle's past exploits, including one case in particular, full, and marble engraved with the winning horse's name for the Corona Crown. Suexliegh admired his collection of gold trophies from every single race the league offered, before leaning in and giving his newest prize a kiss.

"I've wanted to do that for so long," Suexliegh sighed as Quincy Jr. helped his father into the lounging chair. "My collection is finally complete."

"Could I get you a drink, father?" chimed Quincy Jr. as he prepared a plate of hors d'oeuvres. Quincy looked hesitantly at Suexliegh who was busy blowing dust off of the trophy case.

"Go ahead," coaxed Suexliegh, stopping his cleaning efforts as he motioned to the brass faucet. "Be my guest."

"Perhaps just a smidgen of glacier water... just this once," the lines in Quincy's etched face wrinkled as he spoke. Quincy admired the room for the first time from the other side, as someone who was waited on. He had for so long been in the attendance of another's needs that he had forgotten what it felt like to ask for anything himself. At first, Quincy felt guilty. Who was he to make demands? Yet if Suexliegh offered, he would not refuse such a kind gesture. And Quincy didn't.

"Have as much as you like, of anything. What's mine is yours," chimed Suexliegh sparking Quincy Jr. into action who rushed over and began pouring his father a glass. Quincy sighed with satisfaction and looked out the window at the breathtaking view: an emerald oval sitting beneath a pastel blue sky stretched out before them as the ever burgeoning crowd crammed cheek to cheek in their seats. Even the private boxes were standing room only, which would have caused the attendees great vexation otherwise, but today no one seemed to mind.

"Take care of your father," Suexliegh buckled his helmet and whipped open the door, "and make sure he keeps his eye on the lead horse for that will be me!"

"I've heard that Dingle has never lost a show jumping competition... how are you so certain you can beat him?" Junior asked nervously.

"He's never lost, because he's never challenged me."

Chapter The Ninety-Second
High Noon

UPPINGTON DOWNS roared with delight as Dingle raced out of the tunnel and onto the track, riding high in the stirrups and brandishing a crop over his head like a banshee. Winchester appeared staggeringly majestic for the day's event with his mane and tail tightly braided and body attired in the regal red and white of the Dingle family crest. The two raced a pre-victory lap around the entire course making sure to soak up as much adrenaline as possible from the excitement in the air. They sped down the home stretch at impressive speeds before Winchester skidded to a halt and reared up allowing the stands a picturesque view of the horse and rider in all their glory. Dingle scanned the crowd and spied Verena in her box seat right up front, clearly upset to be a part of such a machismo-fueled presentation. Leaning forward in the saddle, Dingle removed a hand from the reins and blew a kiss to her. All the other women in the stands cast jealous stares in Verena's direction, but she just let the kiss land where it may.

By now the stands had filled to capacity and the murmuring of anticipation rose exponentially with every passing minute. Dingle was already at the gates... but where was Suexliegh? Had he forfeited? Had he became party to a horse and horseless carriage accident on the way over? Was he staging a dramatic entrance? A flurry of questions volleyed back and forth between spectators as they eagerly counted down the seconds. Minutes before noon, James Henry, the Scoundrels and the old prison gang sidled into their seats closest to the finish line with the hopes of being the first to see Dingle's look of agony when he lost. True gentlemen they were, for an enemy of their friend, was an enemy to them as well.

The course had been meticulously laid out with a devious set of thirteen fences consisting of double Swedish oxers, triple ins-and-outs, a high vertical, a tilted joker, a fan, a brick wall, open water, and a final hairpin turn into a dead-sprint straight away to the finish. Normally, a time limit was set to further increase the difficulty of the event, but due to the dual riders the first to finish would claim victory. Deemed so demanding and hazardous, not a single soul had attempted the course yet. In fact, two jumpers on the same course had never once occurred in the long history of the sport so many were turning up just to see some guaranteed bloodshed. Dingle looked at the jumps with mild disdain as he trotted calmly to the starting line while swatting at an errant fly.

Suexliegh won't have to worry about making it to the finish, thought Dingle, there's not a chance he will even make it over the first jump.

Speaking of the devil, a hush fell over the stands as Suexliegh emerged onto the field. Besides his conspicuous march through the center of town, no one had seen or heard from Suexliegh since his multiple recent disappearances and they were all eager to catch a glimpse to see if any of the wild rumors were true. Men and women craned their necks, children were placed atop shoulders, binoculars squinted through, but Suexliegh trotted out leisurely without a care in the world looking as calm as ever. Pennywinkle flicked her tail and turned onto the track making straight for Verena's seat. She shrunk back, embarrassed and praying Suexliegh wouldn't make a scene in front of all those people. He stopped Pennywinkle right in front of Verena, looked her in the eyes, bowed, then simply rode away. She blinked in confusion, not sure exactly what had just happened, and watched as the two sped to a light gallop as they approached the starting gate.

"Hello, Suexliegh."

"Hello, Dingle."

"Fine day for a race."

"Indeed."

Chapter The Ninety-Third
Ten Paces, Pistols Drawn

EARS PINNED back against her head, Pennywinkle snorted and stamped threateningly, reaching over to bite the rival horse on the nape. Winchester reared then kicked his legs back as he unleashed a thunderous whinny, nearly toppling his rider. They breathed hot, fiery breath from their flaring nostrils in a show of animalistic intimidation. Whatever hatred these men had for one another, it was even worse between the horses.

"This is a sad day for me, Suexliegh, for in just a short while you and I will have no further bets to make. I will have won your lady fair, fair and square, and will ride off with her into the sunset to start our life together. You, on the other hand, will be laying face down in the mud before the first jump," Dingle reached down idly and tightened his saddle. "I always knew it would come to this: horse to horse, man to man. It was inevitable. Fate. Don't you agree?"

Suexliegh waited a long moment then brushed flat the hair down Pennywinkle's neck, "If you don't mind, I'd rather just sit in silence until the race starts."

Dingle looked at him dumbstruck.

"Come now you must be joking? The great linguist Suexliegh has no use for words anymore?"

"I have nothing further to say to you. I wish you the best of luck in the coming duel," stated Suexliegh as he watched a patterned flock of geese fly overhead. They squawked as they soared out of view.

"Well this is grand, just grand! If I had known a bit of stiff competition would shut you up I would have proposed this ages ago. I just never thought a female would be the final coin that broke the billionaire's pocketbook, as they say. What happened to you, old man? You used to be such a daring gent, always with an ace up one sleeve and a bottle of champagne up the other. I'd hate to think you've gone soft."

Dingle sighed as he leaned over to Suexliegh.

"I'll admit it, for a brief shining moment I used to look up to you. You were my idol. I modeled my entire life after yours, trying to be more like you every single day. You had everything: the elegant family name, royal jaw-line and stature, expansive estate, noble profession, cunning wit and charm, the cars, the yachts, the planes, a full head of hair, everything... except for a wife. I thought to myself, maybe he doesn't have time for one, after all a playboy like him must be in one hundred places at once so there couldn't possibly be time to raise a family. And then one day you found her. No one ever knows exactly why it starts but something did. For a time you were living the life you always wanted but never knew you could have. Though she had everything too, you could have given her the one thing she nor you could buy... love. But it's gone now, she's gone now. And I... I have her. I never really loved her, I only sought her because you did and I knew it would eat you up inside to see her with me. She's a nice enough girl and she'll make a beautiful wife to me soon. Children too, the little darlings will be running hither and thither through the house enjoying their first white Christmas some day.

"Here I go again, daydreaming about the future," Dingle chuckled with amusement as he pulled his gloves on tighter and stuck a hand out to shake. "Let's have a good clean race, shall we?"

Suexliegh shook Dingle's hand with the firmest grip he could muster as the clock began to chime the twelve strokes of noon. One, two. Louder the bells rang, echoing across the field as the two men readied themselves on their horses. Three, four. Reins stretched in their hands, five, six, stirrups pressed tight against the heavily breathing animals, seven, eight, muscles tensed, nine, ten, eyes locked on the first jump, eleven.

Twelve.

Chapter The Ninety-Fourth
The Race Heard Round the World

AT THE FINAL TOLL, the two horses dug out of their starting positions and dashed towards the first fence, hearts pumping with pure adrenaline, the crowd leaping to its feet yelling, cheering, and screaming with all the wind in their lungs as the riders charged and bounded several feet over the first vertical jump, landing on the other side with the earth-shaking force of eight hooves pounding into the ground as they made a wide arcing turn around the outside of the ring towards a joker rail which both horses spotted, lined up, and vaulted once again in perfect unison, stride for stride matching each other through the course as they approached a triple in and out, three fences in a row allowing the horses only a single step in between each before having to jump out again, but Dingle was not fooled one bit, blitzing ahead of Suexliegh to gain the necessary speed as Winchester cleared the first, recovered with two steps, cleared the second, nearly stumbling on the landing, and barely crossing over the third as his heavy back hoof slammed down on the rail causing it to jostle around in the cup, but Suexliegh was not so lucky having never seen a triple before in his life and pulling back too hard on Penny's reins to make her jump high enough which worked on the first two fences, but the loss of momentum sent them crashing through the last rail, obliterating the jump, adding a fault, and putting a large distance between the two competitors which Dingle took notice of and laughed to himself as he easily soared over a triple bar before weaving through the middle of the ring to the hogsback passing by Suexliegh who was determined to cut the lead in half with a daring slanted jump over the triple and a tendon-snapping turn that nearly sent Penny tumbling over but she held on and sprung back to life, blowing hard to catch up as she nicked the front of the cross rail and landed long on the other side which Dingle heard and whipped his head around to see that Suexliegh was literally on his tail as they approached the brick wall which he tried to take too fast and left the ground early causing Winchester to plow through the fence, sending the break away pieces flying into the field as a gasp went up from the crowd, both riders had incurred a fault and now just had to beat the other to the finish in order to win which left Dingle little time to recover as Suexliegh once again pulled neck and neck with him, a bright white smile flashing, which sent Dingle into a fit of rage whereupon he used his crop as a weapon, slashing viciously at Suexliegh and Pennywinkle doing anything in his power to hinder their progress, hoping an accurate blow would send them cascading off course, but Suexliegh moved away at the last second as Dingle swung for a killing blow knocking himself off balance and nearly causing him to topple out of the saddle with only his feet in the stirrups to save him from being trampled but he pulled himself upright and whipped Winchester hard to catch up with Suexliegh who was approaching the open water, closing to within a stride as the two tired horses launched over the water and splashed down on the other side, another fault added for each rider, still tied as they rounded to the oxer which Suexliegh and Dingle took side by side, barely scraping over the rail at the exact same time so they tugged hard on the reins torquing the horses into the final straight away, only a hundred meters between them and victory, the horses heaving and straining as they broke into an all out gallop beneath the two riders who leaned into the wind as the crowd reached a frenzied pitch with the last seconds ticking by in Suexliegh's favor, allowing him to gain a heads-length on Dingle and assuring his victory coming into the final stretch, but just moments from the line, Suexliegh pulled so softly on the reins that no one would ever know except Pennywinkle, slowing his horse and letting Dingle win.

Chapter The Ninety-Fifth
To the Victor

SUEXLIEGH'S ENTIRE LIFE had boiled down to a single moment. A fraction of a fraction of a second. It was Dingle by a nose. By a nose hair. So close it was almost too close to call, but in the end Dingle was declared the winner. The thundering cheer of applause from the audience was deafening; they didn't care who won, they came to see a great show, and a great show they had seen.

Dingle let out a cry of elation as he made another victory lap around the track: flowers, ribbons, confetti, flowing all around. He stood up in the stirrups, both hands outstretched above him, as he slowed to a stop, allowing Winchester a breather for the first time since the start of the race. Suexliegh patted Pennywinkle and bent down to whisper in her ear, "Sorry for ruining your perfect record, old girl. I promise I'll make it up to you."

Pennywinkle didn't seem to mind as she whinnied happily and lifted her head up to have Suexliegh scratch her nose. She squealed with glee as he pulled a peppermint from his pocket and offered it to her. Amidst the whooping and hollering, Suexliegh, and a very content and minty-smelling Penny, trotted over to Dingle by the bottom of the stands who was still being showered by his adoring fans.

"I am victorious! I beat Suexliegh, finally, I beat him!" Dingle cried jubilantly as he blew kisses to women in the crowd.

"That you did," Suexliegh nodded as he stopped beside Dingle. "Congratulations, you are truly a better man than I."

"I'm glad you finally admitted it," Dingle smiled smugly.

"Well, this is goodbye then, I hope to never see you again."

"And I, you."

"Very good."

"Indeed."

"Then we are in agreement."

"Perhaps the only thing we will ever agree on."

Dingle hopped off of Winchester, tossing his helmet to his horses' groom as he dusted down his attire to make himself more presentable. Dingle walked with a royal step up to Verena, who was standing isolated in her private track-side box, and raised a cocky eyebrow.

"Now… to collect my prize," Dingle puckered up for a kiss, but instead was met with a slap across the face.

"I'm not some prize to be won," Verena marched past Dingle who stood nursing his pride and a growing bruise on his cheek.

"What!? How dare you! I won you, you're mine!"

"I was never yours," Verena whipped around with a look of fire in her eyes as Dingle stood there pathetically.

"But, but I… love you," Dingle pleaded with puppy dog eyes, but Verena only scoffed, ripped off her engagement ring and tossed it into the dirt. Dingle watched in horror as she hopped the railing onto the track and hurried over to Suexliegh who waited hesitantly next to Pennywinkle. She crossed her arms and gave Suexliegh the same look of disapproval.

"I should slap you too for this."

"It would only be fair," Suexliegh winced as he offered a cheek, anticipating the sharp sting of her hand. Instead, Verena leaned over to his ear and whispered, "I saw what you did."

A slow smile spread across Verena's face as she offered her hand. Suexliegh waited, unsure if she was using the gesture to lure him in for a backhanded broadside. *It's now or never*, he thought, *what are you waiting for?* Suexliegh reached out and took her hand in his. The two walked, arm in arm, off the field to clamoring applause. Not a dry monocle in the house.

Chapter The Ninety-Sixth
Out to Pasture

PENNY rolled and played in the dirt, squealing happily, as a herd of horses broke into a sprint. She stumbled to her feet and rushed over to join them, pacing one another to see which was the fastest across the open terrain. Suexliegh and James Henry watched the horses turn like a flock of birds and come bounding right passed them, twenty strong, in a blinding blur of brown.

"Plenty of food, open land," James Henry lit a long wooden pipe and shook out the match, "and who knows, perhaps she'll find a mate."

Pennywinkle nuzzled against another horse as she swished her tail with joy. All around, horses roamed wild on James Henry's private equestrian preserve set up for animals too old or injured to keep showing at competitions anymore. Hundreds of acres wove through valleys and forests free from fear of any human presence. Just animals and nature. Though, when the wild pheasant population got out of control every spring, it was James Henry's duty as gamekeeper to thin them out.

"Offspring of the winningest horse in history would fetch quite a price if I were to sell her," Suexliegh contemplated the thought, "but I think I'm getting out of the sport."

"Oh really?" James Henry coughed, cutting short a puff of his pipe.

"Yes really. Betting is a terrible habit and when there are horses around my pocketbook tends to get the better of me. Besides," Suexliegh caught one last fleeting glimpse of Pennywinkle leading the pack, "she will be happier here."

Pennywinkle galloped over the hill, away with her new life, just as the sun slipped beneath the horizon heralding the end of the day.

"Are you sure there isn't another way?"

"Yes."

"So there is another way?"

"No, I've made up my mind, it's settled."

Willard stood on the front porch, handing his suitcases to Baxter, his bald butler, who clunked them down the stairs and into the waiting towncar. He turned back to Suexliegh who seemed on the verge of tears.

"With you, Quincy, Junior, and Verena all living here now this house is full up!" Willard exclaimed as he tightened off the cap of his flask.

"You must be joking, the manor has well over one hundred rooms and I will gladly convert any or all of them into your bedroom. Just say the word," Suexliegh begged.

"The word is 'no.' I don't like saying it to you but you've got a family now. A strange, hodge-podge of a family, but a family none-the-less. I should go home too, get back to the way things were. I've sat on my haunches for too long so it's time to get my hands dirty again."

"Don't tell me you're getting a job?"

"Not on your life! The job market isn't for me, I'll stick with the stock market instead," Willard remarked making Suexliegh laugh. He put an arm around his old friend's shoulder, "Though a liar."

"He was true to his word," Suexliegh's mood brightened significantly as he spoke the end of the quote. The two Scoundrels shook hands. "Genova's tomorrow?"

"The usual," Willard cracked a grin and slipped into the back seat of the car which was soon on its way down the path and out onto the street. Suexliegh held back a single tear as he watched his friend drive away. After leaving the property, the car turned, then quickly turned again into the first driveway for Willard and Suexliegh were next-door neighbors.

Chapter The Ninety-Seventh
Shivering Timbers

THE SEASON had taken a sudden turn North bringing heavy rains and frost to the estate with the days growing ever shorter and the skies ever darker. Yet, inside, the house was bright and warm with Christmas cheer as decorations were arranged amidst the backdrop of a constantly crackling fireplace. Over a mile of lights were strung along the windows and edges of the house continuing out to a criss-crossing pattern down the hedges lining the front driveway. The week leading up to Christmas was Suexliegh's favorite of the entire year for he knew there would always be good food, family, presents, and a new year to start over again. It was a time for warm stews and mulled cider.

"Just a few more whacks and you'll be all the way through! Don't let up, really put your back into it!" Suexliegh's breathy instructions condensed in the frozen forest air as he supervised Junior's chopping of a magnificently tall tree. To make sure he always had the freshest, fullest, most iconic tree on the block, Suexliegh grew a private grove of Douglas Fir which were selectively bred from a healthy lineage of noble Christmas trees. The axe cut deeper with every blow until only a small sliver remained holding the tree upright. It swayed and creaked as a gusty breeze blew past.

"There, that should just about do it," Suexliegh hollered over the chopping, grabbing hold of the branches to steady the tree. "Now, I'll push, and you catch. We don't want this beauty crashing into the ground and breaking all of its branches!"

Quincy Jr.'s neck craned upwards as he took in the full height of the towering fir that blocked out the night's sky with its thickly-pined limbs. He gulped in fear.

"If you insist, sir," Quincy Jr. tramped over into the tree's projected path and stuck out his arms, pinching his eyes shut.

"On the count of three," Suexliegh put his weight behind the tree and began to push. "One... two... three!"

He heaved into the trunk with just enough force to send it wobbling off center on a one-way journey down. Suexliegh jumped back and watched the lone tree lean precariously then tilt off center and slowly fall.

"Timber!"

Quincy Jr. stood his ground and said all the prayers he could think of as the trunk splintered then picked up speed, swinging downwards straight for him. Suexliegh's eyes went wide.

"Look out!"

A split second from impact, Suexliegh dove and tackled the boy out of the way before the tree slammed into the ground, narrowly missing impalement for them both with its prickly branches. Junior blinked at the now horizontal tree, dazed, as Suexliegh helped him to his feet and dusted dirt off his jacket.

"You didn't expect to actually catch it, did you?" Suexliegh mused, stifling the apparent hilarity he found with the near-death situation. "That tree would have smashed you through to China!"

Quincy Jr. stared at his feet, ashamed of his misunderstanding.

"Well... you asked me to, so I did."

Suexliegh looked at the boy in amazement.

"You know, when I tried the same trick on your father he did the exact thing," Suexliegh pulled the axe from the stump and slung it over his shoulder, "Except I didn't get there in time to push him out of the way. I'll thank you for not reminding him of that one."

Junior smiled at the thought. The two grabbed the tree's thick stump and began dragging it home.

Chapter The Ninety-Eighth
Stocking Stuffer

"A FEW MORE ornaments and you won't be able to see the branches!"

Quincy reclined in the armchair while offering directions to Suexliegh, Verena and Junior who placed ornaments on the freshly cut Christmas tree, making sure there was no clumping or empty space. A festive holiday album rotated on the record player filling the house with the magical sound of strings and bells.

"That is the rule: you must put on every single ornament you own," Suexleigh exclaimed.

"Listen to Quincy, dear, he has a better view from where he's sitting," Verena put a loving hand on Suexliegh who was standing on a step ladder hooking ornaments to branches willy-nilly.

"Well, from where I'm standing we need more! This tree is practically barren," he stuck the rest of the sparkling globes and candy canes onto an upper branch then reached down to Junior. "More."

"One more," interrupted Quincy, "and that's it!"

"Who should do the honors?" questioned Suexliegh.

Quincy looked from Suexliegh to Verena and finally to Quincy Jr. "My son."

Verena offered up the box with a golden star which Junior took and climbed the step ladder to the top of the tree.

"You've almost been crushed by that tree today so be careful up there!" called Suexliegh as Quincy Jr. wobbled perilously. He blew a year's worth of dust off the ornament and gently positioned it on top of the tree. After an approving nod from his father, he rushed back down the ladder and cleared it away so they could get a full view of their accomplishment. Quincy Jr. snapped his fingers, "The lights!"

He scurried on his hands and knees behind the back branches, jingling the ornaments melodically, and plugged in the lights which glowed to life. The four stood back and marveled at the nearly twenty-foot tall tree which towered in the living room, the star just barely scraping the vaulted ceiling. Rows of bright white lights twinkled off the hundreds of ornaments arranged all the way from the bottom branch to the tip-top. Suexliegh put his arm around Verena and the two shared a smile.

"This reminds me... of Master Suexliegh's very first Christmas," Quincy sat up, revealing that, though he was infirm, he still wore his butler's uniform. They all gathered round to listen. "It was the very first winter we spent in this house. A howling, frightful winter that snowed us in more than once I recall... up to the second story windows it crept! No matter how hard we tried we just could not seem to keep the rooms warm even with the furnace on full whack and fires in all the hearths. Nothing could break the frost. On one particularly brisk evening, I heard the young master's squeals of joy and ran over to find that he had crawled into a Christmas stocking with his little head poking out the top. He just loved it in that fuzzy red boot, I could hardly get him away from it, so I simply hung the stocking on the mantle where he could swing back and forth, happily warming like a chestnut in front of the fire."

"If I could do it again today, why, I would in an instant!"

Verena tickled Suexliegh playfully as they all chuckled at the image of baby Suexliegh, the stocking stuffer. Quincy Jr. returned to the kitchen to refill the mugs with hot drinking chocolate while Verena creaked upstairs to put on her nightgown leaving Suexliegh and Quincy alone. The young master smiled at his old butler.

"Can I get you anything?" asked Suexliegh softly.

"No no, I'm quite alright. In fact, I'm perfectly content. You've already given me everything I could have ever asked for," Quincy's eyes glistened. "Verena told me what you did. I'm so proud of you."

"To win, sometimes you have to lose."

And with that, Quincy closed his eyes, the lines in his kindly old face creasing into a smile that would last forever.

Chapter The Ninety-Ninth
The Mark of a True Gentleman

ON CHRISTMAS MORNING, before the fire was lit or the presents opened, they buried Quincy in his suit. The sun struggled to break through the ominous clouds, casting the grounds in a pale gray light with no shadows. Patches of cold, misty rain washed overhead creating a dewy fog that hung low on the hills and rolled along with the breeze. Not a single sound could be heard, save for the whistling wind that rose and fell like breath. A shaded oak grove near the lake had always been Quincy's favorite spot where he could watch the birds arrive home every spring, and wish them a fond farewell every fall. The moment he heard them squawking overhead to announce their final descent he would drop whatever he was doing, a rarity for him, and rush outside to watch them splash down in a row.

As with all things in his life, Quincy had planned his death well in advance. He had nothing to leave in his will save for his single spare suit, should the other become tarnished, and the keys to the manor to his son. The unadorned tombstone sitting ahead the freshly packed plot of dirt simply read, "Quincy Tullenshire, a Fond Friend and Helping Hand." Before closing the casket, Suexliegh had placed into Quincy's hands the bell he had used so many times before to call for assistance, hoping now he could ring it in Heaven if he ever needed help from the angels. The three stood in a solemn row, afraid to speak for fear the tears would come rushing out unannounced.

"Would any of you like to say a few words?" Suexliegh said.

Quincy Jr. fought back his grief knowing his father would not have wanted him to cry, but Verena dabbed the corner of her own eyes, overcome by the moment. Though she had been with Quincy only a short while, knowing him a single day was a lifetime of friendship. No one could muster a single sentence.

"I'll go first," Suexliegh peered upward towards the sky. "Quincy, you were a great man. Perhaps I didn't always thank you, or show you the kindness deserved, but you were there for me when no one else was. You asked for nothing, but accepted everything given to you with grace and civility. The mark of a true gentleman. And I might add, though no one ever knew it, you were one hell of a good shot with a rifle."

Suexliegh knelt by the tombstone and whispered so the other two could not hear him, "You made a promise to me long ago that if you were to die before I did you wouldn't haunt me. I'm going to hold you to that promise or when my time comes I will find a way to return the favor!"

Suexliegh stood and buttoned his coat against the bitter wind.

"Goodbye, old friend."

Verena and Suexliegh stepped away leaving Quincy Jr. standing over the grave. He wiped his brimming, teary eyes with the sleeve of his jacket and looked out over the estate in front of him: the lake, the rolling glens, the golf course, the hedgerow, the airstrip, the aviary, the zoo, the tea garden, the pool, the cricket pitch, and the acres upon acres of open land beyond. Not to mention the manor and its one hundred rooms, a garage filled with exotic cars, and the houses on every single continent and in nearly every country around the globe. It was his, all his. His to maintain. His to love. For the first time in his life, he had a purpose, and that was to take care of Mr. Suexliegh, from sun up to sun down and all the hours in between. He thought of everything his father had ever told him about being a butler. How to cook, how to clean, how to hold oneself. It was his turn. He lived for someone else now. The corner of Quincy Jr.'s mouth pulled into a barely noticeable smile.

"Even though we have the same size feet," Quincy Jr. said proudly with a tear, "you left some pretty big shoes to fill."

Chapter The One-Hundredth
Dies Natalis Solis Invicti

RIPPED AND CRUMPLED wrapping paper lay strewn across the carpet as the three tore through the presents that had sat patiently under the tree all day. Suexliegh showered Verena with the usual assortment of offerings, making sure he hit the "big five": bracelet, necklace, earrings, brooch and watch, but she was more thrilled by a smaller gift of olive seeds to plant their own orchard out in the garden. To Quincy Jr. he gave a brand new butler's uniform, fashioned after the model his father wore.

"Thank you, but… you wouldn't mind if I wore his from time to time?"

"Not at all!" Suexliegh hollered jovially. "Now you'll have one to work in and one to sleep in!"

Verena slid a positively massive box in front of Suexliegh whose eyes went wide at the sight. He walked all the way around it, as if stalking his prey.

"This one is something special," said Verena slyly.

"My goodness! Look at the size of it," he bent over and tried to lift the box but gave up at the effort. "Heavy too. Big and heavy are always indicators of a good gift. Perhaps I'll just open it right here."

Suexliegh fell to his knees and eagerly shredded the burgundy paper like a child unable to contain his excitement and making an instant mess that Quincy Jr. scurried over to clear away.

"What's inside, sir?" the young butler asked curiously.

"Why it's, it's!" Suexliegh shouted as he sliced through the tape with a pocket-knife and popped open the top only to be met with a peculiar sight.

"Pieces of wood?"

The box was indeed filled with a dozen hefty pieces of firewood.

"To put into the fire I'm guessing? Or maybe I'm supposed to build a tree from this?" Suexliegh pondered as he scratched his head.

Verena laughed, "You're about as dense as wood I'll tell you that."

The wood had been a misdirection, for the real present was beneath. She helped him clear away the pieces to reveal a large, canvassed square. Suexliegh scrunched up his face, perplexed, until he turned it around to see, staring back at him, a nude woman standing atop a clam shell as it sailed towards the sea-shore, flanked by a man floating in the air and a woman presenting her with a cloak.

"Now that there's a woman living here we're going to need some real art to spruce up the house," Verena took the painting from Suexliegh and hung it delicately above the fireplace.

"This place has always needed a woman's touch."

"And one more thing," Verena reached behind her back and handed a hidden object to Suexliegh. He stopped breathing at the sight.

"Why… it's my face… on a coin!" Suexliegh giggled with glee.

"Both sides. I spoke to the mint and they agreed to print one. Just one. You hold the only coin of this in existence so spend it wisely."

"I don't think I'll spend it at all."

Suexliegh leaned in and kissed Verena on the cheek. His eyes lit up as he peered over her shoulder and quickly rushed towards the back deck where a light snow had begun to fall covering the world in a fresh, white, topping. Verena joined him and the two danced amidst the soft flurry of the season's first snow. Quincy Jr. held back and extended his collar against the frigid draft blowing into the house.

"Wouldn't you two prefer to be in here where it's nice and warm?"

Suexliegh stopped dancing and gestured for Quincy Jr. to join them.

"We should enjoy a bit of fun while we can, don't you think?" Suexliegh took Verena in his arms as they waltzed.

"Come along, Quincy."

And Quincy did.

$206

ZACK KELLER
www.zackkeller.com
@zfkeller

The son of a lawyer and a reading teacher, Zack Keller learned young to keep his nose buried in books and away from the law.

He studied at USC's School of Cinematic Arts then began his career at Pixar Animation Studios. Afterwards, he co-created *Dick Figures*, the most-viewed animated web series on YouTube which earned half a billion views and an Annie Award nomination. Thanks to massive fan support, Zack ran a record-breaking Kickstarter to fund a feature-length *Dick Figures The Movie* which hit the Top 10 Bestseller List on all digital platforms and won Best Animated Feature at the International Film Awards Berlin. Zack's first novel, *The Success of Suexliegh*, became an International Book Awards Finalist and San Francisco Book Festival Honorable Mention.

Most recently, Zack sold his feature animated screenplay *Turner of the Century* to Ghostbot, Inc and his horror series *Death Head* (Dark Horse Comics) will be published Summer 2015.

He lives in San Francisco with his fiancée and two destructive rabbits.

I'd love to hear from you, dear reader! If you would so kindly, please review this book on Amazon or Good Reads or just say "hello" on Twitter. Thank you!
- Zack

"If the world ever ends and we become separated, I want you to meet me at the Falls."

Thinking their father was joking, the Murphy family laughed the idea off that night at dinner. Little did they know that a devastating event would soon topple civilization. But the end was only the beginning of the family's problems.

Now, a mysterious light blazes in the sky dropping metallic pods deep underground. Armed militias roam broken streets for remaining resources, killing anyone who opposes their order. Mankind turns into the monsters they've always feared. Struggling to survive as society unravels into chaos, the Murphy family must find a way back to one another. Their only hope is to do what their father told them that night at dinner: MEET ME AT THE FALLS

$209

ZACK KELLER
THE
Owl's Hare
ZACK KELLER

Endless battles have exhausted the Realm for a thousand years...and the Dark Things have taken notice. Deep in the woods, rumors swirl of an evil wizard rising to conquer the war-weakened land. The only hope for survival is to unite the dueling kingdoms in marriage and combine forces against him. The plan appears promising until Owl, a bard with a deadly secret, sets off on a quest that will ruin everything: kidnapping the princess on her wedding day.

$210

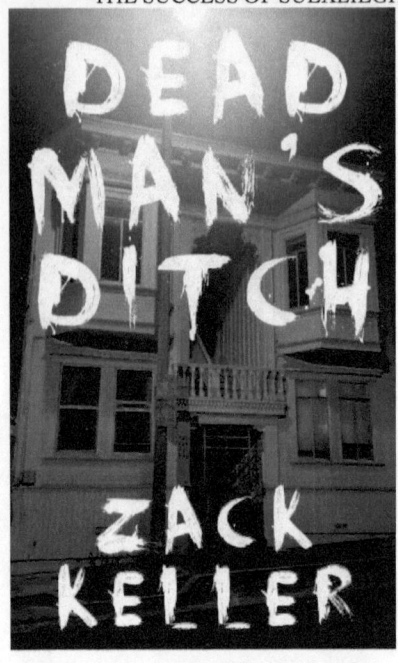

KNOCK. KNOCK. KNOCK. My brother and I used to play this game we called "Dead Man's Ditch". We'd go to this old haunted house in town, knock three times on the front door, and whoever could stand there the longest without freaking out was the winner. We loved Halloween, horror movies, and wandering cemeteries late at night arguing about what was inside that house. The question haunted us. Then, one day, my brother went missing... and I knew just where he'd gone.

"Canyon In The Clouds" twists and turns like a desert rattlesnake and is just as deadly. In this thrilling western tale a moribund sheriff, Clay, discovers the damage done not just to the condemned, but to the man holding the noose. In a desert with no trees, it's hard to find a good spot for a hanging. Even harder to find your way home.

Thank you, dear reader, for sticking with me all the way to...

The End

For more, please visit
www.zackkeller.com